Vianne

Vianne

Hunter Lake

ISBN: 0692890793
ISBN 13: 9780692890790

CORSICA, 1980

EVEN AT THAT LATE AFTERNOON hour, it was hot.

How did I lose her?

He walked quickly, and his shirt stuck to him—soaked through from an equal measure of jogging in the summer heat and a nagging realization that his target had somehow eluded him.

The sun was low, and the last of the sunbathers had left the beach hours earlier.

Every hundred yards he slowed down to scan his surroundings, nervous that he had lost his quarry. *Not good—not good at all.*

He plodded on, ignoring the sweat and the gritty distraction of the sand accumulating in his shoes.

Once again he looked back, and this time his steps faltered. He came to a stop and rubbed his eyes with the back of a hand. *There she is. Back there.*

In the distance, in line with the lowering sun, a hazy female figure jogged at a slight angle to the shoreline. Her body moved in silent deliberation. On a low dune a few yards from the water's edge, she slowed to a walk, the brilliant ball behind her imperceptibly but inexorably closing the short gap between itself, her silhouette, and the sea.

It occurred to him that somehow their roles might have reversed. *Is she following me now?*

The man's eyes narrowed at the vision of the slim, young woman—a distant wraith against the bloated Mediterranean sun. His nerves thrummed with caution, though he was certain she was unarmed, harmless. *She's got nothing.*

The figure came to a stop near a scattering of almost-buried rocks, and then stood still—a monochrome ghost against the sun's violent orange.

She wore a short, loosely fitting tan dress. Some of its sheer folds of silk floated around her—shimmering coronas in the hot breeze. A few sparks of reflected light winked from the edges of her hair.

The indistinct outline of her slim curves excited him on a base, primal level. More and more, over the past seventy-two hours, he had found himself thinking about her in that visceral way.

He had been watching her from afar for the last three days, waiting for the right time and place—the best moment for the kill. It would come when she was away from her well-protected house. When she was out of her comfort zone and off balance.

Now they were both alone on this deserted stretch of beach. Now she was *his,* and as often happened when he was about to execute a woman, his target had taken on a fantasy persona in his mind—an insistent erotic image that stirred him.

I hate to kill this one—this particular girl at this particular moment—but I must.

Now.

He pulled an automatic from its belt holster at the small of his back, cocked the slide, and started walking toward her through the sand. He was confident that she had no means to either attack him or defend herself. The unsettling rumors about her were surely just stories, speculation. But he was cautious in a methodical, professional way, and didn't take his eyes off the ghostly figure in the distance.

Down the beach, the hints of silk swirled around the silhouette.

He walked a dozen more steps—close enough to be within killing range—and realized that now she was facing him, watching him.

He narrowed his eyes to slits. *Damn this glare.*

She placed a foot on a low beach rock, and his eyes were drawn to a point between the silhouette's thighs. The intense light of the sun behind the woman was almost too bright to endure. A single harsh ray shot through the gap where her legs met, and it burned his eyes.

His breaths became shorter.

His endorphin levels soared.

The far-off intersections of light and dark coalesced, and he shook his head in a double take as he saw her smoothly, quickly, bend at the waist and run her hands down to the sand. He lifted his free hand to shade his eyes.

She brought the Beretta up in a single sweep from its hiding place in the rocks.

What's she doing?

She swept it up in two hands, now standing, now aiming.

Is that a gun?

She shot at him three times in quick, measured succession.

Before he could fire his own pistol, the rounds slammed into him. One of them skewered his heart, another a lung. The third scorched through his stomach and smashed into his spine so violently that two vertebrae split apart.

He was dead before his body hit the sand.

The sweltering hush that followed the gun blasts held only a single, far-off cry of a seabird and the rhythmic *shh* of tiny waves at the water's flat edge.

The light dress whispered gently against smooth skin. She slowly lowered the gun and studied her would-be killer's dead body from afar. Tiny bright flecks in the irises of her eyes glinted in the day's fading light.

For a moment she thought about letting the Beretta drop back to the sand, near the spot where she had hidden it when she had learned that her executioner had arrived in Ajaccio. But the gun was hers, a gift from someone special. It had just saved her life—it wasn't the first time—and she wouldn't leave it there on the beach.

She didn't approach the corpse, preferring to stand in silence several feet from the water's edge.

After a few seconds, a familiar voice in her head whispered, *Time to go.*

Vianne

Her hands absently smoothed her billowy dress as she cast a final, confirming look at the lifeless clump in the distance: it had already become dusted with a powdering of blown sand.

Then she turned and walked toward the sun.

Part One

Only when you drink from the
river of silence shall you indeed sing.

—Khalil Gibran

CHAPTER 1

Sirocco

SHE SPOKE ONLY WHEN WORDS were unavoidable, and then her whisper was muted, barely audible—a quiet sotto voce by-product of her breathing.

She listened to the voices of everyone around her with calm deliberation, concentrating on the purities of tone and the shadings of timbre rather than on the careless and dangerous chaos of their words.

And with unerring prescience, she would read the hidden truths in others' faces.

She had learned to communicate with startling, silent effect—using her breathy whispers only as complements to small shifts of her hands, subtle movements of her body, suggestive tilts of her head, and the clear, silent voice of her star-flecked, midnight eyes.

Her father had been a freight handler from Perpignan, a stevedore who made himself transient homes of convenience along the Mediterranean coast—anywhere there were ships with cargo to load and bars at which to drink. And it was in one of those Marseille bars where he had found her mother—had been struck by the woman's shadowy beauty and the attractive hard edges chiseled into her personality.

"What's your pleasure?" she had asked automatically from the other side of the noisy bar on the day he had first wandered in.

His laughing eyes had waited until she had had enough time to size him up. Then he had said, "More than you can supply."

She had snorted. "I doubt that."

Gaston told her he had gotten a long-term job at the docks, hinted at a reliable income.

Corinne was twenty, an orphaned émigré from Algeria, and she soon liked him, and he looked as if he had a bit of money. After a month or two, he moved into her tiny apartment in a run-down section of the teeming port city.

And within a year, in spite of halfhearted efforts to prevent it from happening, Corinne gave birth to a girl.

The newborn was flawed—her vocal cords were so atrophied that they were essentially useless. To make up for the odd shortcoming, she had Corinne's glowing, cinnamon skin, ironic moue, and startling thick and shining black hair, which had begun to grow before she had even opened her eyes to the world.

And those eyes were the color of midnight skies, the large irises sprinkled with tiny splinters of stars.

Though the infant was born into the dull chaos that lurks at the edge of poverty everywhere, the day of her birth was undeniably beautiful—a warm, crystal clear morning in Marseille—the first day of summer, 1960.

Corinne herself chose the baby's name, *Vianne.* It reminded her of *vie,* life. And its sound, softly spoken, was like that of the wind—the Saharan sirocco that blew over Algeria, bringing its swirling fragrance across the sea to the South of France.

She would sometimes call her quiet baby *Sirocco* when she sang her the soft lullabies she had learned in the country of her birth—a country she was certain she would never see again.

When Vianne was less than a year old, Gaston disappeared on a ship bound for Yugoslavia. He left Corinne and the baby with a few broken promises and a fifty-franc note placed alongside the cracked porcelain kitchen sink.

It was the start of Corinne's plodding but determined effort to raise Vianne alone while life in its mocking harshness continued to quietly whittle away at the single mother.

A year later she heard that Gaston had been killed in a bar fight in Dubrovnik, but the news hadn't upset her very much, though any hopes of her daughter one day seeing her father again were forever gone. She shrugged, and hugged Vianne, who looked at her with large eyes and was silent.

"The future will be bright for us, for you, *mon petit,*" she told Vianne that night in a lullaby voice. She waited for the baby to fall asleep, then put her hands to her face and sobbed quietly.

When Vianne was six, Corinne managed to register her at primary school. By good fortune, Chloé and Emma, two slightly older girls in the run-down and often unsafe neighborhood, walked with Vianne in the early mornings. It was a little under a mile to the school, and Vianne enjoyed listening to her two companions as they chatted and navigated the teeming Marseille streets.

At first those companions thought the younger girl was deformed—some kind of mute—but they learned that if they cared to listen, she said just enough in her low, soft whispers.

But school wasn't made for Vianne. Although she took to reading with amazing speed, the other children, most of whom seemed loud and careless to the quiet girl, tended to avoid her. At home, she would look at her reflection in Corinne's small mirror. *I am ugly. And I don't care.* But she did care. And for a time she couldn't understand why she was shunned.

Vianne didn't realize that the other children at the school, especially the girls, resented her strange, unfamiliar beauty and her novel, barely audible voice, which they interpreted as haughtiness.

But she concentrated on what everyone said and how he or she said it, calculating that it might be hurtful in some vague way for her to miss something important.

Before bed each night, she would listen to stories about her mother's life in North Africa, which Corinne told in a quiet, desert voice. As the dark woman carefully brushed Vianne's thick, gleaming black hair, she would gently and endlessly remind Vianne that she would always be different, special.

But Vianne was most intent on Corinne's description of the future. She would silently concur as her mother insisted that for the two of them—but especially for Vianne—there was a bright world ahead, a world without struggle. There in the small, dark room it sounded like a fairy tale, but a convincing one, and she loved to hear the not-so-hidden hope at the back of her mother's voice.

"Somewhere ahead, *mon chéri,* you will find a carpet of stars to take you wherever you want to go," Corinne would say in the soft tones of the night. The vision never failed to soothe Vianne, never left its secret place in her heart.

On some afternoons, Vianne would walk home alone from school, Chloé and Emma being occupied with other missions that took precedence over keeping company with the odd, silent girl. It was on these solitary walks through some of the harsher neighborhoods of the rough and masculine port city of Marseille that Vianne augmented her true education.

As time went by, she tended to spend more time near the docks, gradually enlarging the rough, urban circumference of her world, her meanderings taking her from the myriad of small merchants with their tiny shops and rickety street kiosks to the large, ominous freighters that crowded the port. She liked to sit on a dock piling and study how hard men, with the help of hand trucks and forklifts and cranes, moved tons of everything imaginable on and off the ships.

And she silently and carefully watched those men in the streets, observing how the beats of life flowed between them, sometimes in good ways, sometimes not. Marseille was home to many people who acted badly.

Vianne observed how a class of grown-ups intermingled amid the fractured harshness of the port city, going about a life that seemed richly extravagant and imbued with power. These adults were exclusively men, some of them rough and loud, some of them suave, with hooded, cunning eyes. The former were generally part of the world of ships and shipping that dominated Marseille. The latter were cogs in the large and dangerous drug-smuggling machine that defined the roots of the infamous French Connection.

The massive multinational scheme was responsible for supplying the vast majority of heroin destined for the United States. Huge quantities of the white powder were smuggled from Turkey to Marseille, and thence to the United States through Canada. The complex logistics of illicit shipping, and the darkly clever use of a hundred smuggling techniques, were second nature to the powerful bosses of the operation.

The far-flung and violently dangerous industry was headed and financed by an impenetrable cadre of French, Sicilian, Turkish, and Corsican criminals, whose names were obscure, and justifiably so—smart people didn't want to know those names.

It was said that the Unione Corse, the Corsican version of the Sicilian Mafia, was at that time the most vicious criminal organization in Europe, perhaps in the entire Free World. And their employees—mules, couriers, shills, enforcers, hit men, and heavies of all stripes—had made the streets of Marseille their home away from home.

On her solitary afternoon walks through these same streets, little Vianne, twinges of hunger in her belly, roamed through that dark tableau like a charmed wraith. The occasional presence of the wandering, black-haired, silent *petite fille* became part and parcel of the landscape. She was soon a familiar talisman to the hard criminals on the streets.

The windows of the small shops she passed in her daily travels provided a form of education and entertainment as well. She enjoyed watching the activity of buying and selling through the glass, pretending she was part of the people's action, their small dramas.

One afternoon she stood mesmerized in front of the window of a store that sold women's secondhand clothing. It wasn't the selection of slightly used dresses that had caught her attention. Instead, it was a man installing a carpet inside the store. The rail-thin worker was working his way around the perimeter of the front room of the tiny establishment, a black band of protective rubber tied around his right knee.

Qu'est-ce que c'est? She looked on, fascinated.

As the man pulled a part of the new carpeting up against the wall, he would kneel and carefully position the flat front of a thick metal spatula. Then he would check that the border of the carpeting was in perfect position.

When he was satisfied with the angle, he took quick but careful aim, pulled his right leg back as far as it would go without losing his balance, and then jam his padded knee like a pile driver against the butt of the spatula's handle. A small edge of the carpet was driven hard into the join between floor and wall, and the man would back up, appraise the result, and quickly hammer in an anchoring nail.

Then he moved the tool six inches to the right and repeated the process over and over as he worked his way around the room.

Vianne watched.

It took the carpet layer an hour to complete his job, systematically knee-butting and then nailing the carpet into place.

Très drôle, she thought, and she smiled, having enjoyed every minute of the performance. She felt an inexplicable fascination with the man's arcane demonstration of the hidden power in a humble knee.

When he was finished, he got slowly to his feet and looked up to see his young audience outside the plate-glass window. He made a salute with his metal spatula, and bowed with a flourish.

Vianne gave him a pure smile, clapped her hands, and mouthed the word *merveilleux.*

A dull hunger would often gnaw at Vianne on those afternoons.

Through simple sleight of hand and clever misdirection, she found that she could silently acquire a pear or a fig from a street vendor, or an apple from a distracted fruit-stand owner. She was good at it—had to be—as times were such that getting caught, even for a minor crime like lifting a tomato from a cart, was something to avoid.

One autumn day, as she walked down a narrow alley near the docks, she heard footsteps behind her. She thought of the stolen peach for her mother, tucked in the pocket of her worn jacket, as she felt a strong hand on her shoulder. Expecting to find one of the dark men of the wharfs, she whirled to see a *policier* instead—a stout cop dressed in uniform and flat-topped képi, staring down at her from what seemed a mighty height.

"Give it here, *cochon,* little pig," he ordered. He held out his other beefy hand, palm up.

Vianne's eyes moved, and she saw there was someone else there as well, a huge and ominous man, standing and watching from several yards away. It seemed as if the dangerous-looking giant in his broad black suit was enjoying the little drama.

The ten-year-old quietly took the peach from her pocket and held it out to the policeman. He bent and took it with his free hand, and with his other released her shoulder. A second later he slapped her full and hard across her face.

Her world shook—it felt as if something in her head had snapped. She fell to her knees in stinging shock. Blood beaded on her split lower lip, and a few drops fell to the gutter near the carcass of a dead rat.

"*Voilà*," the man said with level malice, sneering down at the child from his full height. "You are lucky I am in a good mood, little thief, or it would be much worse."

She looked up at him, and the tiny stars in her midnight eyes flashed—stars that now spoke of a silent, blossoming hatred.

"What's your name, *sale môme?*" the heavy-gutted cop demanded in a voice more suited for questioning a murderer than a ten-year-old girl. She dropped her gaze to fix on the gleaming drops of red in the filthy street in front of her.

"Well, what is it?" he repeated, impatience fraying the edges of his demand.

Vianne was about to whisper her name but stopped short. A silky voice from a deep well inside her that she hadn't known was there spoke quietly in her mind: *Don't tell him.*

She pursed her lips, pressed her eyes shut, and after a few silent seconds felt a hard, painful kick to her side.

"Go back to your rat hole," the policeman said in dismissal, and he looked away from the kneeling, breathless girl.

She opened her dark eyes and watched as the man casually raised the peach to his mouth. He took a big, dripping bite and started walking away down the street.

I hope the pit sticks in your throat, she thought.

In his heart, said the inner voice.

From her kneeling position in the gutter, she saw the other man—the huge observer who was obviously enjoying the malicious diversion—chuckle and fall into stride alongside the policeman.

Which one is worse, she asked herself: *the cop or the criminal? And is there a difference?*

She heard the strange, silent voice again: *You'll see.*

CHAPTER 2
Fish Knife

———

CORINNE WAS BARELY ABLE TO make the rent on the sad, second-floor flat over a *poissonnerie,* a fish store several blocks from the docks. But she did spend a few precious centimes once a week for a bit of sweet incense to counter the smells wafting up from the establishment beneath her and Vianne's feet. The apartment was small and spare, but she had succeeded in giving it a subtle aroma that carried faint, elusive shreds of childhood memories.

It was to the flat that Corinne brought her "man-friends."

The woman's heart ached every time her empty purse and her daughter's empty stomach forced her to do so. And the painted plywood wall with its open door frame that bisected the small apartment gave neither mother nor daughter much privacy.

But Corinne understood that in spite of her brave stories to her daughter, her own future would be bleak, and both hers and Vianne's survival would hang by a very slender thread if they were ever put out on the street.

So the men and their thin wallets kept coming sporadically, and the young Vianne got used to the sounds of sex and learned to ignore the fake moans of her mother and the real ones of the men on the other side of the thin plywood wall.

On a cold November night when Vianne was ten, her mother brought one of those "friends" to the tiny flat. This man hadn't been with Corinne in that way, but she had seen him from time to time in the bar.

His name was Marcel, and Corinne had initially liked his rough face and lanky black hair. He was a longshoreman and had come off one of the ubiquitous cargo ships, and that night he wasn't completely drunk. But he wasn't completely sober either.

She had warned him that if he wanted to be with her for a time, her daughter would likely be in the next room, and to just ignore the little girl if he happened to glimpse her. In the neutral ground of the hustling bar, Marcel had seemed calm and safe to Corinne, and at the end of the night he had left with her.

When she took him into her quiet flat over the fish store, he looked at the girl who was sitting in the part of the room that served as a kitchenette, and immediately laughed. He was surprised that the child was reading. It was a book with pictures of paintings in a museum in Italy.

Vianne had found the book in a trash bin, and was transfixed by the strange power and emotion of the works of art in the book when her mother and the man quietly entered the apartment.

"And what are you?" Marcel said, towering over Vianne. "A librarian?"

The girl looked up at him with startled midnight eyes from beneath her thick hair. Though her hearing was acute, she hadn't heard him or her mother come in—she had been mentally submerged in the artwork. She quickly closed the book, stood, and, not looking at her mother, disappeared through the doorway in the thin dividing wall.

"My daughter, as I said," Corinne said warily. He had been warned, she said to herself, and the men who had come this far with Corinne had only one thing on their minds anyway. If there was a child a few feet away, well, *c'est la vie.* That was just the way it was, the dark woman had reminded herself bitterly each and every time. The men would always quickly forget about the proximity of the little girl.

But this man was different, and Corinne saw something in his face that she suddenly didn't like, a feral streak that she had missed, that the man had somehow masked with irreverent drunkenness. She had made it a point to be highly in tune with men and their states of mind, but this time her guard had been down.

He looked at Corinne. "Your little one," he said. "She is included in the price?"

In a frightful second of clarity Corinne knew that her lack of discernment had exploded into a fatal mistake and that any more talk was out of the question. Within a single beat of her heart she turned all her focus to getting Marcel out of the flat.

"*Non,*" she said, quickly moving to the door, which opened to the hall outside the apartment. She stepped into the poorly lit corridor and turned back to him. "Come out here," she said, fingering the top of her blouse. "I—"

The man moved quickly, and he slammed her up against one of the dirty hallway walls with the full weight of his body. His face was in hers, and his breath was warm and smelled of whiskey.

"*Non, putain,*" he taunted. "*Non,* that young one *is* part of the sale." His savage grin burned into Corinne's eyes. "You stay here." He took his weight off her and turned to walk into the flat.

Corinne pushed off the wall and lunged at his back. He tripped forward, and the two crashed into the apartment and onto the worn wooden floor of the tiny kitchen area. She clawed at him like a street cat, but he was hard, tough, and his arms were strong. A moment later he had flipped her over, trapping her on her back on the floor beneath him.

His grin twisted into a sneer. "All right. In that case, the girl will be next," he hissed into her face. "Right after you."

He kept her pressed to the floor beneath him. With one powerful hand he grabbed both her wrists. With the other he ripped at her blouse and tore at her skirt and then grabbed her throat. Corinne tried to kick and bite the man while yelling for Vianne to run, get out of the flat, *hurry.*

She squirmed and tried to hurt Marcel any way she could, but he was too powerful, his mass too heavy—his body and his psyche far too warped by a life on the docks to be swayed by anything as insignificant as a woman.

"*Run, Vianne!*" Corinne tried to cry out, her constricted throat making her words unintelligible. She couldn't see her daughter from beneath the crushing Marcel, but was certain the girl must still be in the apartment. Her heart was bursting with hatred for the beast, hatred for herself, hatred for God for letting these sorts of things happen in her world. *"Run,* chéri," she tried to yell to her daughter, but now the man's full weight was on her, and his free hand squeezed her throat harder.

Then Marcel decided that events had indeed gone as far as they could and that the only way to end it would be to take her life. His alcohol-addled subconscious stirred with the single visceral imperative: *kill.*

He searched Corinne's feverish eyes with a growing madness that screamed, *This woman doesn't count in the world, so I can do as I please.* He looked up for a moment, his eyes searching for the girl who had been at the far end of the apartment. She was nowhere to be seen.

Surely she's hiding close by, he said to himself. *There is no way she could have run past us. Her mother and I are blocking the door to the outside hallway.*

"Nmph! Nmn!" Corinne choked through her pain as the man's hand squeezed her neck harder, and her eyes began to bulge.

He looked at the woman's face and grunted. "Say goodbye to your life and to your little girl, *chienne.* Bitch."

Corinne's desperate eyes began to defocus, and her mind cried out, *Vianne, run!*

"A few good squeezes, and you will be gone," the man hissed.

He knew that by now the daughter must have fled the apartment. He didn't hear the soft sound coming from behind the rusted pipes beneath the counter sink behind him—the sound of a little girl wedged into the small space, in her hand a long filleting knife that she had stolen the week before from the fish store.

Corinne couldn't speak with the man's rough hands clasped on her throat. She tried to scream a final *Run, run, Vianne,* but it came out as a low garbled groan.

Marcel savagely bounced and crushed his bulk against her body and reveled in the satisfying knowledge that he was killing her. He had felt this power before when he had murdered at close quarters. He loved it.

"Who are *you* to deny *me?*" He hissed a whiskey-stinking spray onto her graying face, into her open mouth.

Vianne's inner voice reminded her: *carpet layer.* It was all the explanation she needed. As the monster was steeped in his assault on her mother, the girl quietly unfolded herself from the crawl space under the sink, took two careful steps, and crouched silently by the side of the heaving, distracted man's legs.

She gently touched the stiletto tip of the foot-long fish knife to the back neckline of Marcel's work shirt and, remembering the carpet layer, took quick and careful aim.

Feeling nothing past a grimly besotted triumph, Marcel stared into the dulling eyes of the woman under him, and a black, raw, howling thrill clasped his heart. He opened his mouth to laugh.

The carpet layer, Vianne reminded herself one last time as she pulled one leg back as far as she could without losing her balance. Then she jammed her knee with all the power she had like a pile driver against the butt of the knife handle.

Marcel's face froze, and his mouth shot open as he heard more than felt the grinding, crunching sound of the long steel blade stabbing through the hair on the back of his neck.

The blade rammed straight through his cerebellum, medulla, and brain stem, arrowed through his pituitary gland—slicing it into two pieces—then burst into his mouth from the back. It amputated his tongue and came to a stop.

The tip of the red-gleaming blade poked eight inches out of his mouth.

The man's jaws opened still wider in a mangled, sodden scream, and his severed pink tongue fell out like a bloody pig's liver and landed between Corinne's breasts. His eyes crossed as they looked down his nose in disbelieving panic and focused on the protruding, scarlet-wet spike.

Marcel's iron hands relaxed and fell from the woman's throat as his eyes jittered crazily in their sockets. He choked on a maelstrom of his own blood, and after a long second that framed his last heartbeat, collapsed like dead weight on the breathless woman's motionless body. The jutting, crimson-drenched knife just missed cutting Corinne's turned cheek, and his face fell to the side, as an exhausted lover's might.

A final surge of blood blurted out of his throat and around the blade, and the dwindling cascade flowed over the woman's shoulder and arm. Dark liquid rubies splashed and dribbled onto the floor, and the man's severed tongue rolled off her chest and landed in the red pool with a small *plop.*

His body slowly slid off Corinne and then was still.

The only sound in the room was a faint *drip-drip,* but it slowed and finally ended, and then there was silence.

The quiet that had fallen over the room was thick and even, and it suited Vianne, who felt no need to utter a word. She knew her serene face alone spoke to her mother.

It should be quiet here now, the ten-year-old's eyes said.

But her inner voice whispered that from this moment onward, wherever the rush of life would take her, nothing would be the same ever again.

CHAPTER 3

For Her Sake

———

CORINNE SAT ON THE FLOOR, her eyes fixed on Vianne.

After a time she got shakily to her feet, washed up as best she could, and put on a clean blouse. Then she and Vianne went quickly through Marcel's clothes. The man's front pants pocket was stuffed with a thick wad of hundred-franc notes and US hundred-dollar bills. Drug money. There was a single, worn identity card in an otherwise empty wallet, indicating that his name was Marcel Bronté from Banyuls-sur-Mer, a fishing town near the French-Spanish border.

Corinne's eyes widened, and she unconsciously turned her head away when she glimpsed a tattoo on his right forearm. It was a dark cross with a flaming dagger across it. The bluish-black image was instantly and ominously recognizable as a gang initiation symbol.

She looked at Vianne and nodded as she pushed the dead man's money into a pocket of her skirt. Then she went to her mattress and stuffed the wallet into a hiding place she had hollowed out deep in its ancient tangle of old bedsprings.

Mother and daughter managed to wrap the corpse in a well-worn sheet and drag it out into the hall and through the stairwell door. It was difficult to pull the body down the two flights of steps to the building's dank and abandoned basement, and it took a long time to clean up the blood in the apartment.

And Corinne knew that now their hours and minutes were numbered.

Marcel undoubtedly had a complement of friends from the ships, some of whom had been drinking with him when he had propositioned Corinne, and they had surely seen him leave the bar with her. She had to count on at least one of them missing him and his money after a time, and when he didn't turn up after a day or two, a search would be initiated.

At the very least, the small fortune on his person would assure that.

And dozens of regulars at the bar knew Corinne, and knew she had a young daughter. She couldn't hide for long.

Brought to frustrated exhaustion by the grim prospects that she and Vianne had suddenly found thrust upon them, and reconciled to the fact that the balance of time she had left was extremely finite, Corinne made a hard decision.

The next day, as the rats in the basement below the fish store slept off their meal, Corinne finished her preparations.

She packed a cloth bag of worn clothes, and with Vianne, walked the three miles through the city to the Benedictine abbey on the rue Edmond Rostand.

She stood across the street from the imposing tan stone structure and held her silent daughter's hand. After a minute, she leaned down and hugged Vianne mightily and wiped a tear from each eye.

She clasped Vianne's reluctant hand, and the two crossed the street and went inside the abbey.

Vianne's mother implored the nuns to take over her daughter's education and provide her shelter and food. She herself was being forced to leave for a place that her daughter couldn't go. The nuns, whose authority went only so far, ushered Corinne and her daughter into the office of Odette, Mother Superior of the convent.

Mother Odette was a Parisian who had been transferred to Marseille twenty years earlier. She was in her early sixties, tall and beefy, and peered at her two guests over the top of her gold-framed glasses.

Vianne stood in a silent state of mental agony as Corinne spoke urgently to the nun and then sweetened her pleading with Marcel's thick wad of bills—the small fortune that she had extracted from the dead man's pocket.

Odette pocketed the wad in a fold of her habit, and promised Corinne that the nuns would immediately place her daughter in the convent school. Then she touched the large silver cross hanging on the front of her habit and looked on as Corinne hugged her daughter.

God will provide for all beggars and orphans, the Mother Superior mused to herself, patting the bulge of bills in her habit.

Corinne leaned down and hugged her daughter. "Please understand." She tried to sound strong through the despair that was breaking her heart. "Think of the future."

Finally she stood up and walked to the door, and a minute later, she was gone.

Vianne stood rooted to the spot on the verge of tears. She didn't want to understand, and barely believed that now she was all by herself and might be forever.

Corinne left the large stone building and walked the three miles back to the small, sad flat over the *poissonnerie.* Each lonely step felt as if it were carrying her closer to the gallows.

She let herself into the tiny apartment and forlornly scanned the sorry surroundings. She cursed to herself and thought about Marcel—an evil, violent man with the distinctive, dreaded tattoo of a "made" killer in one of the powerful French Connection gangs. He was likely an important, highly placed, missing cog in the wheel, with friends who were sworn to avenge his death. Quickly and harshly.

Her mind focused on her daughter. "Help her, God," she said out loud, sitting on the edge of the bed. The knife that had been skewered through Marcel's head now rested on the thin blanket beside her, cleaned and gleaming. The dry smell of sweet incense floated like a soft hum in the still apartment.

"I'm sorry, Vianne, my love," she said to an empty point in the air a few feet in front of her.

An hour later, without a knock or a word, a large man with a killer's face broke down her door. For Vianne's sake, Corinne fought bravely with the knife.

But it was over fast.

CHAPTER 4

A Five-Pointed Star

THE BENEDICTINE SISTERS OF MARSEILLE were overburdened and often clumsy in their attempts to raise the many orphaned girls in their charge. And when word reached them a few days later that the mother of their newest arrival was dead, they sent Vianne to Mother Odette.

The well-fed woman's graying hair was piled neatly out of sight under her black-and-white coif. Her small eyes were sharp with the attention and focus demanded of the overseer of an order of nuns and their orphanage. She sat in a large leather chair behind a mahogany desk, opening a small stack of mail.

Vianne watched the woman slice into the envelopes with a long, slim letter opener adorned with a gold crucifix at one end.

Setting her work aside, the head of the convent looked up from behind her desk and studied the girl standing before her. She said, "Your mother is gone. Dead. She has been relieved of this vale of sorrows. We will pray for her soul. Sorry."

Vianne couldn't help but tremble, and she longed for her mother and for the familiar inner voice that sometimes came to her unbidden. But the only sound in her soul was the pounding of her emptied heart.

Mother Odette watched Vianne cry on in strange silence. When she felt enough time had passed, she said, "Calm down, young miss. You should be happy, you know."

Vianne lifted her midnight eyes to meet Odette's dull brown ones.

"You should be happy," the nun repeated with certitude. "Your mother may now be sitting at the right hand of Jesus. That is, of course, if she has avoided hell. I would hope that the former is the case."

Vianne didn't know what she was talking about. That night her tears fell on the thin pillow of her dormitory bed. Her mind had gone blank as an overcast night sky, but finally the trembling in her lips subsided and she made a decision.

I have to live. Mama kept talking about a future, a good one. Somehow, in some way, I'll find it.

She held that thought for hours until she finally fell asleep.

The convent school was a mixed bag.

Most of the other girls and some of the nuns thought Vianne was a mute, and she wasn't quick to disabuse them of the notion. She went about her studies in silence, which suited her.

She didn't care to apply herself to arithmetic and science. But she was exceptionally receptive to and blindingly fast at reading and languages. She was mesmerized by high French and took it quickly as her own. Within a few months the ingrained sloppy slang of the Marseille streets was gone, and now her low, compelling, whispers caressed flawless *haute français*.

And she learned English as well. She found its vocabulary vast, and its grammar and syntax disconcerting at first, with a raft of exceptions proving its rules. But it was still a language with deep Latin roots that Vianne instinctively recognized.

The convent had many books in English, mostly Bibles, and Sister Flora, a plump, middle-aged nun who was born in England, spoke the language fluently. In less than a year, under her tutelage, Vianne knew that if by a miracle she one day went to England or America, she would get along without a problem.

The pretty girl also spent hours alone with the foreign dictionaries in the convent library. She discovered that Spanish, Italian, and Portuguese were a relative snap—intuitively easy if one had a strong base in French and English. She practiced by herself in a whisper only she could hear, but devoted most of her time to listening to her teacher. For Vianne, it was through careful listening that one learned a language—that one learned *everything*. There was little use for words.

As impressed as the nuns were with Vianne's quiet linguistic skills, they were equally frustrated with her ongoing problems with God.

Vianne's mother had been a Berber from Algeria, whose father was a Sunni Muslim and mother a dark-skinned Sephardic Jew. But Corinne had never instilled any specific form of organized religion in her daughter. Although Corinne had a strong belief in a higher power, as a logical offshoot of her blended upbringing she considered herself naturally polytheistic—revering and fearing all gods equally. She hadn't taken any chances, but had covered her bases in case Jesus, Moses, or Mohammed were ever discredited and cast from the divine pantheon.

But now Vianne was alone and in the convent school, where Jesus stood at the center of the universe. The Sisters tried mightily to set her on Christ's path, but from the outset, Vianne found the story of Jesus sometimes charming, sometimes violent, and often confusing. She would kneel in the chapel during *matins* along with the other girls, but her heart wouldn't wrap itself around the Savior's divinity. Nor could she synchronize her soul with the regimented structure of the Catholic hierarchy, headed by a man named Paul who was living in splendor in Rome.

But she did have a strong sense of an unseen force to life. Deep inside she was sure there was some kind of cosmic presence in all things, for better or worse.

As time passed, a certainty grew in her heart that God was above all. But not in a vague place called heaven. *Non, God must be in the stars.*

Alone at night, while the other girls slept in the crowded convent dormitory room, Vianne would gaze at the spangled sky through a single small window.

Sûrement when we die, we go there to be with God and shine for eternity. On the day that I die, I will fly up there forever. Her inner voice assured her beyond the shadow of a doubt that she would one day be there with her mother.

She felt comfortable with her faith in a stellar divinity—it didn't ask anything of her, didn't insist on her obedience to ritual in any form, and was inclusive of all. And it was inscrutable and quite visible at the same time. The stars, she knew, sparkled down on everyone in silent testament to their calm stability, their assurance to all who were living beneath them that there would always be a static, immutable certainty overlying the lives of the people walking the earth. That from the beginning of time to the end of eternity, the carpet of stars would remain.

So that is God, Vianne would think comfortingly at night. *The stars will always be there for me, just as the Sisters say that Jesus will be.*

But I can see the stars.

As Vianne grew, she used every opportunity to spend time outside the convent. The Sisters didn't seem to mind if she wandered off after her lessons were done. She always returned, and besides, the abbey was bursting with orphans.

She was now far more mature and hardened by the violent loss of her mother, which had only made her quieter and more perceptive—and a more adept survivor.

She ranged the streets and the docks, becoming known as the pretty young girl with the heavy black hair who rarely spoke but could hold her own. The rough men noticed her, but only as another anomaly—a poor mute who was part of the local tableau, the Marseille scene.

And as Vianne grew, she became fascinated with men—how they spoke, how they walked, how they were with women.

Over time, the nuns came to the realization that Vianne had become more of a liability than an asset. In most things convent, she rebelled in silence. They couldn't get inside Vianne's head, and the reticent girl was stingy with her whispered words to the point of frustration, putting an ironic twist to the saying "silence is golden."

After a few years of unsuccessful attempts to win over the uncommunicative girl to a life of Christ, the Sisters had a meeting.

They decided to double down on their efforts to place Vianne with a family. Not only did they push her name to the top of the adoption list, but they carefully eased up on some of the strict guidelines they generally adhered to in the already rudimentary vetting of prospective and safe foster homes for the older orphans.

As a result of this relaxation of standards, the rare household who agreed to take in the quiet and comely teenager generally featured a dominant male figure whose actions often tended to conflict with the expected civilized behavior of responsible adults.

Though not an adult herself by any legal standard, Vianne was rapidly turning into a stunning young woman. Not surprisingly, these trial adoptions didn't last long. Typically the woman of the house would become annoyed with Vianne's difficult and irritating silence, and jealous of the pretty girl's slender body and disconcerting eyes. And the dark-haired girl's hushed demeanor was most often misinterpreted by the man of the house as a form of sultry provocation.

At that point it was usually only a short time before Vianne would be returned to the nunnery or forced to take matters into her own hands and orchestrate a timely exit before trouble with the husband reached a tipping point.

I hate this vicious cycle.

Vianne would run away from the foster homes when she got the slightest hint that trouble might lie ahead. Then she would haunt the familiar streets of Marseille, trying with no success to seek out a stable place to stay. But invariably she wound up returning to the convent in a few days, her other options exhausted. Typically she would be thinner and very, very silent.

Each time this happened, the nuns would wring their hands and have yet another meeting with Mother Odette, and then let several months pass. They agreed that they had never had a girl in their charge that so consistently failed at adapting to a foster home.

But they kept right on trying. They were oblivious to the fact that Vianne, whose physical beauty had soared to a far higher aesthetic plane than that of the other orphan girls, would *always* fail at "adapting," whether she wanted to or not.

One night, on the cusp of her sixteenth birthday, she had been sleeping in the tiny bedroom of the latest foster home when she awoke to a new, frightening shock. The middle-aged head of the household, a bland and harmless-seeming pipe fitter from Toulouse, had without warning been transformed into an out-of-control drunk and entered her small room.

It was a close call for Vianne. She rose quickly from her thin sleep to find the drunk kneeling by her bed, his hands awkwardly trying to paw her through her nightdress. Seeing the flushed face and the defocused eyes close to hers, she moved quickly and managed to slip through the man's powerful but booze-addled groping to get herself out of the small apartment.

Still in her nightclothes, she was running full tilt down the outside fire stairs of the three-story walk-up when she felt an odd and urgent wetness. She came to a full stop a few steps before reaching the sidewalk. For a confused moment, she was unable to understand what was happening to her, and quickly glanced down at herself to see a dark spot on her clothes. She had little time to absorb what it meant as the sound of the man's footsteps on the stairs behind her grew closer. Still a few steps above the street, she looked around in desperation—the rain-slick cobblestones and the walls of the low apartment buildings were black and deserted at this time of night.

That brief hesitation was all her drunken attacker needed to catch up to her, and he grabbed her from behind, pinning her slender arms against her sides with his fat, hairy ones. The two stumbled down the last few steps and hobbled awkwardly, locked together, onto the sidewalk.

It was Marcel all over again, she thought in terror. Only this time *she* was the one in the crosshairs of an insane man. And there was no knife to help her.

At that point, any other woman would have screamed— something that the silent Vianne was unable to do.

The pipe fitter was at least twice her weight, and he pulled her with frightening strength into the darkness beneath the metal staircase. The man grunted as he mashed her against the wall with the weight of his body, his intentions frighteningly obvious. Vianne struggled, but the sheer weight of the huge man pressing on her made it impossible for her to move.

A moment later she felt his hand slither down the front of her clothes, but after a moment he pulled it away and muttered something about *les règles*. Vianne tried to twist herself out of his powerful embrace, but was pinned by his heavy, unyielding weight.

His hand disappeared from view again, but in a moment was back, this time clutching a metal tool, a wrench that he had pulled from a loop on his thick canvas work belt. He raised it over her head, his intentions clear—he would knock her out and then ravage her unconscious body.

She made a last twisting, writhing attempt to escape, but he was too strong. Looking up quickly, her eyes searched the strip of star-flashed night sky that peeked between the buildings above her, and her mouth moved in a silent prayer to her mother.

Then she leaned in, almost as if to kiss the man, and a second later bit hard into his left cheek. Her bite took off a small chunk of flesh, and she spat it onto the ground.

The pipe fitter screamed an incongruously high shriek and dropped the wrench. Splatters of blood flew from his ruined flesh, some of them hitting the front of the girl's clothes and mixing with the blood that was already there. One of the man's hands clasped the side of his mangled face, and with the other he pulled Vianne along with him as he collapsed to his knees.

Feeling his grip falter, Vianne shook out of his grasp, rose quickly, and sprinted away down the dark street. It was hard to run on the slick paving stones in bare feet, and she had no idea which way to go. She expected to hear the man yelling or the sound of his pursuit, but after running a long block she turned to find the streets empty.

She stood in the light of a single street lamp, breathing fast and heavily. Then she cautiously put her hand down between her thighs and felt the wetness of her own blood again. She half walked, half hobbled to the door of one of the dark buildings that lined the sidewalk and tried the doorknob. It was open.

She walked shakily into a tiny, dim lobby. A single weak bulb in the ceiling cast a yellowish light, and a narrow staircase led upward through an arch in the far wall. She sat down in a corner and pulled her knees up to her chin, her eyes brimming with tears. For some reason she was bleeding to death, and she was certain that now she would die.

But her inner voice said, *Not yet.*

Vianne was shaken awake by the rattle of bottles and a hand on her shoulder.

The uniformed milkman standing over her had a concerned look in his eyes, and he leaned down toward her. "Are you all ri—" he began, and then he saw the blood on various parts of her torn nightdress.

"*Mon Dieu,*" he said. "What has happened?"

Vianne merely shook her head. She had barely nodded off to sleep, and now she knew what she wanted to do.

"I will take you to the hospital," the man said.

Vianne put a hand to the front of his jacket, shaking her head *no*. In a whisper of bleak desperation she begged him to take her to the Benedictine convent on the rue Edmond Rostand. Her fist gripped his milkman's smock with a plain urgency, and her eyes pleaded with his.

She knew that in a hospital she would die in a strange, crowded room. But she wanted to expire in a familiar place. The convent, for all its faults, would have to do.

He stood up and looked at her in the dim light. Delivering milk in the district for two decades, he had seen far too much of the depths of the human condition and understood that the people of the streets, even at the point of death, had to be left alone to survive the way they knew how. *Who am I to interfere?* he thought.

He nodded and put an arm around her, helping her stand. Then he led her out of the building and carefully helped her up into the passenger seat of the shabby milk delivery van.

He got into the driver's seat and took her to the convent.

Vianne staggered into the nunnery's anteroom, sat down exhausted on one of the wooden chairs against the wall, and instantly fell asleep.

Five minutes later, one of the other orphans who slept in a dormitory bed next to Vianne's walked into view and froze in her steps.

Seeing Vianne asleep with the heavy smears of blood on her clothes, she was tempted to run and get one of the Sisters, but there were no nuns in the vicinity, as prayers were going on in the chapel. She walked up to the sleeping girl and tapped her shoulder until she came groggily awake. Then she put an arm around her, and the two made their way to the dormitory.

The girl's name was Adèle Dupuy, a shy, pale redhead who was a year older than Vianne. Her features were plain, and she had a large, dark birthmark on one side of her neck that disappeared down into her high-collared, buttoned-up blouse.

Adèle eased the woozy girl over to her narrow bed. She helped Vianne strip, throwing the bloodstained clothes into a corner. She brought over a shallow bowl of water and some soap, and carefully bathed the now-sleeping Vianne. Then she gently wrapped her own worn nightgown around the unconscious girl as best she could, and sat down on the next bed over.

Though the two were not particularly friends, Adèle sat and watched the girl, and thought she knew what had happened.

Vianne didn't wake up until late afternoon, and Adèle had since gone out and returned with some bread and sardines from the convent's commissary. She sat with Vianne on the side of the bed.

"I'm dying," Vianne whispered as she stared at the floor. "Bleeding to death."

Adèle smiled compassionately. "No you're not."

Vianne's eyes had lost their luster. "*Je veux me tuer.*"

Adèle was alarmed. She sensed that this girl just might indeed be capable of killing herself. "How old are you?" she asked, shifting the conversation as best she could.

Vianne looked at her. "Fifteen."

"You're a bit later there than most girls." Adèle gave the confused and frightened girl a hug and explained what was happening to her body—what to expect and what to do. She was surprised that Vianne knew almost nothing about it.

Vianne had discussed the topic once or twice with her older street friend Chloé, but she was taken by surprise by the actual event, especially because it had occurred during what could have been a fatal rape.

The two teenagers talked into the night, Vianne's despondency slowly dissipating. She discovered that although Adèle was completely knowledgeable about female anatomy, she sorely lacked even a scintilla of feminine self-worth.

The shy, fair girl believed the convent to be the only escape from another familiar rough life in another familiar Marseille rat hole. And Adèle had finally decided to become a novitiate on the way to becoming a nun.

Vianne listened carefully and realized something was very wrong with the girl. As the night wore on, it finally came out in a sob-wracked story. Adèle herself had been raped when she was very young, and her psyche had been severely wounded and never allowed to heal.

Vianne put a hand on the girl's slumped shoulder and whispered that even though the world outside the convent was difficult at best, deadly at worst, she was special and pretty and smart and had a future.

Adèle touched the birthmark on her neck and looked at the floor. "*Non,* I'll be all right, Vianne. It's orderly here, and I feel safe."

That makes one of us, Vianne thought.

She looked into Adèle's pale blue eyes and smiled. Then she reached into a fold in her worn mattress and pulled out a thin silver chain with a dangling charm on it—a tiny, silver, five-pointed star. She had stolen it from one of the foster homes she had lived in for a very short time, and now she pushed it into Adèle's hand.

"I couldn't take this," Adèle protested weakly, but she instantly loved the bauble, and her eyes couldn't conceal the fact. No one had ever given her anything like it. She clutched it to her chest and leaned forward.

Vianne thought Adèle meant to kiss her cheek, but instead she placed her lips over Vianne's with surprising force. Vianne's eyes went wide, and she gently pushed the girl away.

Adèle flushed with embarrassment. "I'm sorry," was all she could say.

Vianne was silent.

"I … I thought …" Adèle stuttered.

Vianne tilted her head in a question.

Adèle looked down and almost trembled with shame. "I thought that since you've been hurt so much by men, that you … I …"

Vianne gave her a small reassuring smile and whispered, "Everyone hurts you if they can—men, women. It's life."

She put a finger to Adèle's cheek and pressed away a tear. "You saved me, Adèle," she said, her mouth close to the trembling girl's ear. "I won't forget. Ever."

Adèle looked at her with a question in her eyes.

Vianne sighed silently. She was tired of the ghastly results of the nuns' intentions, well meant or otherwise, that had put her in danger more times than not—and this time had almost killed her.

Along her life's path, she had learned some ways to protect herself, most of them usually involving knives and other sharp weapons.

"Come with me?" Vianne whispered, but she knew that the gentle girl would refuse.

Adèle Dupuy shook her head. "Where will you go?" she asked, searching Vianne's face.

Vianne thought carefully before she answered. She couldn't risk anyone learning the small plan that she had been working on, not even this good and kind friend.

She leaned over toward Adèle, and quietly breathed, "*Dans l'avenir.*"

Into the future.

CHAPTER 5

Red and Black and Rat

———

THE FOLLOWING MORNING AFTER PRAYERS, Vianne appeared at Mother Odette's office door.

The nun's reaction to her appearance wasn't what Vianne had expected.

"Back again, eh?" The woman peered over her rimless reading glasses, her mouth bent in sarcasm. "Turning into a real boomerang, aren't you, miss?"

Vianne hadn't actually wanted to say anything to the Mother Superior, just gauge her face, which she did immediately. She stood still and said nothing, and thought, *No surprises.*

"Well," the nun said, sighing mightily. "I guess I have to not only smooth over another disappointed adopting couple, but make room for you here again." She made a face that shouted of the heavy burden that Vianne's return had brought back to the convent and to her in particular.

"Go, leave me now, and try for once to repent for your sins, *Vivienne.*"

Vianne turned and walked out, not dignifying the woman's transparently intentional mistake with any kind of a reaction.

On a sunny morning in July, Vianne informed the nuns that she was going to leave the convent for good. The Sisters wrung their hands and fingered their rosaries in a show of thin concern, but after a meeting with the Mother Superior and a few prayers, they shrugged and found peace in their belief that it was God's will.

The time was at hand to bid Vianne a final *adieu*.

Just as they had noncommittally resigned themselves to the chore of simply showing the girl the door, Mother Odette summoned Vianne to her office. "Stay with us one more day, *Vivienne*." The solicitous words fell from her mouth in surprisingly sincere tones. "You cannot just wake up in the morning and leave us. You have your goodbyes to make, and prayers to say. And I would like you to meet an old friend of mine—someone who will certainly help you."

Vianne hesitantly nodded in agreement, feeling that perhaps she did owe the nuns at least a modicum of thanks for feeding her and putting her through school. And she preferred to err on the side of patience and prudence—to make a clean exit from the convent, leaving no animosity behind.

She was dismissed from the room, and Odette was left thinking about that friend of hers—Zelda.

Zelda lived in a distant section of the city. One telephone call from Odette to the aged woman, and the fragile dowager had happily agreed to take in the fifteen-year-old named Vianne.

Praise God, thought Mother Odette, placing the receiver back in its cradle. She smiled a modest and selfless smile. *When all else fails,* she reassured herself, *it all comes down to Zelda.*

The next day, the old lady was driven up to the convent in a black Citroën and helped up the steps by her new driver and bodyguard, Benito. It was his first week on the job, a job that the large man seemed to relish with quiet attention. He remained guarding the car as one of the nuns escorted Zelda to Mother Odette's office.

The Mother Superior was happy, and she sent one of the novitiates to find and fetch Vianne. The mistress of the convent had gotten to know Zelda well over time, and they were good friends. She chatted with the old woman for a few minutes, and smiled mildly as Zelda reached into her large purse and then gingerly handed over a thick envelope.

Odette discreetly made the sign of the cross in front of her and carefully pushed the bulging envelope into a fold in her black habit. Then she glanced upward to heaven while Zelda turned her watery blue eyes and all attention to Vianne, who had just walked silently into the room.

I know that God works in mysterious ways, the Mother Superior said peacefully to herself.

What Odette *didn't* know was that Vianne, child of the streets and wanderer of the docks, knew with sickening horror exactly who Zelda was. The silent girl took a single look at the aged woman and froze in her tracks.

She had seen Zelda more than one time, and had heard many things. Being the quiet listener that she was, Vianne already knew all she needed to know about Zelda Latour.

For the last forty years, Zelda had carefully nurtured her shadowy reputation as a reliable procurer and provider of girls and very young women to the wealthy underbelly of the South of France and other points on the Mediterranean compass. She was known as the Rainbow Madam, believed to be a reference to her varied, extensive, and available inventory of young women—*very* young women—for rent or for sale.

Now, at eighty-two, she had found that her sex-slave business was better than ever. Vast new quantities of drug cash were pouring through Marseille, and a whole new crop of eager customers for her latest high-quality acquisitions had popped up, making her a busy old *entrepreneuse* indeed.

It had occurred to her that to keep her supply of *product*—young, underage women—from drying up during this seller's market, she should keep an open mind to all sources. Because she was Catholic by birth, the convent had seemed a perfect supplier for Zelda, and she had been nurturing her mutually beneficial relationship with Mother Odette for the last dozen years.

And Benito, stout, muscular, and vastly pitiless, was Zelda's brand new and very capable enforcer in charge of keeping the Rainbow Madam's inventory in line.

Now the octogenarian grinned as her mental cash register ticked off the marketable features embodied so beautifully in the girl standing before her: sparkling dark eyes, luxurious, thick black hair, clear, mellow-taupe skin, ample enough breasts for a girl her age, and a stature that seemed more suited to a woman bred on the Champs-Élysées than a wastrel from a Marseille slum.

As an added plus, the girl seemed mute. *Merveilleux!* What an extraordinary feature, sure to qualify for an extra surcharge to her price.

Zelda mentally rubbed her hands together in delight. Better to get her away from this nunnery, out of these rags, and into some decent clothes *tout de suite. This one's going to fly off the shelf,* the old harpy thought gleefully. The idea of a spirited bidding war between a few of her wealthiest clients sprang happily to mind.

"I'm so glad you're coming to live with me, *chéri,*" she rasped as they headed for the door.

The Rainbow Madam smiled, demonstrating that most of her teeth were still in her head and capped with gold. Then she walked out carefully, one hand clutching the arm of the black-haired girl with the marketable dark eyes and the very valuable speech impediment.

The heavy door to the convent shut behind them with a decisive slam.

Vianne held Zelda's arm as they came down the steps of the convent to the sidewalk. Her adrenaline level had soared, and her eyes darted to the left and right. She was about to let the old lady go and take off running when she saw the car.

The black Citroën waited on the street, motor running, a menacing brute of a driver standing by its open door, an ominous look in his flat-black eyes. Vianne nearly gagged in the grip of blossoming fear, but the germ of a tiny strategy had grown quickly in her head. She decided to play the part of solicitous young helper until the last possible second.

Benito watched balefully from the sidewalk as the old lady and the striking young woman approached. The man needed to demonstrate to this latest piece of good-looking meat that from this moment onward her life was no longer hers. He shifted his weight from one leg to the other, and his lips tightened.

Vianne studied the bodyguard for another long second, and her heart nearly stopped.

I recognize him.

A few more steps, her mind screamed as she and the old madam slowly approached the black Citroën. *Three more steps to go. Two … one …*

They had almost reached the car when Vianne abruptly stopped, stepped behind Zelda, and pushed the old lady into Benito.

The move was so fast that the big man could only grab at Zelda while trying to stay upright. The old pimp made a startled crow-like sound and clawed at the surprised bodyguard. It took the man a few moments to get his balance back, see that the girl had taken flight, and quickly manhandle Zelda into the backseat of the Citroën.

When he straightened up, he saw Vianne at the end of the block. She was running flat out and in a moment had quickly veered to the right and disappeared around the corner.

Benito got behind the wheel of the car, put it into gear, and took off after his employer's property.

Vianne zigzagged through the few clots of pedestrians on the sidewalk. She could easily have ducked into one of the alleys or doorways that she passed but knew that it would be safer if she could reach the docks. It was an area she knew well, and it was the best place in the world to hide.

And the wharfs and the ships were at the crux of the small plan she had been nurturing. She reasoned that if she stood any kind of a long-term chance, it was there on the docks that she would be able to truly find a doorway to a new life. It would be a huge risk, but she was ready to take whatever came next.

Halfway down the next block, she looked to the left and saw a worn bicycle leaning unattended against a dusty storefront window. With hardly a thought, Vianne ran to it, took its handlebars, swept one leg over the frame, and aimed the bike out into the street.

She pedaled hard, her soul burning. Her brain was working fast, but kept circling back to what had just happened at the convent.

She sold me, she said bitterly to herself as she zoomed between honking cars and across intersections. *I should have left yesterday. By trying to do the right thing, I gave Odette time to arrange to sell me to that* maquereau, *that vile old pimp woman.*

I should have seen it coming.

Behind her she heard the sound of a car horn and screeching tires, and at the next corner she took a hard right and guided the bicycle across the busy rue de Lyon and down toward the wharfs.

She pedaled a few more blocks and had almost made it to dockside when a roar on her right made her turn her head quickly. The Citroën pulled up, screeching, in front of her, blocking half the sidewalk. She couldn't stop in time, and ran the bike straight into the driver's door, which Benito had quickly swung open.

Vianne's head smacked hard into the car's bodywork, and she saw stars as she was knocked off the wrecked bike onto the pavement. She landed on her stomach on the concrete, but her animal sense of survival took over, and she quickly pushed herself to her knees. She shook her head, and a moment later saw that the large man was now out of the car and reaching for her.

She saw his lips move in a strange grin, a grin she had seen before—six years before. He was the huge man who had accompanied the vicious cop those six long years ago—the cop who had slapped her to the gutter for stealing a single peach for her mother. The man had laughed along with the policeman, and Vianne had immediately seen that he and the filthy cop were fast friends, peas in a pod.

That he would remember her now—remember the insignificant street animal she had appeared to him to be—was unlikely. And she was now six years older.

Vianne saw that the deep trouble she was in had immediately expanded to the next level.

His thick arms went around her waist, and he lifted her off the ground as if she weighed nothing.

She twisted with all her strength and clawed viciously at his face. One of her slender fingers gouged his right eye, and he bellowed. She pushed the finger as far into the socket as it would go and then hooked it out.

One or two pedestrians turned their heads at the sound of Benito's unearthly scream as his eyeball was dislodged from its socket.

As they were locked together in a bizarre and desperate struggle, the giant reared up bellowing like an enraged beast, the slender, frantic girl trapped in his powerful arms. He snarled ferociously as a torrent of blood from his eye socket splayed across and down his face and into his open mouth.

He spat a loud obscenity and threw Vianne as though she were a rag doll. The girl flew a dozen feet and crashed onto the pavement. She felt bolts of pain in her left arm and right leg, and sprawled, dazed, on the sidewalk.

Benito was standing, his legs apart, howling at the sky above the buildings. Then he lowered his red-splashed face and looked at Vianne. The mad stare from his one good eye was like the flame of a blowtorch—a blowtorch burning out just one word: *kill*. He pulled a gun from beneath his jacket, and the few pedestrians who had gathered at a distance scattered like frightened mice.

Vianne tried desperately to stand, but her right ankle gave way. She made a feeble effort to lever herself up against the brick wall of a nearby building but succeeded only in kneeling. She looked down. Between her knees on the filthy pavement lay the stiff body of a dead rat.

Her inner voice: *Do it.*

Benito had abandoned any lingering resemblance to a rational human, and in a blind rage raised his gun at Vianne from the short distance between them. He flicked the safety off the automatic and squeezed the trigger at the same moment the rock-hard rat carcass hit him in his dangling eyeball.

It was enough. The bullet smashed into the wall behind Vianne, missing her by a few inches. The sound of the shot was so loud that for a moment she thought she had gone deaf.

She fell back to the ground and tried to pull and roll herself down the street away from the killer. Her ankle and her left arm were afire with pain, and her head ached mightily.

What was left of Benito's sanity exploded like a grenade, and in the next moment he was above her, a dark, towering figure blocking the sun. He leaned down, and with one giant hand firmly held her shoulder while the other pushed the muzzle of the gun to her temple.

She looked up and saw the insanity in his ruined face, and knew that she was going to die and see her mother again in the next few seconds. She tried to shake her head, the stars in her dark eyes flashing in hopeless defiance, and in the last and final seconds, thought she saw a man in a business suit a dozen yards away. He was running toward her.

But he was too far and too late.

She tried to turn her head a last time and spit at the monster, but the pistol's steely barrel pressing at her temple made her too dizzy to move another inch.

She closed her eyes tightly as Benito twisted the muzzle with a savage finality, and heard him holler the Sicilian word "*Mortu!*" at the top of his lungs. And then the sound of gun blasts filled the world.

Her eyes remained squeezed shut, and she felt the steel drop away from her temple and then a thick splash of hot rain on her face and arms. Reluctantly she opened her eyes.

Benito still loomed above her, but there was something wildly wrong with him. She blinked in terror-filled disbelief, and her eyes went wider. It seemed as if the man's head was almost falling off his body. A huge chunk of his neck was missing. Blood was hosing and spurting out in all directions, splattering her and the brick wall and the sidewalk and the side of the Citroën with hot bright red.

Benito froze in place for a second, the gun still clutched in his fist, and then he suddenly crashed down on top of Vianne like a felled tree. His massive body sprawled across her, arms and legs jerking violently.

Her breath was knocked out of her, and she was on the verge of fainting. She tried with waning strength to crawl away to safety. But her arm, stuck beneath the heavy, heaving man, was ablaze with a fiery agony and her ankle was shot through with pain.

I'm at the end. Her head pounded and her heart was nearly exploding with fear as the man's immense body twitched out even more blood. *What's happening? Why am I alive? What should I do now?*

Her inner voice said, *Nothing.*

And in the next moment, the street, the buildings, the sky itself, began to shimmer and turn to water as her vision faded to a flat, dark void.

As her arms lay outstretched on the rough pavement of the filthy Marseille street, Vianne's gleaming black hair slowly fanned out across the shining river of Benito's red blood.

CHAPTER 6

Broken Savior

———————

SHE SWAM UP FROM A dark well and took a few deep breaths.

Her head hurt, but not as much as her left arm, and her right ankle was also pounding. She thought she heard faint noises of faraway cars, and the basso *moo* of a distant ship's horn, but the sounds were muffled. She realized that she was no longer on the street, and it slowly occurred to her that she hadn't yet gone to the stars.

Vianne opened her eyes.

Around her was the white of a hospital room: white ceilings and white walls and a single white sheet to cover her. And her hospital gown was white, as were the bandages on her head, her arm, and her foot.

She was in a bed with her head raised on a disinfectant-smelling pillow. She cautiously let her eyes scan down her body and saw that her left arm from her hand to elbow was now in a stiff cast. She worked her legs out from under the sheet to find her right ankle was wrapped as well, but just in soft bandages.

She raised her good hand to her forehead and felt a wide, tight swath of gauze. She assumed it was white as well, that it matched everything else. She looked to the left and right, at the other three beds in the room. They lay perfectly made up and empty.

Who brought me here?

She lay still, waiting.

As if in response to her silent confusion, an austere, hatchet-faced nurse appeared at the door. She had a faint mustache, and her dark hair was drawn back under a starched white cap. She walked into the room and stood at the foot of the bed.

"You are awake, young lady," she announced unnecessarily in a dry voice. "*Bon.*"

Vianne looked at her and cautiously whispered, "*Qu'est-ce qui s'est passé?*"

The nurse snorted. "It seems you were in a bad accident. And if it weren't for your guardian, it could have been much worse for you, Isabelle." The woman gave a grudging little smile.

Who? Isabelle?

Then she nearly retched when she realized that the *guardian* was Zelda Latour, who had certainly seen everything that had transpired from the backseat of the Citroën. The girl's empty stomach turned at the thought.

But the nurse went on. "Monsieur Duval left us with instructions to contact him the moment you regained consciousness." She studied her patient for another few seconds, turned her back on the injured girl, and left the room.

Vianne's eyes narrowed. *Who's Monsieur Duval?*

Her inner voice said, *Stay alert,* but she was suddenly overcome with fatigue and closed her eyes for what seemed a minute.

It was an hour.

Her insistent bladder finally woke her, and she managed to swing her feet off the side of the bed. She gently placed them on the floor, and quickly discovered that it would be a while until she could put weight on her right foot. She hobbled across the room to the loo.

Coming out of the bathroom she saw a handsome, middle-aged man in a business suit standing near her empty bed alongside the starchy nurse. He looked at Vianne and quickly crossed the room.

She expected him to either hold her elbow or perhaps put an arm around her shoulder. But instead he swept her up off her feet as though she were weightless, and carried her in his arms to the bed. He set her down gently and stepped back a few paces.

Then he gave the nurse a severe look, and the woman haughtily adjusted her cap and made a quick exit.

The room was still.

Vianne studied the man. *Is he a doctor?*

He looked to be in his late forties and had a head of thick salt-and-pepper hair. His gray eyes were the color of an angry sky and shone with intelligence. A strong Roman nose, tight, thin lips, and a natural tan gave him a roguish look, and he radiated a relaxed but unquestionably dominating presence.

He looked at Vianne with obvious concern. "How do you feel?" His deep voice was overlaid with a faint and unfamiliar accent.

She nodded and softly whispered, "*Bien.*" She looked at him for half a strangely uncomfortable minute, and then breathed, "*Merci.*"

The man nodded and pulled a chair up to the bed so he could sit next to her. Vianne noticed that he smelled fresh, as if he had just come down from a high mountain.

He looked at her and said, "You are one of Zelda's girls?"

The question jolted Vianne, and she lowered her head slightly and slowly shook her head.

He studied her midnight eyes. Finally he said, "My name is César. César Duval." He watched her face and waited. Then he said, "What's yours?"

She hesitated but then felt her inner voice: *Tell him.*

"Vianne." It was the faintest of breaths.

He smiled. "That's a beautiful name."

She watched him. There was little else to do, nothing else to say.

"You've been here for over a day. I brought you here." He paused for a moment. "I had no way of finding out who you were, so I called you Isabelle. It was the first name that came to mind."

Vianne nodded.

The man got up slowly and paced next to the bed for a few moments. He stopped, looked at the girl again, and said, "You left the convent with Zelda. You are an orphan?"

Vianne felt sick. *What does this man want from me?*

She nodded.

César walked over to the window and distractedly watched a tanker out at sea making its glacial approach toward the busy port. Without turning to her he said carefully, "Vianne, have you ever seen me before?"

Vianne was about to whisper *non,* but suddenly stopped. Something in the back of her mind clicked.

The events on the previous day came flooding back: She had lain injured in the street, and the insane Benito had pushed his gun at her head. Through the terror, she had seen someone running toward her from several yards away.

Vianne realized with sudden clarity that without a doubt, it was this man, César.

"*Oui,*" she whispered to the man's back.

He didn't move, and Vianne couldn't see that his eyes had closed.

He had followed the black Citroën in his Alfa Romeo for the better part of the previous day, and was puzzled when it had pulled up in front of the Benedictine convent. He had parked at a safe distance down the block and watched the old pimp enter the building. But more important, he watched the driver, Benito.

Got him, César thought, seeing the hulking man take up a position outside the nunnery. But it was too open, too public for César to take advantage of the opportunity. So he waited and watched.

After the better part of an hour, Zelda emerged from the building with a young woman by her side. César squinted through his sunglasses at the girl with the shining black hair, and his mouth opened in shock.

And in soul-shaking disbelief.

But there had been little time to organize his emotions. As the two approached the Citroën, the girl had suddenly shoved

Zelda into Benito and sprinted away down the block. César saw that she was running for her life.

He saw the bodyguard manhandle Zelda into the backseat of the Citroën and get into the driver's seat.

César started the Alfa, put it in gear, and pulled out into the street. He was in a quandary. *Which one do I follow?* he asked himself: *Benito, or*—*her?*

Reasoning that now both he and Benito had an interest in the girl, but that the burly bodyguard was a dangerously capable aggressor, he opted to follow the Citroën as it took off through the streets of Marseille.

In a matter of a minute or two, César spotted the girl. Now she was a block ahead on a bicycle. *She's resourceful,* he thought to himself as he watched her cutting off traffic and making for the docks.

He dogged Benito's car as it slalomed through the streets, but two minutes into the chase, he was suddenly cut off by cross traffic for what seemed an eternity. Finally breaking out of the jam, he thought he had lost the Citroën, but a few seconds later he saw it was just a block ahead of him—parked at an angle, halfway up on the sidewalk.

César quickly stopped the Alfa and jumped out. He started walking toward the black car, but froze at the sight of the tableau unfolding in front of him.

Benito was out of his car and had the struggling girl in his arms. One of the man's eyes had been levered out of its socket and was hanging down obscenely against his blood-wet cheek. As the girl struggled to free herself from the man's grip, the huge man bellowed in agony, and a moment later, flung her through the air.

César saw the girl's black hair gleam in the light as she flew. She hit the ground hard, in obvious agony, and at that moment something inside César Duval's brain exploded. He surged forward. As he ran toward Benito, he pulled a Colt .45 automatic from the inside of his suit jacket. Not a moment too soon.

Benito, in his blinding rage, had fired a single wild shot that had missed the girl, but then he pushed the muzzle of his revolver against her head. The one-eyed man screamed once like a wild animal, and the injured girl shut her eyes.

César, now just a few yards away, squeezed off two fast, deafening shots.

Both bullets blasted through Benito's neck, almost decapitating him. The large man dropped his gun, and a second later crashed to the ground amid a powerfully violent spray of arterial blood. The girl lay beneath his convulsing body, and as César approached, he saw her try to crawl away and then finally lie still.

He took a quick, hard look at the bloody mess that was Benito's neck, and in the grip of a red fury kicked the dead man's head hard. The last damaged cervical vertebra parted, and the head detached from the body with a *crunch* and rolled into the gutter, coming to rest facing the carcass of a dead rat.

César disregarded the screams of a few horrified onlookers, and kneeled down at the unconscious girl's side. "It's all right," he whispered as he carefully lifted her in his arms and walked quickly to his Alfa Romeo.

Gently placing her limp body across the backseat, he got in behind the wheel, heedless of who may have seen him but oddly confident that he would not be followed or found. He knew where the hospital was, a matter of a mile or so.

Not again, he said to himself over and over as he drove with a mad urgency through the streets of Marseille.

Not again …

He turned from the window and studied the girl lying silently in the white bed. She was watching him, and the uncertainty and loneliness radiating from her eyes was almost palpable. *God, she looks so much like* her, he thought, the sting of a familiar yearning piercing his heart.

He walked over to the bed and looked down at the girl. "I spoke to the doctor," he said. "Your wrist is broken, and he assures me that he's set it properly. The cast will come off partially tomorrow and then completely in a week or two."

The girl just looked at him as he went on. "Your ankle, it is very bruised, but only sprained. Not broken. You'll be walking on it in a few days. Running, a bit later."

Her eyes tugged at him.

"And you have a bump on your head like an egg." He saw her furrow her brow. "A small egg," he added quickly. "A sparrow's egg."

He slowly sat down on the end of the bed. After a few moments his face got serious and he said, "That nunnery is your home?"

She shook her head slowly and in a voice no louder than a breath said, "*Je ne sais pas.* I can no longer go back there." She thought again about Mother Odette, the woman who had sold her to Zelda, and her eyes narrowed.

A few seconds went by. Then she whispered, "I have no home."

"Mother, father?" César asked quietly.

Another slow shake of the head. "*Morts.*" Dead.

He stared at a spot in the middle distance, obviously deep in thought. After a long minute he leaned closer and gently took her uninjured hand in his large dry one. "I imagine I saved your life, did you know that?"

She nodded.

"Some say that by doing that, I have interfered with the will of the gods." He raised his eyebrows for a moment and continued. "And that would mean that from this point onward, I am responsible for you, for your safety—your life."

Her face had calmed, but inside she was torn. *Where is the man going with this? Whichever way I turn, I'll be in danger.* She gently pulled her hand out of his.

But she had listened very carefully thus far, not so much to what he was saying but to the tone, the timbre—the shadings of his voice. And she had watched his eyes with even more concentration. They were truthful, without hidden meanings or artifice, and in a dark place behind those eyes was a strange sadness.

Vianne waited in silence.

Finally he said, "I have a home for you. A good one, a safe one."

She whispered, "*Pourquoi*? Why did you save me?"

He looked over his shoulder at her and narrowed his eyes, but said nothing. The air in the room was still.

"Tell me."

The man stared at her for a minute, but stayed silent.

"*Vous devez,*" she whispered. You must.

César stared at her. No one dared tell him what he must or must not do. *Refreshing, from this girl,* he thought. A small smile crinkled his eyes, a smile bittersweet with her soft command and with the painful knowledge of what the answer would reveal.

"Not now." The words were freighted with a subtext that Vianne couldn't grasp. He looked at the floor, seeing something that wasn't there.

Vianne pushed herself into a sitting position, the pillows at her back.

She breathed hard. So far, the man had been honest, she knew it—his face, his eyes couldn't lie.

After a minute went by, she whispered as soft as the wind, "César?"

He looked up at her at the sound of his name, spoken with the quietness of an orphan's smothered heart.

"You would protect me." It was more a soft statement than a question. The man stared at her, at the silent intensity in her eyes. Were there tiny stars in them? He nodded.

"Teach me."

"Teach you?" he asked.

"To protect *myself.*"

César nodded again. A long silence hung over them in the white hospital room.

Finally, watching his face intently, she whispered, "You won't hurt me." Once again a statement of fact as her gaze bore into his, scrutinizing his reaction to this, the most critical of her concerns.

The man suddenly became who he had been when he had first entered the room. She saw the strong confidence and power flood back into his face.

"No one will hurt you. I swear."

Vianne knew he was telling the truth. She heard it clearly in the landscape of his voice—saw it in the windows of his eyes.

After a moment she whispered, "Where are we going?"

He hesitated for a few seconds. "Corsica."

Vianne knew that many of the rough men in Marseille had ties to that island, but it had little effect on her. *Where are people not rough?* she asked herself. Her inner voice offered an answer: *The stars.*

What should I do?

Seeing the concern in her face, César said, "Not to worry. In our household we speak French almost exclusively. We revert to Corsican only when we're telling secrets." He winked at her.

She felt as if her world were balancing on the cusp of a seminal moment that would have a profound effect on her life ahead. She whispered so low that it sounded like a faraway breeze, "Do you know what today is?"

He looked at her quizzically, and said, "The first day of summer."

She smiled for the first time, and the white room around them was suddenly dull by comparison. "*Mon anniversaire.*" My birthday.

He laughed softly and marveled at the good omen, this final auspicious sign—it was someone else's birthday as well. Today *she* would have been twenty, had she been alive …

The Corsican sun was warm, and the blue sky infinite.

He and Isabelle had been spending that sparkling day in the port city of Ajaccio.

She had been the same age of the girl in the hospital bed, and on that sunny summer day her father had taken her into the capital resort to spend an afternoon together. He traveled much in his line of work, but made sure to spend time with his only daughter at every opportunity. They had a small lunch at a café near the docks where the yachts were lined up at gleaming attention.

They spoke of Isabelle's mother, who had died four years previously. The dark, exotically beautiful woman had been thrown from a horse in the rough hills of the Haute-Corse, and her neck had broken instantly.

It hadn't been easy for Isabelle, and for a year after her mother died, she wouldn't speak. Her father and her two older brothers had tried to compensate as best they could. One morning she had simply walked into their large kitchen and told them that she loved them.

From that point on, the healing had commenced. Life had been slowly returning to normal.

Until that single day in Ajaccio that changed everything.

After leaving the café, César indulged Isabelle with a shopping spree. At around three in the afternoon, the two came out of a woman's fashion shop, César's taupe-skinned, black-haired daughter radiant and happy with a shopping bag swinging from each hand.

In front of the store, Isabelle stopped walking and started to say something to her father. As he turned to look at her, at the face that was his legacy—the living memory of his darling wife—a car roared by on the street and a fusillade of ratcheting shots rang out. Dozens of rounds from a submachine gun slammed and ricocheted everywhere, crashing into the windows and façades of the stores behind them—into parked cars and a few innocent passersby.

César was slammed halfway around as one of the rounds smacked into his shoulder, and as he fell, he saw Isabelle collapse in a heap.

The two bodyguards who had accompanied him and his daughter at a short distance opened fire on the retreating car, but it was too late.

As he lay bleeding in the Ajaccio street, hugging his dead daughter, César's soul ignited like a bonfire and his heart felt on the verge of exploding. It was a long time before the police were able to pry his hands from Isabelle's lifeless body.

At the girl's funeral, César stood dressed in black with his injured arm in a sling, and made an oath. He swore to both God and Satan that he would dedicate the rest of his life to finding and killing whoever was responsible. And he would make any deal with whichever deity would accommodate him and somehow bring his daughter back.

He was forever and profoundly broken.

Someone had killed César Duval's daughter. And the bloodbath that ensued was one of the worst in the history of European organized crime.

He stared at the girl in the bed. He could not save his daughter, but he would save her.

"How old are you today, Vianne?"

In her almost inaudible voice she breathed, "*Seize.*"

Sixteen.

Boat

———

The next afternoon César returned with a large, paper-wrapped parcel. He put it on the hospital bed and pushed it toward the girl. *"Joyeux anniversaire,"* he said in his odd accent. Happy birthday.

Vianne smiled hesitantly, carefully tore away the wrap, and opened the box. Her eyes widened.

Inside was a neat pile of folded clothes. There was a deep red skirt, a few tops, a pair of low pumps wrapped in tissue, and ... *could it be?* Not one, but *two* pairs of Jordache jeans. *Il est impossible! I've never owned any clothes like this.*

"*Merci,*" she said, her whispering voice alight with happiness. "*Mille fois merci.*"

César summoned the starchy nurse, and he left the room while the woman helped Vianne dress. He sat outside in the hall, leafing through a copy of *La Provence de Marseille,* but he was distracted. The matter of the girl had hijacked his mind.

After a few minutes Vianne limped out into the hall, holding on to the nurse's elbow while awkwardly working a crutch. She wore one of the pairs of designer jeans and a loosely fitting white blouse. Her eyes gleamed, and her thick black hair tumbled over her shoulders.

His heart caught in his throat at the girl's similarity to Isabelle, both in her dress and in her smile, and a carefully guarded love stirred in his heart.

He rose and stepped up to her.

"Here," he said as he carefully took Vianne's good arm. The other was in a sling, but the heavy cast had been replaced by a shorter one that wrapped her wrist and lower hand.

César ordered the nurse away with a nod of his head, and in a few minutes he and Vianne were on the street in front of the hospital

In a moment a dark Mercedes-Benz pulled up at the curb in front of them. The Alfa Romeo had vanished—it had been at the scene of Benito's demise, and César didn't want to press his luck. The Italian car was now resting quietly at the bottom of the Mediterranean, a few hundred feet from the docks.

A slim, middle-aged man in sunglasses and a black suit was behind the wheel of the Benz. He jumped from the car and helped César carefully guide the injured girl into the backseat. Vianne thought the two were overdoing it slightly, but she had little experience with gentle men who gave a damn, so she kept silent.

"Let's go, Eduard," César said to the driver.

They headed toward the port, and in less than twenty minutes the car was making its way along one of the industrial wharfs where large freighters were loading and unloading their container cargo with the assistance of huge metal cranes. The scene was a familiar one to Vianne, who had walked these docks innumerable times over the years.

Eduard guided the Mercedes onto a concrete jetty, and there, hidden behind the bulk of a giant, dark gray tanker, was a sleek, white, seventy-foot Hatteras motor yacht. The area below the stern rail, which would normally display the name of the vessel, was blank—plain white.

As César helped Vianne up the short gangway, he said, "I hope you don't get seasick."

Vianne smiled slightly. *I wouldn't even know what that feels like.*

An older man standing at a break in the rail reached out to take her good hand. He had a trimmed white beard and wore a captain's hat.

He eyed Vianne curiously and touched César's arm. "She looks just like—" he began to say.

César interrupted him. "Take it slow, Gerard. I don't want you to get there until tomorrow."

The captain nodded and headed off to the bridge, glancing back one more time at the eerily familiar girl.

Vianne was trying to put the events of the last few days in context, but was coming up short. The men, the boat—it was jarringly different from anything she had known—intimidating and alien. She didn't trust what she was seeing, but didn't shy from it either.

I let this happen. This man César left the decision up to me. Now I have to make the best of things.

César took her down a narrow staircase to one of the cabins. It had a window with curved corners, a neatly made bed, and a few prints of famous paintings on the walls. There was a bathroom with a sink and shower, and a sideboard jammed with toiletries. It was clean—immaculate—and Vianne liked that immensely.

While César was putting her few things in the cabin's small closet, a woman appeared at the door behind him. She appeared to be in her forties, tall and slim, with highlighted auburn hair cascading to her shoulders and deep, smiling brown eyes. She wore a stylish, knee-length shift and smiled at Vianne.

"*Bienvenue*," she said.

César turned at the sound of her voice. "This is Jacqueline," he said to Vianne. "Whatever you need, just ask her."

Vianne was surprised, and her eyes asked César, *Where will you be?*

He was momentarily nonplussed by how the girl could ask a question with no words. The expression on her face alone—a shifting of her eyes, a tiny move of her mouth—had seemed to frame the unspoken request unequivocally.

He put a hand on each of her shoulders. "I'm going to the airport to fly on ahead. There are preparations to be made in Corsica." He smiled. "And I have business I need to take care of there."

Seeing the look of apprehension on the girl's face, he said, "Don't worry. I'll be waiting on the dock at Ajaccio when you arrive tomorrow." He smiled. "And remember: I made you a promise that I intend to keep."

He said to Jacqueline, "I don't think Vianne knows Corsican." He looked over at the quiet girl and tilted his head as if to say, *Do you?*

She shook her head. She knew nothing of the language.

César gave them each a light kiss on both cheeks, and a few seconds later he was gone.

The night before, César had told Jacqueline that he was taking this girl in, at least for a while. It hadn't surprised the woman—she had watched as her lover did many strange things, many things out of character for a man who led the kind of life he did.

But what was César expecting to accomplish? Jacqueline had asked herself. She knew that in this case he had let his heart rule the day, but had he thought it through?

Who was this girl—*woman,* almost—who looked so much like Isabelle? Jacqueline marveled at how César had a secretive yet outsize capacity for charity, but if his enemies saw what was going on here, they would think he had gone over the edge—become soft, maudlin, careless—crazy.

But he *was* César Duval, so his word was the law, she thought resignedly. And she trusted his judgment.

As she looked at the girl, she couldn't help thinking that through a mix of profound emptiness, rage, and the best of intentions, César had probably signed this unlucky orphan's death warrant.

"You must be hungry," she said to Vianne.

Vianne sat on the edge of the bed and nodded.

"So am I. Famished, in fact. Do you need help with that crutch?"

But Vianne was already standing without it and shook her head. Then she smiled and Jacqueline thought, Mon Dieu, *this girl is truly beautiful.*
There will be trouble coming.
Much trouble.

The sun streaming into the small window woke Vianne early. She had slept a dreamless sleep, lulled by the distant, steady hum of the boat's engines.

When she had dressed, she went up on deck to lean against the V of the yacht's bow, holding the railing tight, her eyes wide open. Ahead, the once-empty horizon had filled with the slowly approaching island that was Corsica.

The beaches, the protected harbor with its breakwater, its hundreds of boats, and its ocher-and-orange-roofed buildings were mesmerizing. In the distance, behind Ajaccio and its port, rough mountains dominated the horizon.

Vianne, who had never before left the city of Marseille, was spellbound.

Corsica is a territorial collectivity, a part of Metropolitan France, though Marseille lies around 250 miles across the water from Ajaccio.

The rough beauty of the island is undeniable. It is the most mountainous island in the Mediterranean. Thick forests and deep valleys dominate the interior, and half of its 3,300 square miles are wild, untamed nature preserves.

When Vianne set eyes on the island, it was home to around a quarter million people, two-thirds of them native Corsicans, with the rest being mostly displaced French nationals.

And among the Corsican natives was a small but powerful group of international outlaws, men who ruled their far-flung criminal organizations with iron fists, men who were rivaled in their ruthlessness only by their hated Sicilian Mafia counterparts.

One of those men was César Duval.

Vianne spotted César as the yacht slowly approached its dock at a stone jetty. He was leaning against a gleaming silver Maserati Quattroporte, wearing tan slacks and a black, open-collar shirt. Behind the wheel of the low-slung sedan, the driver, Eduard, sat watching everything carefully through his wraparound sunglasses.

When the boat had been tied up to the long stone pier and its short gangway lowered, César pushed himself off the car and strode up the ramp onto the deck. He saw Vianne at the bow and walked over to her.

He took her slim shoulders in his hands and said, "No seasickness?"

Vianne shook her head.

"How was the voyage?" he asked, stepping back a pace.

Her freshly washed hair was shot through with the sun's gleaming, and her dark eyes almost seemed to sparkle. "*Merveilleux.*" She gave his face a deep, searching look and whispered, "Is everything all right?"

He looked at her for a few seconds, surprised at the question, and then said, "*Oui,* nothing that can't be handled later."

Jacqueline, just coming on deck, looked at Vianne and said, "How was your sleep, *chéri?*"

The girl nodded. "*Bien.*"

Jacqueline turned to César. "She is a woman of few words."

Vianne shrugged, pushing out her lower lip.

"Silence," César said. "It's a vastly underrated character trait, much to be treasured." He looked at Jacqueline and raised an eyebrow. "Especially in a woman."

Jacqueline gave him an arch look. "*Bâtard!*" she said in a chiding voice.

"I missed you too," he said through his smile.

Then to both of them he said, "Let's go."

CHAPTER 8

Two Brothers

THE DUVAL ESTATE WAS TEN miles east of the city of Ajaccio.

It nestled in one of the valleys in the foothills of the mountain chain that ran north to south through the island. Deer, rock sheep, and boar roamed the thick cover of oaks, woodland, and pine forest.

The estate consisted of a large Tuscan-style home surrounded by seventy-five cleared acres with purposely unobstructed views. Bordering one edge of the property, at the base of the close, steep mountains, was one end of a half-mile-long lake—deep and indigo, clear and cold from the mountain streams that fed it.

There were a couple of smaller houses down the road from the main house and a low, reinforced concrete building with a metal roof that looked like a warehouse or a bunker.

A thousand feet up the steep, nearby mountainside, a modern single-story glass-walled building poked off the side of a pine-covered cliff. It was a contemporary, elegantly appointed villa, accessible only by an unpaved road, best traversed by one of the Duvals' four-wheel-drive all-terrain vehicles.

Vianne took it all in from the backseat of the car but found it difficult to put a meaning to what she was seeing. The scene was completely new to her—exciting and unsettling at the same time.

The Maserati pulled up at the main house, and a dark-haired man wearing casual but obviously expensive clothes came out the front door and stood, watching them. He stopped and waited while César, Jacqueline, and Vianne got out of the car.

Two large brown-and-black dogs shot out of the door and ran past the man.

César watched intently as the German shepherds made a mad dash for the newcomer. A few feet from their target they slowed down and approached the stranger warily.

Vianne stood calmly looking at each in turn. She had no fear, had experience with the semi-wild street dogs of Marseille, and knew what to do. She held out a closed hand to each of them. They approached her and took in her natural scent with obvious pleasure, and each gave her an appreciative lick.

Vianne looked up at César.

He scowled. "Solomon and Sheba. They guard against strangers. Very effective, as you can see."

The man at the front door walked toward them. He was six feet tall and in his late twenties with thick dark hair and gray eyes. As he came up to them, Vianne saw that he was almost too handsome to be real and was obviously fit, a product of careful bodybuilding. His only visible imperfection was a small, faded scar on one cheek.

He stared at Vianne with a look of mild amazement.

"Where's Bernard?" César asked him.

The man smiled out of the corner of his mouth and seemed unable to take his eyes off the girl. Finally he said, "Who knows? He wandered away to attend to something or other." Then he shrugged. "I guess he didn't care that you wanted him to stay around."

César ignored the comment and turned to Vianne, who was massaging Sheba's forehead. "This is my son Luc," he said.

Luc smiled, and Vianne saw his perfect teeth. "*Bonjour,*" she breathed.

He chuckled as he stared at her, white smile flashing. "*Salut,* Vianne. My father spent the better part of yesterday evening telling me you were coming." Finally he tore his eyes off the girl and glanced at César. "Unbelievable."

César scowled at his eldest son's lack of tact. He said to Vianne, "He's struck by how much you resemble my daughter. Please forgive his bad manners."

But Luc wouldn't be stopped. To Vianne he said, "My sister, Isabelle, could have been your twin. How old are you?"

"Sixteen."

He looked at César. "As old as *she* was when …"

"Luc!" César's voice was sudden and imperious. "That isn't why Vianne is here."

Luc rolled his eyes slightly and nodded. He turned to her and said in an even voice, "*Bienvenue.* Welcome to our home." Feeling his father's stare on the back of his head he added, "*Your* home now, I guess."

Vianne's eyes narrowed a millimeter as she felt the lightest chill in her spine. She wasn't sure of its nature or meaning, and stood perfectly still.

Jacqueline walked up from behind and took her hand. "I'll show you around," she said, and she sensed the girl's immediate relief. The two went into the house.

Luc watched them go, then threw a look of scorn at his father. "You're too sentimental, Papa. That girl is not Isabelle, never will be."

"Nevertheless, she is going to be a part of this family, at least for a while, until she can survive on her own. And you're going to help. Your sister was taken from us, and nothing will change that. I saved this girl's life on an impulse that I can't explain—only that Isabelle somehow directed me to do it. I believe that it is fate."

"Fate or otherwise, we have to address our latest problem. Randazzo called again while you were away."

César grunted. "You're going to tell me that the Sicilians will wait no longer." His voice was uncharacteristically hesitant.

Luc nodded.

César looked at the nearby mountains on the other side of the valley, and seemed to make up his mind. "We'll have to finish the trade and pay them soon. I need to talk to old man Randazzo himself in Palermo."

Luc started toward the house. "I'll get him on the phone."

His father followed, lost in thought.

In the large, country-style kitchen, a short, squat woman, her thick, gray hair done up in a chignon, stood by the sink, intent on her work. She was smoothing a large oval of dough with a wooden rolling pin, but stopped when she heard the door open. She looked up and wiped two strong, floury hands on her apron.

"Marta, this is Vianne," Jacqueline said as the two came into the room.

The woman's black eyes widened. *"Dio mio! Questo è Isa—."* She stopped midsentence, not taking her eyes from the girl, and the rolling pin nearly fell from her hands. She crossed herself in earnest.

Jacqueline walked over to her and said in Corsican, "She's our guest." She looked back and added, "I hope for a long time."

Marta fussed with her apron for a few more seconds as she looked frankly at Vianne. Then, as if coming to a decision, she said, *"Benvenuti."* Welcome.

Vianne smiled and whispered, barely above a breath, *"Merci."*

Marta looked at Jacqueline, her doughy face freighted with questions.

"She can only whisper," Jacqueline said. "In French."

Marta nodded slowly and turned back to Vianne, not sure if the inability to speak in a normal voice was the mark of a devil or an angel. The old cook looked intently into the starlight eyes, and her thick fingers closed around Vianne's hand, deciding it was both. She said in bad French, *"Salut,* Vianne. The quiet is the blessed thing, eh?" She smiled broadly, showing Vianne that she still had every tooth in her sixty-five-year-old mouth.

Then she turned to Jacqueline and ordered in rough Corsican, "Now get out of my kitchen, strumpet, and take our new guest as well. I am making you and *il Bosso* your favorite bread, which *you* never seem to eat. While it's baking, I'll fix something special for Vianne."

She released the girl's hand, winked at her, let her black eyes travel up and down the girl's body in a critical way, and continued in tortured French, "You are needing something solid—you look as if you could faint from hunger. Prepare yourself for real food."

A small sense of relief began to worm its way into Vianne's deep and natural nervousness. The old woman's worn face was guileless, transparent as a mountain stream, and Vianne was quietly moved by the plain sincerity she saw flowing from it. She liked Marta instantly, and vowed to spend time with her. *Maybe she would help me learn Corsican,* she thought, shrugging inside. *Yes, probably, whether I want to or not.*

Jacqueline helped Vianne put her few things away in an upstairs bedroom, then led her through the house. Back on the main floor, they wound up in the large, sunny living room. Its opulence and size, like most of the house, was intimidating to Vianne. And she was feeling tired—her arm had started aching badly, and she was having a bit more trouble walking.

"May I rest?" she asked Jacqueline in a barely audible voice.

They sat on a long leather couch and looked out the tall French doors onto the forest and mountains. Vianne turned to Jacqueline and was about to whisper something more when a man walked into the room. He came to an abrupt stop, a look of shock on his face.

Vianne knew at once that this was Luc's younger brother, Bernard. He had many of Luc's features, and he was an inch or two shorter than Luc, a bit under six feet tall. He was likewise very fit, but unlike his older brother, he was muscular from what was obviously hard, outdoor work—not from preening with barbells in front of mirrors.

His face was slightly off: his cheekbone and jaw had been broken sometime in the past, and had healed unevenly. And he had the same Duval stormy-gray eyes.

He stood rock still in well-used work clothes and stared in openmouthed confusion at the girl.

After a few uncomfortable seconds, Jacqueline said, "Bernard, this is Vianne."

The young woman was instantly aware that his face wasn't the only thing slightly off about Bernard. His eyes traveled hesitantly to Jacqueline, and he mouthed the name *Isabelle*.

The woman slowly shook her head. "No, this is *Vianne*. Remember what your father told you. She'll be living here."

It seemed as if Bernard was thinking this over with a grave intensity. Finally he lifted his head a bit and took a few steps toward the couch until he was towering over the two women.

"Vivienne" he said, his voice low and steady. He looked at the girl for another moment, and then quickly cast his eyes downward.

She stood up slowly, mindful of her ankle, and breathed quietly, "*Bonjour,* Bernard. Not Vivienne, *Vianne*."

"Vi-*anne,*" he said softly and carefully, still looking at the floor and mimicking her whisper.

She nodded and smiled, an uncertain fear in the back of her mind.

But he lifted his eyes, and his ruined face lit up in a huge, open smile. "Vi-*anne,*" he repeated with quick and obvious joy. "*Vianne.*"

Before she knew what was happening, Bernard had put a hand on either side of her slender waist and lifted her three feet straight up as if she weighed nothing. She looked down at him and felt a bit relieved. Though this man was obviously damaged, she realized, there weren't going to be any problems.

He just kept looking up at her and smiling. The emotion in his eyes was happily crystal clear, and Vianne immediately understood that her similarity to his dead sister was affecting him hugely and in a good way. In a soft, almost intimate whisper, she said, "Careful, *s'il te plaît.* My ankle is sore."

Bernard was suddenly aghast at his own clumsiness. He lowered Vianne with exaggerated gentleness and glacial slowness. After a full fifteen seconds, a toe of one of her shoes gently touched the floor, and a moment later she stood looking up at him.

She smiled again and whispered, "*Merci,* Bernard."

"Vianne," he said again, loving the way it resonated in his clear and simple mind. "Vianne."

Vianne looked over at Jacqueline.

The woman smiled ironically and said, "Welcome to the family."

CHAPTER 9

Lycée

"STAY HERE WITH US. MAYBE until you are eighteen or nineteen. However long you like."

Vianne knew that although César's request for her to stay was sincere, he didn't expect her to decline or to protest. She laughed to herself. *Where would I go, anyway?* But neither did she feel that she was a prisoner in a velvet jail.

César regularly traveled out of the country on business, which gave Vianne time to assess her new situation. The estate in the valley was beyond anything she had ever experienced, but she slowly adjusted from a life of paucity to one of comfortable sufficiency.

And she loved the small, modern glass villa that jutted out from the steep mountain cliff a thousand feet above the property. Because it was hardly used by the family, she staked it out as her own private place, sometimes spending nights on its patio, cantilevered over the valley, gazing at the stars.

She wasn't at all bothered by some of the oddities of life at the estate, especially the unconscious but pervasive emphasis on security that everyone lived with on a daily basis. Guns were secreted around the house, under couches and beds—even Marta had a loaded automatic hidden in her kitchen.

As her first year in the Duval house progressed, Vianne developed a huge liking and a tremendous respect for César. She finally decided that he wasn't trying to replace his lost daughter after all. His motivations were clearly those of a man who felt an imperative to save someone whom he saw would have inevitably perished if he hadn't stepped in.

Perhaps, by saving me, he was atoning for past sins.

He had automatically understood Vianne's initial fears, and had given her the space she needed to assess her life and come to her own decisions. And he possessed the understanding, uncommon in many men, to recognize that the girl's blossoming beauty could be more a hindrance to her than an asset.

At first Vianne had a problem with Luc.

Luc lived at César's house on and off. He had a flat in Ajaccio near the beach, which he used as a base for entertaining a flock of generally opportunistic girls who bought into his exaggerated stories, empty good looks, and seemingly endless supply of cash.

And though he had more or less ignored Vianne when he was at his father's estate, there was a moment or two in the first few months when his behavior seemed too flirtatious and inappropriate.

Vianne had been watching out for it, and felt that she should err on the side of caution. Her experience with men up to that point had been nightmarish in general, and though she was approaching her seventeenth birthday still a virgin, she was on constant alert.

When Luc had started in with innuendos and slick suggestions that were too intense to ignore, she had complained in her low whispers directly to César, who listened and nodded noncommittally. But later, in private, he had taken Luc to task.

"Just keep your eye on other things, Luc. Vianne is in our protection—*ours*. If you have an itch, go to your beach apartment and let your *putains* scratch it."

Luc had bridled at the comment, but César had doubled down immediately. "In fact," he said in a threatening voice, "in fact, from this point forward, if something untoward happens to Vianne, you will be the one to blame for not watching out for her."

"But the guards—"

"Are also your responsibility."

From that moment on, Luc had given Vianne few problems, but his frosty attitude around her was slow in dissipating and made her mildly uncomfortable. His face told her of his resentment. If something happened to César, she wondered more than once, what would Luc do?

Well. There's still Bernard.

The twenty-seven-year-old had been seriously injured three years earlier. No one in the household, even Bernard himself, would talk about it, but he had been hospitalized for two weeks. It was unspoken knowledge that the mob war that erupted after Isabelle's death had been in the process of playing itself out across the island at the time. Bernard had been caught in the crossfire.

As time went by, Vianne concluded that Bernard was probably a participant, maybe even an instigator in that crossfire himself. But now he was reduced to being a person of simpler mind. *No, not reduced,* thought Vianne—*elevated.*

Since his physical recovery, Bernard had been in perpetual motion from dawn to dusk. He was a friend to all, and self-appointed guardian of the estate. César's heart had at first ached at the pronounced dulling of his son's intellect and the diminution of his previously sharp mental abilities. Everyone knew that this had forced Bernard's exclusion from the intricacies and nuanced strategies of the family business. But those thoughts were tempered by the way Bernard had become a strong, simple man with a broad range of basic capabilities. His hunting instincts and motor skills had improved dramatically since his injury.

And Bernard's kindness toward Vianne was broad and pure. He smiled at every one of her quiet words and rejoiced in her presence, which he couldn't get enough of. And it had been an absorbing game for him to communicate with her, in her language: with whispers and signs and the words of his eyes.

He has a lot of his father in him, she thought. *Certainly he has César's energy and a hard claim on life. What was he like before he was injured? I would like to have known him then, but I suspect that he's even better now.*

And he's amazingly fast at learning to speak without words. One day neither of us will need any words at all.

Jacqueline Murat was full of secrets, and Vianne admired that. She knew that keeping quiet and holding things away from view was the essence of survival.

What must have been deep disappointments in the woman's past were balanced out by César's obvious affection and love for her. It seemed to Vianne that the only thing that kept César from marrying Jacqui was some kind of obscure loyalty to his deceased wife.

Vianne began to like Corsica—its mild and sunny weather and its generally happy, earthy people. Ajaccio was a prominent Mediterranean tourist destination, and cruise ships steamed into and out of the busy port twelve months a year. Vianne liked it— she was used to being near the water.

But there were detractions about the country itself.

It was insular, and if it hadn't been for César's commitment to her protection, it would have proved challenging for Vianne to create a life in the tightly knit, family-based society. But to those members of certain families who pulled strings in Corsica, she was afforded the compliment of being courteously respected from afar as César Duval's "stepdaughter."

César asked Jacqueline to enroll Vianne in an exclusive *lycée,* a private high school in Ajaccio.

Vianne was cool to the idea, but reasoned correctly that there would be no getting around it.

Eduard, César's head bodyguard and his best driver, chauffeured her into the city every morning and waited for her each afternoon on the street outside the impressive French colonial building.

Vianne was surprised that a number of the other teens at school had setups that were similar to hers. It seemed that a surprisingly significant part of the local wealth was concentrated in the "shadow" families—crime families—of Corsica. And many of them sent their children and teens to private and very secure schools.

Her new school was the polar opposite of the convent school in Marseille. The Benedictine Sisters had run a tight, dry ship concentrating on the basics, with a thick overlay of religious and biblical admonitions.

But the curriculum of the *lycée* had a contemporary structure, stressing the arts above the sciences, and the virtues of unrestricted thought. This was fine with Vianne, who naturally soaked up languages, literature, and art.

But at the *lycée* she encountered a new set of problems.

Although Vianne's soft whispers, intense eyes, deep complexion, and radiant hair were violently exciting to the boys at the school, the whole exotic package was gratingly, *inexcusably* threatening to the girls.

En masse, the young women of the private school thought of themselves as gorgeous ingénues and examples of the sexiest and most desirable that Europe had to offer. Their strutting demeanor and carefully crafted hauteur may well have meshed with their financially highborn yet unearned status. But when the strange, dark outsider arrived on the scene, the security of their small world was shaken.

None of them were willing to concede that Vianne was more striking than any of them. And they bristled like cornered cats at her silky, almost inaudible voice, which they interpreted as her way of luring males—if musk had a sound, it would be her whisperingly soft, auditory pheromone that seemed to drive the boys at school over the edge of sanity.

As such, the young females, gathering in ever tighter cliques, felt their hatred for the interloper was well justified and was to be nurtured and expanded upon by means of the salacious lies and unfounded gossip that have been features of this kind of situation since the dawn of time.

The boys were the other side of the same coin.

From the day the exotic girl first entered the school, the testosterone levels of the healthy young males who came into contact with her elevated exponentially.

Vianne seemed immune to their frenzy, and she was soon labeled as a haughty, stuck-up bitch. But it was merely her hardwired caution in play, especially when it came to men. She had nurtured the hope throughout her difficult life in Marseille that there existed at least some men who were good—who were not animals who pushed women to the floor and tried to choke them to death. Or kill them in the street.

She didn't commiserate with the feelings, whispers, or posturing of the other students at the *lycée*. Both male and female alike seemed to her to be generally clueless about life's basic imperative: survival. Though she had no sense that she was better than any of them, neither did she feel inferior in any way—just different.

As time went by, her uniqueness at the school faded to the point where she made friends with a few girls who were not part of the nose-in-the-air crowd. Yet she still presented an image of a sexy, unobtainable goal in the boys' eyes.

Whispers in the school were that she was César Duval's mistress or sex slave or both. That rumor canceled out all but the bravest boys' forays into breaching her silent reserve.

One afternoon Eduard drove up to the school with Jacqueline in the seat next to him. The woman had been doing some shopping in Ajaccio, and Eduard had been the careful and watchful chauffeur that he always was.

As the two drove toward the *lycée,* Jacqueline spotted Vianne speaking with a boy at the bottom of the building's steps.

"Stop here, Eduard," she said to the driver, and he pulled the car into a parking spot a few dozen yards down the block within sight of Vianne.

Through the windshield Jacqueline watched the classic pas de deux of two young people with a secret. She recognized the looking, the hand touching, and the interestingly familiar expression on the face of the obviously inexperienced fair-haired boy.

"Have you seen that boy before, Eduard?" Jacqueline leaned over slightly and asked the driver.

Eduard nodded. "I asked her once about him and she ignored me." His eyes looked over at Jacqueline behind his wraparound sunglasses, and he smiled out of the corner of his mouth.

Over the boy's shoulder, Vianne spotted the car waiting down the block, and Jacqueline saw a sudden annoyed flare in the girl's eyes. She watched as Vianne said a quick goodbye to the boy, who gave her a fast kiss on the cheek.

As Vianne stalked down the street toward the car, Jacqueline smiled. When the girl dropped herself into the backseat, she pointedly glared out the window, and her body language dared anyone to talk to her at their peril.

Jacqueline was no fool, and she knew that Vianne wasn't one either. She thought back to the time when she herself was seventeen, and saw with clarity what nature in its unstoppable irony was up to. The boy to whom Vianne had quickly said goodbye on the street had the look of a young man who had just returned from an adventure in an exciting, unexplored country.

Jacqueline smiled inside at the girl's silence and resourcefulness—how had she found the time or the privacy?

She turned once in her seat to look at Vianne. The girl moved her head, and their eyes met for a second of woman-to-woman confirmation and conspiracy.

Then Vianne turned back to look out the window, and not another word was spoken on the trip home.

One afternoon, when school had ended for the day, Vianne, wearing her required blazer and skirt, walked out of the *lycée* at the edge of a group of students.

She slowed, glanced to her left, and in a matter of a few seconds sensed that something was wrong. There was a tension in the air on the edge of her consciousness. *Where's Eduard and the car?*

She looked through the people to her right. Half a block away, a man in dark slacks and a gray shirt was striding toward her. She saw his face, its clear and obvious intentions, and her throat tightened.

He's here for me, she knew instantly. *Where's Eduard?* Her eyes moved everywhere and then snapped back to the man, who had closed most of the distance between them.

Vianne ignored the rapid beating of her heart and the bustle of the high school kids milling around her. She was rarely distracted by anything when it came to the street. In the face of the man approaching her, she saw the look that she had seen those seven years ago in Marcel's eyes. Her mind suddenly shot back to that black moment when the man had his hands wrapped around her mother's throat.

As she ran at the approaching stranger through the throng of teenagers, she worked a short kitchen knife out of its hiding place in her clothing. Out of the corner of her eye, she saw a second man, equally ominous, crossing the street toward her.

Deux d'entre eux, she thought. *Two of them. And in the next few seconds we will all collide.*

She ran harder.

As the three converged on the sidewalk, neither of the men expected the teenage girl to attack. But she was sprinting fast, and they were a moment late reaching for her as she flew between them, knife in hand. The second man who had crossed the street saw a glint of sun on metal and too late realized everything was wrong. She slashed hard, feeling the blade cut into the man's thigh. He yowled in surprised pain, and dark red spread quickly down his pants leg.

He stopped short and stood bleeding, his face a mask of painful indecision.

The first man frowned at him—a mistake, because if he hadn't been distracted, he might have ducked in time.

Vianne whirled again, shifting the grip of her fist on the knife handle, and with every ounce of her strength sent her arm in a swinging backhanded arc that punched the blade like a railroad spike straight into the man's head through his ear.

His last thought: *She's only a girl!*

His body hopped once violently, blood sprayed in the bright sunshine, and he slammed down to the ground.

The other man remained frozen to the spot, clutching his leg. A harsh growling noise finally came from between clenched teeth, and he stared at the girl and the downed bleeding man.

Vianne looked to the left and finally saw Eduard limping down the street toward her. In the sunlight, she could see a scarlet stain on his shirt and jacket. A dozen yards before he got to her, he collapsed on the hot pavement and was still.

The man with the injured thigh pulled a small revolver from one of his pockets, and Vianne knew he would shoot her. But he glared at her for three long seconds, and then stumbled across the street to a dark gray Opel, trailing a thin line of red drops. He managed to get into the car, sat heavily behind the wheel, and drove away.

The sidewalk near Vianne was filling with stunned passersby, most of them her fellow students who were leaving the school. But she stood in the center of a wide circle that no one seemed to want to enter. The shock on the onlookers' faces was almost comically broad. And the tableau before them would remain in the minds of the witnesses for some time to come:

A man lay on the sidewalk, a knife sticking lewdly out of the side of his head, blood dribbling in a thin stream into the gutter. Eduard sprawled on his back a dozen yards down the block, un-moving, possibly dead as well. And in between stood Vianne—motionless, outwardly calm, but piano-wire tense inside.

After a few long seconds of stunned silence, people started screaming.

CHAPTER 10

A Certain Napoleon

———

Gᴜsᴛᴀᴠᴇ Mɪɢɴᴏɴᴇ's ʙʟᴀᴄᴋ ʜᴀɪʀ ʜᴀᴅ been receding for the last few years, but a wide, pomaded lock hung forward, covering most of the center of his skull. Flanking his long, straight nose, his intelligent eyes looked out from under heavy lids and short black eyebrows. His lips were pursed in an oddly feminine way, and his cheeks were full. His height of five feet, six inches finished off his almost comic similarity to Ajaccio's favorite son, Napoleon Bonaparte.

Now he was pushing fifty and had been inspector in charge of the high-crimes department of the Ajaccio police for the last ten years. His long, impressive record of fearless willingness to confront the highly organized and vicious criminals that infested his beloved homeland of Corsica was the stuff local legends were made of.

But what many of the citizens didn't realize was that it wasn't so much raw confrontational courage that kept Inspector Mignone ahead of the curve. Instead, it was his realistic accommodation with the right players involved in the convoluted power games played in Corsica and most of Europe. The innocent and the guilty often merged into a blur, and under Mignone's careful watch, shadowy and illegal political sleight of hand generally ruled the day—as long as he was included in any excess profiting resulting from those activities.

And César Duval was one of those players at the top of Gustave's list of allies of convenience.

Two hours earlier, the inspector had watched silently as a couple of his men brought a lifeless body into the morgue. A knife had been extracted from the deceased's skull with not a small amount of difficulty.

The police had quickly identified the dead man as a midlevel Sicilian "contractor" with a long record of crimes in his home country. Gustave had thought it over for a few minutes and then phoned Gino Murano, his counterpart in Palermo.

When the Sicilian policeman heard the news of the man's demise, he gave a sigh of relief over the phone. *Buono,* thought Murano. "Keep him," he said to Mignone. *Not only is another Mafiosi thug crossed off my list, but it happened in Corsica.* "Let it be Mignone's problem for now," he muttered in Sicilian to one of his detectives. "If the dead piece of trash belongs to the Randazzos, the Castigliones, or the Gianvicenzos, let them all fight it out across the water."

But Inspector Mignone had little patience with Sicilian mobsters who overstepped their bounds by operating in Ajaccio, and he made a quick push to have the corpse exported as quickly as possible.

The girl's other assailant was still at large, but Mignone had no idea of his identity. The second thug was likely planning to never return to Sicily if he knew what was good for him. He had botched his job—an odd and embarrassingly easy job that for some reason had targeted this girl. And if the man showed up back in Palermo, he would be certainly be dealt with by his boss. *I'll wager that boss is Giuseppe Randazzo.*

Mignone snorted, certain that the injured man's expected life span had been suddenly, critically truncated.

But the thug was just a sideshow—Gustave was far more interested in the girl.

Vianne had immediately been taken to the police station and placed in a cell under the watchful eye of a heavyset female officer. Also in the cell were a few local prostitutes, who looked at Vianne with appraising disdain for around a minute, but then went back to their desultory gossip.

It was almost two hours until Vianne was ushered out of the cell, up three flights of stairs, and into the office of the inspector.

He sat in his leather office chair, smoking a cigarette, seemingly lost in thought, and when she was ushered in, he looked up from his desk and stood.

"*Bonghjorno,*" he said, with a slight bow.

Vianne had been mostly silent since setting foot in the police station, and had given only her name to the sergeant at the booking desk—her first name and the surname under which she was registered at the school.

"*Cumu sì?*" the inspector asked.

"I don't speak Corsican." An almost inaudible whisper in French.

He eyed her for a moment, and then sat down. Leaning back in his office chair, he laced his fingers behind his head and said in French, "You killed someone, miss." He looked carefully at the girl's face and waited for a reply.

Vianne was silent.

Mignone suspected that she must be César Duval's French prostitute, the one he had heard rumors about. She supposedly was living at the man's estate, and was a close lookalike to César's deceased daughter. Mignone had seen Isabelle once or twice some years ago, and he had to concede that the girl before him could have been her identical twin.

He also had to concede that this wasn't going to be simple—the fact that Duval was somehow involved lent the case a complex, delicate, dangerous slant. And he knew that if a mob war resulted from today's incident, it would get very bad very fast.

"Did you kill that man"—he looked down at the girl's new record sheet on his desk—"Vianne?"

She stared at him, and her inner voice said, *Careful.*

"*Oui,*" came one soft breath.

He looked up. "Why?"

"He was going to kill me."

"Why would he want to do that?"

"*Pourquoi tu lui demandes pas?*" Why don't you ask him yourself?

The policeman's face seemed to close upon itself. "You're in my world now." The timbre of his voice dropped to a rough hiss.

"You don't seem an idiot, but appearances can be deceptive. Now tell me what really happened."

Her eyes burned into his, but she didn't get the chance to whisper a word. In the next second, the door to the inspector's office was flung open on its hinges and slammed into the wall.

Framed in the doorway stood César Duval. Vianne looked over at him and felt a sudden relief course through her body. A relief and a small, puzzling chill.

A plainclothes detective, gun in hand, was right behind him. The man pushed himself in front of César in a clumsy attempt to keep the man from entering the office, but César stood his ground.

The detective was rail thin and wiry, and he pointed his Police Special at Duval. Mignone threw his underling an annoyed glare, and tossed his head a fraction of an inch in dismissal. "Leave it be, Philip. And get out."

The detective, a man named Philip Jouet, went silent, gave his boss a crooked, frustrated stare, and then pushed himself past César and out of the office, muttering under his breath in Corsican.

César, dressed in a tailored dark navy Brioni suit with a white, open-collared shirt, dominated the door frame. He stood with his legs apart, his arms slightly away from his body, his head high.

His angry gray eyes were alive with electric aggression, and Vianne watched the man in silent fascination.

Although she lived in his house, had spent much time with him, and had seen him behave in many different situations over the last year, this was something new. She had never come across the kind of raw, latent mayhem that darkened his face at this moment.

The inspector had pushed his chair back against the wall, not speaking.

César was a ticking time bomb.

Vianne was still as a statue.

No one moved for half a minute.

"Hello, César." Gustave finally tried to break the tension, his eyes level and appraising. He made sure not to blink. "Do you have an appointment?"

César hadn't looked at Vianne yet, but glared at Mignone, his face immobile.

After another fifteen seconds, the inspector let out a short, audible breath. "It appears that there is no short supply of silence today. I feel like I'm at a Sicilian funeral."

"What are you doing, Gustave?" César finally spoke, his voice low, his stance in the doorway unmoving.

Mignone snorted quietly. "My job, what do you think? There has been a murder on my streets and what seem to be at least two other assaults. And a crowd of witnesses, and …"

The inspector paused and turned to look at Vianne. "And a suspect."

The girl hadn't moved a millimeter, and her face was unreadable.

He returned his attention to César. "Who is this g—" he began.

"The girl was attacked," César interrupted. "And then she solved the problem. Your crowd of witnesses saw exactly what happened." He still had not acknowledged Vianne's presence in the room, though he stood less than ten feet from her. His voice tightened and lowered at the same time, and his eyes narrowed. "You had her put in a cell like a common criminal."

Vianne shifted in her chair, about to whisper something, but her inner voice said, *Wait.*

Mignone stubbed out his cigarette in an overflowing ashtray, got up, and walked around his desk toward César. He was a good six inches shorter, but had the presence of a man who knew he was master of his turf. "Giuseppe Randazzo is going to want answers," he said, his eyes looking up at César's stony face.

"He won't," César said quickly. He let the two words linger in the air for a few seconds, and then said, "But I will."

Gustave gave an exaggerated Gallic shrug. "César, in this instance, revenge from Sicilians is not my problem, it's yours. This seems cut and dried. These men were sent for this, this ..." He looked with exaggerated interest at Vianne, who had been sitting silently watching everything. "Who is this girl again?"

The inspector's eyes narrowed for a few seconds, and then he looked back at Duval and stepped forward another step. Now he was so close that César could smell the man's inexpensive cologne beneath the omnipresent reek of cigarette smoke.

"What are you up to, César?" Gustave asked in a low, almost conspiratorial voice. "People are talking, and most of them are people who you would do better to keep a fair distance from."

"Talking about what?"

Without breaking his stare, Mignone inclined his head in the direction of the girl. "How did you find her?"

"Find her?"

"This girl, she looks exactly like Isabelle. Anyone can see it. Where did she come from?"

"Marseille."

César finally turned his head slightly and looked at Vianne. She sat still as a statue in the chair, her hands peeking from the sleeves of her navy school blazer, her slim legs crossed at the ankles.

Her lips were tight, and her midnight eyes bore into César's. The eyes said, *I trust you.*

Watching her at that instant—almost reading her mind through her flashing eyes—César knew for the first time, and with laser-sharp clarity, that the girl was a full adult, a complete woman, regardless of her age. He resolved that from that moment on he would treat her as such.

"Marseille," he repeated, without looking back at the inspector.

Mignone reached out, took César's elbow, and walked him out of the office and into the hall. "All right—no more questions about her, but we must come to an understanding." He let his hand fall from the arm of the man's expensive suit jacket. "This is *your* problem, and I would advise you to end it right away, right now. I'm shipping the body, which has already begun to stink up my morgue, back to Sicily. As for the other one, the one who got away …"

"I'll take care of him. And my driver as well. Eduard was lucky."

Mignone nodded and inclined his head toward Vianne, who was sitting in the office watching them through the open door. "I'll let this girl—whoever she is—go with you now. No one will come forward to press any kind of charge—we both know that. But …" He let his voice trail off.

César stood waiting.

"Be careful," the inspector said, lowering his voice with a conspiratorial urgency that surprised César. "There has been an increase in the whispers about you."

"Whispers? From whom?"

"Different sources. There are hints that some of your competitors are looking to move you out. To take over your, er, banking operation."

"Nothing new there." César's voice remained flat. "The price of popularity. I ask again, who's trying to climb over my wall now?"

Mignone made a face. "Not sure, César, but I wouldn't tell you if I didn't think these threats had meat on them."

"Occupational hazard, Gustave. That's all."

César started to walk back into the office, but the inspector's voice stopped him. "I don't want a repeat of what happened three years ago, Duval. The streets of Ajaccio are a nice neutral color now. I don't want them running red again."

"I'll handle it," César said. He walked back into the office, looked at Vianne, and nodded.

She rose slowly from the chair, shook her head once as if to free up her hair, and smoothed her blazer and skirt. Her eyes were locked onto César's, and the tiny flashing stars in the deep, dark pools said, *Let's go.*

César took her cool hand in his and shot the inspector a hard look of finality, and he and Vianne left the room.

César drove the Maserati, his eyes on the road, but his mind was elsewhere. *Now there is something new going on,* he thought.

Or rather, someone *new—someone who has specifically targeted Vianne, for whatever reason.*

His eyes narrowed to slits as he drove. Why? Who?

Vianne sat silently in the passenger seat, her eyes worried, the passing scenery leaving little impression on her.

After a few miles, when the traffic had thinned to only an occasional car or truck, César said, "Are you all right?"

He turned his head to look at her, and she nodded.

The car worked its way into the steep foothills to the east of Ajaccio, and after a few more minutes he said, "I'm sorry."

She shrugged, but inside she was shaken and angry. *Just wait,* her inner voice counseled.

"You're sure there's no problem?" he repeated as he drove.

"*De rien,*" she whispered at the windshield in front of her. No problem.

But it is *a problem.*

Vianne watched the steep forested mountains on either side of the valley and considered how to broach the conversation. "What happened today," she began to whisper. "Why—?"

"Not now."

She looked over at him, and saw that his angry eyes were far away.

CHAPTER 11

Ultimatum

———

THE NEXT DAY César was in his office off the large living room when the phone on his desk rang. He had been standing staring out the window lost in thought. He let the phone ring a half-dozen times. Finally he picked it up and merely listened.

"You owe me, César," a familiar accented voice said without preamble.

"What do I owe you? A bullet in your fat stomach, Giuseppe?" César automatically lowered his voice with malice. He was half expecting the call and the lies or revelations that it would hold. He made sure that he sounded ready to explode—Giuseppe Randazzo would understand that. The old Sicilian don was a ruthless survivor armed with the cunning and fearlessness of seventy dangerous years. César knew that the mafioso could smell another man's lies, fear, or treachery a mile away. Or his power, for that matter.

Randazzo made a guttural sound. "You owe me for bringing your vendetta to a close, César. That *testa di cazzo* your little girl canceled on the sidewalk near her school. You know who that was?"

When only silence was forthcoming, Randazzo said, "The corpse belonged to Benito Scapalone's brother."

César was silent. *Now, that's interesting.*

"I had no quarrel with Benito's brother," César said evenly. *But I didn't even know he* had *a brother, and that's bothersome.*

"I didn't care that you killed Benito in Marseille," Randazzo went on. He smoothed the few straggling hairs on his liver-spotted scalp. "That wasn't my concern. He and his brother were both contract labor—no blood ties to me, nothing."

César listened carefully for hints of ulterior motives and hidden treacheries.

Randazzo went on. "But when I found out that his brother was going after that girl, I figured it would set you off and stir the pot for no good reason. I'm too old for those kinds of games, Duval."

"It took the brother long enough. Benito died two years ago." César frowned at the realization that the devious old man had nurtured the knowledge that it was he who had killed Benito. Information and secrets were the most valuable and the most dangerous weapons in the worlds of both men, and César couldn't afford to ignore anything, no matter how small or seemingly inconsequential.

"So I sent Braggia to, uh, defuse the situation."

César remained silent. *So that's* who the second man outside the lycée was—the man who ran back to his car and drove away. I know who this Braggia is—one of Randazzo's button men—good at what he does, but obviously not that good. César rolled his shoulders to ease their tension. *All right, Giuseppe,* he said to himself. *Keep talking.*

"But your *volpetta,* that little fox of yours"—Randazzo chuckled with irony—"she seems to have handled the problem all by herself, and nearly killed Braggia in the process. Impressive girl you have there, César. *Brava.*"

César let a few seconds pass. Then he muttered in a low accusation, "You let that man, Benito's brother, get close to her."

"Unclog your Corsican ears, Duval." Randazzo's voice was flat and threatening. "I didn't let anyone near your *girl.* Benito's brother was a loose cannon, not my employee. I sent Braggia to *prevent* her death." He thought carefully about his next words. "I sensed an advantage to keeping her alive."

"For the sake of your life and your family's, Giuseppe, you'd better be telling me the truth." *But I don't think you are, you old Sicilian killer, at least not all of it. Something else is going on here.*

Randazzo's voice sounded like gravel. "Don't doubt what I say, César. Ever."

"Don't doubt what I can do." César's was the voice of death.

Giuseppe Randazzo went silent and waited for César to say something else, but after a few seconds he heard a dial tone. He frowned, hung up the phone, and idly ran a hand across his belly.

He was suddenly tired and irritated. *No,* he thought nervously. *A war with César Duval I don't want. But if that Corsican prick wants to fight, then the Randazzos will fight.*

And we'll win.

Vianne lay awake at night, tossing and turning.

She wasn't concerned with the fact that the man on the sidewalk was dead. She rubbed one of her wrists—she had sprained it when she drove the kitchen knife into the man's skull through his ear.

Only one of us was destined to live through the day. It turned out to be me.

It was Eduard's condition that kept her from sleeping. The careful middle-aged driver with his ubiquitous wraparound sunglasses had always treated her with calm courtesy and a dignified respect. The bullet he had taken in the abdomen wasn't fatal, but his healing time would be weeks. Vianne felt responsible, and was determined to visit him in the hospital as often as possible.

Wide awake in the dark, her thoughts turned to César's lack of any explanation for what had happened. When she had confronted him, he had told her firmly that he was taking care of the problem.

This whole life here in Corsica may be the problem.

It was a long time until she fell asleep.

Each morning for the next few weeks of school, Vianne was literally escorted to the door of the *lycée* by one of the family's other bodyguards. It annoyed her immensely, but she bided her time, carefully considering what her course of action should be.

Her clandestine trysts with Laurent, the shy boy in her class, had come to an abrupt halt. He had cautiously tried to skirt the issue of the violent incident outside the school, but Vianne felt a nervous uncertainty in his words, in his eyes, in his touch.

To make it easier on him, she told him it might be a better idea to put their relationship on indefinite hold. She understood with stark clarity that she herself could be a danger to him.

She thought about his calm ways and their few but exciting times together. He called her sirocco, like the wind—the term of endearment her mother had called her when she was a child.

Vianne sighed. *It would be wrong to bring a gentle innocent like Laurent into this life,* she said to herself dismally.

Into this damn life of mine.

She decided to wait out the time until the end of the school year, and then tell César what she was going to do.

The day after the school year ended, she approached César.

He was sitting at the butcher-block table in the large kitchen, having just returned from a business trip to Switzerland.

She poured a cup of coffee from the small percolator near the sink. Then she came and sat next to him, took a careful sip, and whispered, "We have to talk."

Chewing a bite of the bread and hard cheese that Marta had set out for him, he looked at Vianne's sparkling eyes. He thought he saw a storm among the stars.

"I'm leaving." Her words were softer than a breath of air.

César had known that something like this was coming. *It's not fair to ask this young woman to live her life with danger waiting around every corner. I told her I would protect her, and I meant it. And if that protection involves setting her free, so be it.*

But as he looked at her, he couldn't deny his affection for her natural equanimity, her clear-eyed street smarts, and her incredible bravery. And he knew beyond a shadow of a doubt that another unseen threat to her could be just around the next unguarded corner. She didn't deserve to be exposed the danger, but she was, whether she sensed it or not.

"I'm leaving," she repeated softly, reaching over and touching his hand. "Unless …"

He lifted his chin. "Unless what?"

She straightened up and narrowed her eyes. "Unless you let me in."

His eyebrows shot up.

"Into all of it," she whispered.

"All of …"

She suddenly stood and looked down on his surprised face. "You promised me," she hissed softly.

He remembered all too clearly what he had said before taking her from the hospital in Marseille. "Yes, I promised to teach you to protect yourself, but—"

She shook her head decisively and glared at him. "This is my family now." The whisper was suddenly urgent. "Let me in. Or I go." She felt an unbidden flush in her face, and it angered her further. "It will be two years next month." She ran the back of a hand across her eyes, and composed herself.

"Your birthday," he said.

She nodded and whispered, "I want a gift."

"*D'accord.*" He was about to say something else, but she interrupted.

"The gift I want is to be part of it all." She made a vague gesture with one hand. "A part of all this."

As he looked at her, something in his heart began to hurt, but she whispered on, "Then *I* can protect *you*."

César blinked. No one had said that kind of thing to him for as far back as he could remember. He was always the one offering protection to so many, for better or for worse—not the other way around. And her quiet statement had a strange intimacy that was almost that of a lover's. He studied her face.

Please, her eyes said in silence.

"Knowledge is dangerous, Vianne," he said. "And this life is a Pandora's box that once opened can't be closed. I don't think—"

"You wouldn't keep me here if I wanted to leave," she interrupted. "To make my own way out there in the world." Her voice had become so soft, it could hardly be heard—all the words had almost used up any sound she could make.

After he didn't respond, her eyes changed subtly, and with the last of her faint breaths she said, "Which is more dangerous— here or out there?"

He pressed his lips into a hard line. He knew the answer only too well. For all its peril, the life he had carved out for himself and his family was one in which he had control, in which he called the shots. What better definition of safety is there than that?

He nodded slowly, got up from his chair, and faced her. Something told him that in spite of the risk, in spite of the danger, he was making the right decision. He looked straight into her face—the face so like Isabelle's. Sparkling midnight eyes looked back from their heavy frame of gleaming black hair.

For the first time in his life, a shiver ran up César Duval's spine, a tremor of destiny that he was unable to deny.

"Very well, Vianne," he said. "On your birthday."

Her eighteenth birthday fell on the first day of summer, 1978, exactly two years since César had gently lifted her unconscious body off the bloodstained streets of Marseille.

Now the family gathered in the living room.

Vianne hugged César, looked into his eyes, kissed him on both cheeks, and whispered, *"Toujours."* Forever.

He knew she meant it—knew he would trust her now as he did his other children, his two sons. He thought about Isabelle and took both Vianne's hands in his. He held them to his chest for a moment.

"Je t'aime," she whispered, feeling his heart beating. I love you.

Jacqueline stood across the room, alongside Luc and Bernard.

Vianne went to each in turn, and kissed them as she had César.

Bernard was plainly happy, but the other two nursed differing brands of misgivings.

Jacqueline's eyes spoke of hesitant acceptance.

Luc's face was unreadable.

"Now we are yours, Vianne," César said. "And you are ours."

"Merci," she whispered, so low that the movement of her lips told more of the word than the light breath that it floated on. She turned slightly to hide the tears that came unbidden to her eyes.

Then Vianne whispered to her family, *"Dans l'avenir."*

Into the future.

In the darkness César spoke toward the ceiling, "What are your thoughts on what happened today, with Vianne?" He turned to look at the dark silhouette next to him in the bed.

Jacqueline pulled the sheet up to cover her breasts, not so much from modesty as from the chill night air coming through the large window, which was open a few inches to the night sky. She was silent for a while, and then said, "She loves you, that's clear. And I trust her, and I've always liked her. I'm glad for what you decided to do in spite of the danger. It means everything to her."

After he didn't say anything for a minute, she continued. "César, there was never a mature man in Vianne's life until she came here. No father figure, no brother—just a hard young life on the streets and in a convent school. What she knew of men as a child were the longshoremen and drug people of the Marseille docks that she came in contact with. *Horrible.*"

She waited a few seconds. "And her life in that convent was very difficult, according to her."

"Then I made the right decision? To let her in on things, as I have with you?"

Jacqueline frowned in the darkness and said in arch tones, "That's different, and I'm certain I know less than half of everything anyway, César."

He was silent.

"Perhaps if you married me someday, I might know a bit more, eh?"

"Calm down, Jacqui. You know that—"

"I'd rather talk about Vianne now. I've heard this conversation about us for years. It goes nowhere."

As César seemed to have nothing to say, she sighed loudly for effect and continued. "Vianne is very strong. She hides the bad things away in a secret place." She paused for a moment and said, almost to herself, "She's told me things."

"Such as?"

She hesitated a moment. "She killed someone when she was ten. She was protecting her mother."

"I know," he said, surprising her. He continued to look at the dark ceiling. "I found it out recently—what happened to her, to her mother. Despicable, unforgivable. And the man Marcel may have had a connection to the Unione Corse. If the man were alive today, I would take joy in killing him myself."

His words made Jacqueline uneasy, but she let it go. They were the words of a hard man who had a strong grip on his tough world. And she shuddered at the mention of the Corse. It was assumed by many on both sides of the law that César was heavily involved with that deadly organization. She knew he wasn't, at least directly.

Then Jacqueline said, "She's not a virgin."

At that César sat upright on his pillow. "What?" he said. "What do you mean?"

"She lost her virginity to a young man—another student at the *lycée*."

"Impossible!" he said in a too-loud voice. "How did that—"

"*Shh*. It happened, that's all, and it isn't any of your business. But I did do a bit of snooping. He's a good boy from a place on the outside." *On the outside* was rough code that meant he came from a family that was on the safe, clean, lawful side of the tracks.

"You won't tell me his name, will you?"

From what she had quietly confided to Jacqueline, the boy Laurent had been as inexperienced and naïve about sex as Vianne was. They had been equally curious about the technicalities, and thankfully he was very gentle. That tenderness had helped Vianne past some of her strong, ingrained cautions, and was as integral and erotic to her as the physical experience.

"If she wants to tell you about him, it's her business," Jacqueline said.

When César made no reply, she went on, "But I doubt she will mention it, and neither will you. She's been very secretive about it, but confided in me that it's over." She looked at him with a dark sarcasm. "Likely a casualty of the attack on her life."

She heard him breathing, and after a minute she said, "César, Vianne is an adult now. She has all the needs, wants, and emotions of any woman. Let that part of her life be hers, please. You couldn't control it if you tried, not with every ounce of your power. And if you pressed the issue, you would only compromise yourself in her eyes." She paused for a moment. "The woman has adopted you as much as you have her. Go easy."

He closed his eyes, mildly aggravated that he hadn't known about the girl's tryst with an outsider, but oddly proud of the initiative and ingenuity it had taken on her part to keep it a secret.

A cool wind breathed at the edges of the window.

He looked over at Jacqueline in the darkness and considered his affection and respect for her. The woman was an important part of his life—not only as his lover and confidante, but also as a sorely needed voice of female reason. And she had become a touchstone in Vianne's shifting world. Her advice counted.

"Any more commands, comments, or critiques?" he asked with a feigned exasperation.

She let the whispers of the darkness settle on both of them for a few moments. Then she smiled and shifted her body until it was snug against his. "Not tonight."

CHAPTER 12

Training Program

———

IT'S INCREDIBLE.

Incredible that a seasoned Mafia killer was unable to perform a task that I was certain he could do in his sleep: murder a clueless schoolgirl in broad daylight.

Well. It seems that mongrel Vianne isn't all that clueless after all.

And to add surprising insult to injury, old Giuseppe must have contacted César and somehow prevented the war I was counting on. César seems to have kept his hand off the throttle that would have surely destroyed him. With all his brains and resources, he could never take on the full force of the Randazzos.

It was a beautiful plan, a perfect situation, pitting those two men one against the other while I remained in the shadows. And I must remain in the shadows in order to survive.

But that girl! Her vicious reaction to the attack was a complete surprise, and now my opportunity has passed. It's suddenly become far more difficult—César will be on high alert for the foreseeable future. And he's not about to wait for another shoe to drop.

I'll just have to find another way to line up the dominos again so I can smash César down once and for all. And this time I'll make sure that the girl dies.

It may take some time, but I won't fail again.

Your days are numbered, César Duval, and so are Vianne's. Especially Vianne's.

"You're trying to kill us!"

Luc's face was a study in broad fear as Vianne downshifted, the tires screeching in protest. She blasted the Alfa down the rue du Fort, braked at the last minute, and half slid the sports car around a corner and onto the Cours Lucien Bonaparte, right in front of the Hôtel Les Mouettes.

She gunned the motor, and the roaring car accelerated up the palm-tree-lined beach road.

The sounds of the white convertible's engine made it impossible for Vianne to whisper anything back at her stepbrother, and she liked that.

The "training program" she had embarked on was one that César had devised for her. It consisted of important skills with which she had hitherto been unfamiliar, the first of which was driving.

It was completely new to her, and Luc was charged with her education in that department. Now, after just two days, he sat in the passenger seat of his Alfa Romeo Veloce Spider, his knuckles white, while Vianne blithely ignored most of his instructions and all of his hollering.

She took to driving the car naturally and aggressively, and was secretly flattered by the looks she was getting from men walking on the sidewalks of the city—men who appreciated the stark contrast between the car's hard white bodywork and the stunning driver's windblown black hair.

Behind the wheel she felt oddly safe and free. One hand on the wheel, the other on the gearshift, she chuckled inside at Luc's unending instructions and imprecations. She would purposely turn to look at him as she made the car hurtle toward an intersection or veer momentarily out of a lane, and his handsome face would invariably cringe as his voice rose in alarm.

You're not that tough, Luc, she said to herself happily, nearly sideswiping a car coming from the other direction. She enjoyed the interplay with Luc, and the small but sweet power she had over her older stepbrother.

She let her eyes snap back to the terrified man, and mashed the gas pedal to the floor.

As for self-defense, César decided to take on that critical aspect of her education himself.

The first day of her training, the two stood in the low, reinforced concrete warehouse on the periphery of the estate. The structure was used to store everything from toilet tissue to a trio of all-terrain four-wheelers, as well as doubling as a strong bunker if needed. César had set up a table at one end of the long, spacious interior with a few handguns and a dozen boxes of ammunition. At the other end, he had had several large bales of hay rolled in, stacked in an impenetrable barrier, with targets sporting human silhouettes tacked to their fronts.

Vianne already knew that everyone in and around the family, including Jacqueline, carried a gun somewhere on their person most of the time, and those were usually automatics—Colts, Rugers, Walthers.

She listened carefully to César's serious tone as he went through the basics of handling and loading and holding guns. He taught her how to stand, how to use the sights, how to make herself a small target.

She wore black jeans, a black, high-collared shirt, earmuffs, and clear shooting goggles. Holding a Ruger .45 at arm's length, legs apart, she looked dangerous and strangely erotic, dark eyes blazing in concentration.

César and Vianne fired a couple hundred rounds, shredding dozens of targets until Vianne's hands and arms hurt mightily.

The next day, after the last of another dozen salvos had been blasted into the hay bales, Vianne held up the Ruger she had been firing and asked César, "Jacqueline carries this every day?" She stood at the table near one end of the long room.

"A somewhat lighter model," he said, nodding that she should put the gun down. "But you have to keep practicing with heavier guns for now. Trust me on that."

She nodded, placing the Ruger on the table amid a jumble of shell casings. That Jacqueline carried protection with her at all times made perfect sense, and the vision of the fashionable older woman packing serious firepower didn't strike Vianne as odd or out of character.

She looked from César's face to the gun and back again, her eyes reinforcing the point that the pistol was still too big. She didn't need to use any more words for him to understand.

No words, her inner voice counseled for the hundredth time.

A couple of days later, as she sat reading at the large kitchen table, César appeared in the doorway. In one hand was a plain box of the kind used to hold cigars. He placed it on the table in front of Vianne.

She looked up at him, and her face asked, *Pour moi?* He nodded.

She opened the lid and saw, positioned in a square of cutout foam, a blued-steel Beretta 3032 Tomcat .32 caliber automatic. It seemed half the size of the handguns she had been practicing with, and she picked it up, hefted it for a moment, and smiled.

She got up from the table and leaned toward him until she was almost touching his face. Her eyes gave him a knowing look, and she whispered. "*Parfait.*" Perfect. She kissed his cheek.

"Come, let's see how it works," he said.

Vianne quickly put something into her pocket that César didn't notice, and they left the kitchen and headed across the estate to the warehouse bunker.

She was delighted. The Beretta worked like a dream— seemed to come to her hand with a mind of its own. It had less of a devastating punch than the other, larger guns, but that was just a matter of negligible degree—it was certainly deadly. And she already possessed the rare, coveted combination of an excellent eye and an almost preternatural inner calm so necessary in an effective shooter.

César was confident as he stood back and watched her run through a dozen clips. *She's already past me,* he thought contentedly, and turned to walk out of the bunker.

She tapped his shoulder. Wait.

He looked back and watched as she gently placed her Beretta on the table. From her jeans pocket she pulled out a short knife with a flat plastic handle. Its blade winked in the overhead light. He tilted his head as if to ask, *Where did that come from?*

"Kitchen," was all she whispered.

Then she looked at the mangled remains of a silhouette target tacked to one of the hay bales at the other end of the long room. She stood with her feet apart, her eyes gauging the distance. Suddenly her arm was a blur and the knife was gone.

The slender blade's trajectory was so fast as to be all but invisible, and by the time César's eyes had moved to the target, the haft of the knife was sticking straight out from the center of the silhouette's head, right where the nose would be.

"What?" was all he could say, and he tore his eyes from the target back to Vianne. She stood relaxed, hands on hips, staring at him frankly. He could see the flash in her dark eyes from where he stood.

"Practice," she breathed, answering the next question that she saw forming in César's eyes. "Secret."

He snorted a short, ironic laugh, and shook his head.

She touched his sleeve and whispered, "Am I ready now?"

He smiled. "Not quite. Come with me. We have to find Bernard."

With Vianne at his side, César carefully explained to his younger son what he wanted him to do.

Bernard listened intently, and as he learned what his task would be, his eyes almost glittered in happiness. He looked at Vianne with a wide smile.

"Of course!" He paused with uncertainty and looked at his father. "But it will take a while."

Knowing that his damaged son worked best with clear outlines or goals, César said, "I think if you work with her until Christmas, she'll have it down, Bernard. She's quick to learn. Two months from now." His eyes flicked to Vianne, who seemed to have taken to the idea as much as Bernard.

"Christmas," Bernard said happily, looking at her. "For you, Vianne, that will be more than enough time."

Vianne was about to whisper something when César said, "As soon as you're finished with this last part of your training, you'll be ready."

On their first day out, Bernard took one of the ATVs from the warehouse and drove Vianne up the steep dirt track and past the villa on the side of the mountain. The trail meandered through the trees another mile before petering out in a small clearing. Bernard brought the four-wheel-drive vehicle to a stop and shut off the motor.

Immediately, the huge stillness of the pine forest made itself known. Vianne was calmed by the sounds of soft winds and tiny animals that she alone could hear.

They got out of the ATV, and Bernard handed her a new, matte-black compound bow. She looked it over carefully—she had never held a bow before, and Bernard knew it immediately.

"Why this?" she whispered, hefting the serious-looking weapon with its skeleton grip, crisscrossed cables, and small idler cams at each end. "Why not a rifle?"

"Papa is smart," Bernard said, grinning. "If you are going to really learn to hunt—animals, enemies—bow hunting is the best way. It's quiet. And you and your target become more … uh …" His face showed that he was looking for the right word.

"Intimate?" she whispered.

"Yes! Intimate is good. You and the animal become kind of … uh …"

"One," she whispered.

Bernard nodded vigorously. "You're going to love this, Vianne. It's all about keeping your head and staying still and quiet until the right moment."

Without another word, Bernard set out into the trees, and Vianne followed.

They spent the morning walking the forest, Vianne watching with eyes wide and listening to everything around her. She had been born and raised on city streets, and this was her first taste of nature untamed. It was exhilarating, thrilling—a rapture for her acute senses.

Bernard obviously knew the woods, and at noon they came to a clearing where they sat on boulders and ate mutton sandwiches that Marta had prepared for them that morning. A few jays complained from the nearby trees.

"No shooting?" Vianne whispered after a bite or two.

"Just walking around with the bows," Bernard said around a mouthful of mutton. "You have to get used to the trees being in control. And they have to get used to you."

Vianne tilted her head in a question.

Bernard swallowed. "Out here the trees make the rules. So do the sky and the wind and the rain. They all let us come here and hunt if they like us. And they'll like us only if we're quiet and humble and respectful. Then they will give to us whatever we want."

Vianne nodded at the explanation. *I feel that way about the stars.*

"So for the first day or two we just walk. The forest knows we're here. When it's gotten used to you, you'll know it."

Vianne's eyes went to the bow resting against a rock.

"Next week I teach you to shoot straight," he said. "When you've learned that, we hunt."

The edges of her eyes crinkled in delight.

Corsica was rarely cold enough for snow to fall, but this year was an exception.

It was four days before Christmas, precisely six months since Vianne's eighteenth birthday, and tiny snowflakes zigzagged down from the iron sky that brooded above the mountains and the lake and the Duval estate. The hushed forest surrounding Vianne and Bernard was dusted with twinkling sugar.

Over the last two months she had soaked up long days of practice and had cherished the quiet, careful way in which Bernard had taught her to shoot and to stalk. She found there were clever ways to melt into her surroundings and move through the woods without making a sound.

This forest, these mountains are so different from cities or towns, she thought. *Out here it's all about care and quiet and finding my exact right spot in the forest—my exact right spot under the sky, the stars.*

She wore a black windproof jacket with its collar up, a dark blouse, and tight, black chinos with low boots. She and Bernard held their compound bows as they worked in tandem—silently— each knowing almost by instinct the other's location as they slowly made their way in parallel paths through the dense tracts of laricio pines. Between them was a small, steep, open area of scrubby greenery.

As the light snow silently drifted down, Vianne spotted an antlered deer at the edge of the meadow, sniffing at some wet grass. She and Bernard exchanged practiced glances from their places on either side of the clearing.

Bernard held his bow down at his side and moved his head slightly, indicating that the next move was up to Vianne.

She turned her full attention to the grazing buck.

Bernard watched his stepsister in simple fascination as her slim body in the tightly fitting clothes cautiously moved between the trees like a flowing, dark wraith. More snowflakes swirled in the gray silence.

She found the right spot to make her stand, her lips compressed in a tiny lotus of concentration. She stood as still as the rough pine tree that partially shielded her, and rested one foot on the edge of a moist rock.

The deer was nibbling on some grass at the base of a tree when it suddenly raised its head, ears flicking.

With both eyes wide, Vianne smoothly brought up the bow and carefully pulled the nock of the arrow to her chin with her right hand.

The buck froze.

She sighted, waited a full second, took in a deep breath, held it, and slowly let the tips of her fingers open.

The arrow was a whoosh and a blur, and a fraction of a second later, it smacked loudly into the tree next to the deer. The feathers at the end of the quivering shaft vibrated against the front of the animal's black nose.

The startled buck reared back, sneezed once, and leaped off into the forest.

Vianne lowered her bow and stepped into the clearing.

Bernard appeared from the trees across the clearing and walked toward her. As he approached, he saw her wink at him.

Driving the ATV back down the mountain, Bernard said, "You're only teaching the animals to be more cautious and smarter by missing them on purpose, Vianne."

She leaned over and whispered in his ear, "Good."

He laughed again, overjoyed as usual with his stepsister. He turned his head, gave her a quick kiss on her cheek, and said, "You're too soft, too kind."

No, I'm neither, she thought. *But I am ready, and Christmas is here.*

Now César has to fulfill his promise.

CHAPTER 13
Pandora's Box

———

VIANNE'S THIRD CHRISTMAS EVE IN the house was traditional: a monstrous dinner prepared by a grumbling yet happy Marta, endless glasses of superb wine supplied by the Cappucci vintner family across the valley, and a pile of wrapped gifts under a freshly cut tree garlanded with pinecones and tinsel.

Vianne had spent the better part of the previous two days in the more fashionable section of Ajaccio carefully selecting presents for her family: a pair of Orsini leather driving gloves for Luc, a shearling coat for Bernard, a Hermès handbag for Jacqueline, and a pair of silk Sulka ties for César. She also found gifts for Marta, Eduard—even for the dogs, who now sported red-and-green Christmas bandanas around their necks.

"Vianne," César said, standing near the tree.

She turned to face him.

"For you. Happy Christmas." He held out a small gift-wrapped box.

She came to him, and he took one of her hands and lay the present in her palm. Then he stood back a pace and winked at Jacqueline.

Vianne looked at their faces, carefully removed the slip of wrapping paper, and opened the box's hinged lid. Her next breath caught in her throat.

The diamond on the small velvet square was two centimeters across, almost an inch. It was flawless, and cut in the shape of the letter *V*. One leg of the *V* was slightly longer than the other, and its cleverly cut facets directed flashes of blue-white light through the whole stone and upward to the apex of that longer leg. It gave the illusion of a bright star glittering at the tip of a blazing checkmark. The diamond was attached with cleverly concealed, minuscule loops to a thin platinum chain.

Vianne had never seen anything like it.

The uniquely shaped stone had been fashioned by one of the greatest diamond cutters in the world—the father of a friend of Jacqueline's—a man known for taking on impossible cutting jobs like this one.

Vianne could only shake her head, but her eyes spoke gracious volumes to César.

"It was Jacqueline's idea," César said gruffly, hiding a smile. "She noticed you had no jewelry, not a single piece, and chided me about that sad state of affairs until I couldn't stand it any longer."

Vianne's eyes slid to Jacqueline's.

The older woman took the diamond pendant from its velvet box. She stepped behind Vianne, spread the thick black hair, and fastened the tiny clasp behind the girl's neck. Then she stood back a few feet to appraise the way the jewel looked.

The glittering diamond checkmark stood out like the point of an evening star. It sparkled silently between the gentle, half-hidden swells of Vianne's breasts, framed by the edges of her slightly opened white blouse.

"*Magnifique,*" said Jacqueline. All the faces in the room showed their appreciation at the sight of Vianne—a daughter, a stepsister, and a woman—no longer a girl, no longer a stranger.

Vianne had never had anything made with a diamond, let alone something like this. She came to César and gave him a light kiss on each cheek, and then did the same with Jacqueline. Then she turned away, so that no one would see the wetness in her eyes.

The next day, César and Vianne took one of the ATVs up the mountain to the villa.

Vianne loved the small, modern house that jutted out over the steep mountain cliff. She cherished its solitude and its incredible views, and had secretly staked it out as her own—a place where she could go to be alone, to think, to listen to the silence.

She stood with César on the villa's balcony, the two leaning against the slim metal railing, drinking in the view. A cloudless azure winter sky ruled above the deep green and browns of the mountains on the other side of the valley.

The air held a sharp chill, but they didn't mind. Vianne had made a pot of coffee—Kenyan blend, her favorite. They both wore cable-knit sweaters that Marta had knitted for each family member as Christmas gifts. Beneath the heavy wool, Vianne felt the light touch of her diamond *V* pendant on her chest.

César looked at her. "You like it up here, eh?"

She nodded and whispered. "*D'accord.*" Of course.

He looked at her calmly, loving and hating what he had promised her. But his gut told him that against all rational reason, it would be all right.

Finally he said, "What about our life would you like to know, *ma fille,* my daughter?"

"Everything," she whispered, her eyes searching his. He felt the heat in their glittering imperative. He had known only two other human beings whose eyes had such depth. One was his wife, and the other was Isabelle. But they were both gone.

Nature was just about finished with the subtle changes that had been turning Vianne into a deeply beautiful woman. She hadn't gained an ounce since coming to Corsica, her cheekbones were a bit more defined, and her thick hair seemed impossibly fuller—now it was a cascading avalanche of gleaming, blue-black, overlapping commas.

And the tiny splinters of starlight in the irises of her eyes seemed even sharper with the glow of her new life and its new secrets.

He walked over to an old-fashioned telescope at the end of the balcony. It was positioned on a metal tripod and aimed across the valley. Vianne liked the instrument, and used it to look down on the large house and the lake, and at night, up at the stars.

He grunted. "I won't deny the bad things I've done, which were—are—many. But I learned early on that the other bad survivors in this business, the other so-called mobsters, had the help, the aid, and even the encouragement of equally bad men in positions of authority."

Vianne's face said, *Go on.*

"Those people hold real, legitimate power: officials, policemen, politicians who run their own games in the shadow of the laws they pretend to uphold."

César was silent for a few seconds. "Those dangerous, powerful individuals seek out people like us who they can collude with, who do their dirty work for them, and who they can eventually point fingers at if things go wrong. They need 'bad guys' to take the heat, to keep the spotlight away from them. And they also need us to find novel ways to hide their own bloodstained secret wealth."

Vianne was stone still, enraptured.

"We Duvals are the bankers to these people, the facilitators, and we are often the ones who are blamed in the newspapers. In return we are left alone to a large degree. We know these people's secrets, so they ultimately can't hurt us without annihilating themselves."

"And we ..." her whisper prompted.

"It's almost impossible to stop them, Vianne, but we can at least control them. We move gold, diamonds, and money around the world for these people for a well-earned commission."

He paused and stared at her. "And I know how to quietly remove these bad players from the chessboard if and when it becomes necessary." He made a face that she couldn't read.

Vianne had never heard César speak that way, and she was taken aback. *Oh God, what is the man doing? What kind of tightrope does he walk, what kind of chances does he take?*

César's tone changed, and his face darkened. "I'm certain that Isabelle's murder was not collateral damage of an attack on me. No. It was intentional. Someone powerful was sending me a message, the worst message imaginable. I've yet to find out who, but one day I will. Until then, I have my fingers on many buttons. If I push those buttons, many heads will roll." He looked out over the valley and was quiet.

After a while Vianne whispered, "We are all criminals then?"

He looked at her for half a minute, watching her face carefully. Then he said, "We operate outside of the law, so technically the answer is yes. But I don't consider myself a criminal, and neither are you. We're imperfect people trying to do the right thing and stay alive at the same time."

She marveled at what must be going through César's mind, and breathed deeply of the clear mountain air. *How lucky I am that the stars brought me this man—this man who rescued me from evil. Rescued me from death.*

My broken savior.

Vianne inclined her head, but decided not to pursue the next obvious question. Instead she whispered, "Someone wants to punish you by hurting, killing me."

She's right, of course, he said to himself, unable to control a scowl. *Gustave Mignone almost told me as much. Whoever murdered my innocent daughter is still alive and is part of what's happened with Vianne. And has led me, led us, to this juncture.*

"People will keep coming after you and me and the family," he said. "One of them killed Isabelle."

He watched Vianne's face and saw agreement and determination. A dark dread rose within him, and in an even voice he said, "Now you know everything. You can still opt out, go anywhere in the world with my protection—out of the line of fire."

Hearing no reply he said, "What are you going to do?"

She stood up and walked to the railing. The sky seemed brighter now, and there was a light, almost fragrant wind. She remembered how she had wandered the docks of Marseille feeling and smelling the subtle wind of the sirocco long before all this began. Remembered the love of a mother whose life was cut short by revenge. Thought she could feel the cold outrage of Benito's gun barrel on her temple.

Well. Now I'm here and free to choose my life, thanks to this man and his family. Who am I to judge this world of his?

He stood next to her at the railing, and repeated, "What are you going to do?"

She leaned one shoulder against his.

"I'm a Duval now," she said in a whisper, without taking her eyes off the endless sky.

He knew then, beyond question, that his rescue of this girl— this woman—had come full circle. He turned his head and examined her close profile, the dark confidence of her face, the familiar silence in her eyes.

Yes, you are, he thought.

You're one of us.

Part Two

Deep vengeance is the daughter of deep silence.

—Vittorio Alfieri

CHAPTER 14

A Trade

It was early spring, and the city of Ajaccio knew it.

The port was already busy handling its barrage of tourists from all over Europe, most of whom arrived on cruise ships and yachts from Italy, Greece, and mainland France.

The morning sun was still temperate and benign when Vianne walked into the Commissariat de Police on the rue Général Fiorella. The heads of the uniformed and plainclothes policemen in the main lobby turned as one to ogle the young woman who had just strolled through the station's double doors—who had just stepped onto their turf.

She wore a fitted, sleeveless, cream-color dress, cut a few inches above her knees. The three-inch heels on her matching pumps clicked on the tile floor.

The men in the large room couldn't help but stare at the way she walked with her head up, the clear dark eyes almost sparkling, the cascade of blue-black hair gleaming. The normal background noise of cop conversation lowered to a murmur.

She walked to the information kiosk.

"Yes?" The woman behind the shoulder-high desk looked down at her.

Vianne pretended not to notice the air of vague resentment. "Inspector Mignone," she whispered.

The woman almost laughed. "He's very busy. You can't—"

"I have an appointment," came the breathy but firm interruption. "My name is Vianne."

With a glare and a snort, the woman consulted her thick logbook for a long minute. Finally she raised her eyes and said, "Very well. His office is—"

But Vianne was already heading for the elevator.

Five officers, who a moment before seemed to have little to do, quickly jammed into the small lift with Vianne. The trip to the third floor gave each one a chance to bump and jostle against the girl, and all breathed deeply her faint natural scent of dark spices and unattainable possibilities.

She was silent as always, her face impassive. As she got off the elevator, she reminded herself to change her clothes when she returned home.

She stood in the open doorway of Inspector Gustave Mignone's office.

He sat at his desk, a cigarette jiggling from his lips as he spoke rapidly into his phone. He looked up, took in the vision of the girl standing before him, and made a quick end to his call.

He didn't stand up, but stubbed out the almost-done cigarette in a jammed ashtray and made a beckoning movement with his hand. "Please come in. Close the door behind you."

Vianne pushed the door closed with two fingers, walked into the cluttered office, and sat down in a chair across from the desk.

The inspector leaned back, eyeing her in silence. *Ouah,* he thought, *this is no longer the disheveled schoolgirl whose* beau cul *César pulled out of the fire that day. Oh no, what has happened in the last year?* He grinned inside, answering his own question: *life kept moving along.*

Vianne was silent, her hands in her lap.

"When your guardian told me—"

"Stepfather," she whispered quickly.

Mignone pushed out his bottom lip. *"Je suis désolée,* sorry. When your *stepfather* told me that you would be coming here, I was surprised."

He picked up an almost-empty pack of Gauloises and held it out to Vianne, who waved a hand in refusal.

"You're smart," he said as he extracted a cigarette for himself and put the crumpled blue box on his desk. "Nasty habit, but it calms my nerves. Do you mind?" He flicked his lighter open.

Vianne shook her head.

He straightened in his chair and got down to business. "César said that you have replaced him."

"Oui." It sounded like a breath of spring air.

"That is very implausible, young lady."

"Vianne."

The edges of Mignone's small mouth turned down in mild annoyance. "Of course. *Vianne.* Now that we have sorted that out, César told me you have a message."

She ran a slim finger over the V-shaped diamond glittering on her chest. "We want to trade," she whispered.

"Trade? Trade what for what?"

Mignone saw her eyes carefully scan the room. *Smart girl,* he thought. "No microphones or cameras," he said. "It's only you and me."

Her expression said, *I doubt it.*

"You have my word," he added.

She watched him closely as she leaned forward slightly.

Mignone had a better glimpse of the sparkling diamond checkmark.

"Kemal Zorzo," she whispered.

Mignone's face blanched, and his cigarette nearly fell from his mouth. He stared at Vianne.

Her face was impassive, but she smiled inside. *César was right.*

Composing himself, Gustave narrowed his eyes. "What about him?"

"I'll give him to you," Vianne whispered. "And one hundred kilos of China White."

Mignone sat frozen for a few seconds, then pushed his chair back and stood up. *If she weren't César Duval's daughter, I would lock her up now.*

"Zorzo," he said firmly. "Where is he? He is in Corsica?"

She gave an innocent shrug.

Mignone mentally scratched his head in wonder. *Is César Duval truly in bed with a Satan like Zorzo?*

Looking at the silent girl sitting in the chair in front of him he said, "What do you want in return?"

She whispered, "A blind eye to Duval business."

Mignone made a gritty laugh. "Impossible."

She stood up. In her heels, she was six inches taller than the inspector. She moved around the desk until she was so close that he could see minuscule tiny flashes in the dark irises of her eyes. Her scent was distracting.

His eyes went wide when she whispered, "If there is a war here, keep your police out of it."

The corner of Mignone's mouth twitched. *Not another mob war, damn it.*

"I can't do that," he said.

"It may not happen."

Merde! Of course it will happen. "I can't," he repeated at lower register.

She studied his face. Vianne's inner voice: *Yes, he can.*

She took a step back, shook her head without taking her eyes off him, and held out her hand. "Very well," she whispered. *"Au revoir."*

He looked hard at her face, scowled, and took her hand in his. But instead of a shake, he held on to it. "Helping or hiding a man like Kemal Zorzo is an offense in this country that carries the maximum penalty, young woman."

She felt a chill of secret power. César had told her he would say that, almost to the exact words. She let a light smile shape her lips and in a whisper repeated, *"Au revoir."*

"What César is asking for is impossible." Mignone continued to grip her hand, but she could feel the touch of acquiescence flow through the man's fingers. "His request is an affront, a betrayal of my people, my country—Corsica itself."

She shrugged and waited. Patient. Silent. Finally she whispered, "Deal?"

He let go of her hand and after half a minute said in a low voice, "Very well."

She put her hands on her hips and didn't move.

"You have my word." He sounded like he would spit.

She nodded and let a calm smile shape her lips. Pointing to the phone on the desk, she whispered, "*Puis-je?*" May I?

He hesitated for a few seconds, and then made a motion of acquiescence with his hand. She leaned over, picked up the receiver, paused, and with her fingers hovering over the dial, looked back at him hard.

"Private line," he said. "No one is listening in."

She lifted the receiver to her ear and dialed. After one ring César answered.

"He gave his word," she whispered into the phone.

After a few seconds, César's voice said, "All right. Tell him."

She whispered *ciao* and hung up.

Vianne turned to face Mignone and breathed softly, "A yacht. The *Crescent Rose* from Malta." Her eyes flashed. "Docking here in Ajaccio this evening. Zorzo and the heroin are on board."

Mignone almost held his breath. The whispered information rocked him. If what Vianne was telling him was true, he himself could personally deal a crippling blow to a significant conduit for the European heroin trade.

Then she closed her mouth firmly as if she had used too many words, startled Mignone with a conspiratorial wink, turned, and walked toward the door.

"I don't suppose you can save us the trouble and tell me where the drugs are hidden on the boat?" he said to her slim and shapely back.

She opened the door and turned to face him for a final time.

"Floor panel beneath the captain's bed." Her whisper was low but clear.

Inspector Gustave Mignone stood in one place and watched the woman leave.

Then he reached for his phone and started mobilizing his men.

César sat behind the wheel of a black Mercedes a few blocks from the police headquarters and saw Vianne walking toward him. He also saw the plainclothes detective following her and trying to be invisible.

As Vianne approached the car, her follower stepped up to the pay phone that César had been using to speak with Vianne. The cop's charade of distracted nonchalance was far from convincing.

Vianne let herself into the passenger seat, closed the door, and lowered the window on her side.

She was about to whisper something when César said, "Let's get out of the city. Then we'll talk."

Fifteen minutes later they were driving into the steepening foot-hills east of Ajaccio. Vianne never tired of the rugged scenery.

How easy it was to manipulate that police inspector. How good it felt to be in control, to make things happen like that. Just like placing one of my arrows to tickle a deer's nose.

After a few miles, when the traffic had thinned from little to none, Vianne broke the silence. "You were right," she whispered. "You know Mignone well."

César drove quickly, his mind on this new strategy. *I also suspect that at least one or two of the policemen in that station will remember Vianne, and at some point will gossip as all cops do. And that her presence, her involvement, will reach whoever has been planning her doom.* Our *doom.*

She stared through the windshield and whispered, "Luc knows about this?"

César let out a long breath. "Luc's perfectly all right with this. As much as the two of you grate on each other, he cares for you."

The expression on her face showed that she wasn't convinced.

"Luc is just fine," César repeated.

Vianne let out a short, quiet breath, and filed away the problem of her stepbrother in the back of her mind. She knew their sour relationship would one day have to be addressed, for better or worse.

"What now?" she asked in a small breath.

He didn't take his eyes off the road. "Now we wait."

That night the sleek power yacht *Crescent Rose,* registered in Valletta, Malta, approached the port of Ajaccio from the south.

When two fast police boats made for her, she tried to alter course and make a run back out into the Mediterranean. The *Rose* was very fast, but gave it up when an armed helicopter swooped in and fired a volley of warning shots across her bow.

Mignone himself was on one of the patrol boats, and he was the first to board the yacht. The Corsican police swarmed the luxurious Benetti and rounded up the small crew with little resistance, and the hundred kilos of heroin was quickly found exactly where Vianne had said it would be.

Kemal Zorzo had pushed his muscular frame into a specially made compartment in the control room, but one of the drug-sniffing dogs brought on board found the man in his hiding place easily and set up a howl. The powerful Turk burst through the room's fiberglass wall, .45 caliber automatics roaring in each hand.

But Mignone had his best men with him and was prepared.

In the ensuing gun battle, three cops were injured, but Zorzo was mortally wounded, two bullets in his chest.

Mignone leaned over the large, rough man as he lay dying on the messy deck, air and blood escaping from his ruptured lungs. "A nice bit of justice, yes, Kemal?" the inspector said. "So it goes."

"*Anani sikirim,*" the rough man cursed through the pain. "I was sold to you, wasn't I? *Seni degersiz pislik!*"

Gustave merely shrugged at the incomprehensible epithet, saying nothing, waiting for the man to expire. He knew that trying to extract information from the drug lord would be futile, even in the grasp of doom.

"*Tabi,* of course I was sold," Zorzo continued on, starting to gurgle on his own blood. "And I know who the seller is. It's ..." His voice faded and his body shuddered and was still.

The inspector straightened up and had turned to leave when he heard a few more words grind out of the drug lord's mouth.

"It was César Duval," the weakening voice rasped. "It had to have been him."

Before Gustave could reply, Zorzo said, "That Corsican *bok* is in for a surprise before he gets sent to hell ..."

Then his eyes opened wide, his lips pulled back in a ferocious smile, and in the next second he was dead.

CHAPTER 15

The Calm Before

IT WAS VIANNE.

From her description it could be no other.

I've vastly underestimated her. How on earth did she ingratiate herself so deeply and so fast with a man like César Duval? Is she that good in bed?

The audacity of walking straight into Ajaccio police headquarters by herself is huge. If my contact in that building weren't so completely reliable and so completely corrupt, I would never have believed it.

But there is no doubt—it was Vianne.

And lo and behold, not more than twelve hours after her visit with Inspector Mignone, the legendary Kemal Zorzo himself is cut down in the Ajaccio harbor. Imagine the coincidence.

Well. I don't believe in coincidences. I smell César Duval all over this. He's up to something, and it will certainly affect my movements, my plans.

If he hasn't figured out my intention to destroy him by now, he will soon.

Sorry, César, but you have to die.
And so does that girl.
So does Vianne.

Four weeks later, on a beautiful day at the end of May, the phone in César's office rang.

"*Salut,* Duval." The words were in smooth, dark gutter French.

César recognized the voice immediately, and felt a sudden adrenaline surge throughout his body. "Quentin."

"You heard about Zorzo?"

"I did. Congratulations."

Quentin chuckled. "Funny how the Turk was brought down on your quaint little island last month, César. By your quaint little policeman."

"So?"

A few seconds of silence. Then, "Did you trade Kemal Zorzo for something, César?"

"I didn't know Zorzo. If I had, I would have given him over for free."

The man laughed out loud. "Then you would have left millions on the table." His voice suddenly got serious. "Surely you've done some, uh, funds transfers for Zorzo. You're everyone's money manager, César."

"Never for the Turk." César's voice was low and hard. "You have my word on that."

Quentin stroked his carefully shaped mustache and ran a hand through his wavy mane of dyed black hair. *Duval's word,* he thought with a shrug. *True, he's never broken it. So far.*

At forty-five, Quentin Maillot oversaw the underground network known as La Chose with a focused brutality that gave even the Sicilian mobs pause. His tightly knit gang provided the backup muscle to a number of the most powerful players at the pinnacle of the French Connection.

"*Bon,*" Maillot said finally. "Now, on to other things. A dead Turk is not what I called you about."

César listened carefully as the man continued.

"I'm absorbing Zorzo's business, staging a sort of 'hostile takeover.' Can I count on you to move yellow for me now?" It was a code for smuggling gold.

"When?"

"As soon as possible."

Duval narrowed his eyes. "I've raised my rates, Quentin."

A smooth chuckle. "Whatever you say, César."

Without letting a single second intrude on the flow of conversation, César said, "Who tried to kill my daughter last year?"

Silence on the phone.

Finally Maillot said, "I heard about that." Then, without skipping a beat, he said, "It wasn't me."

"I've heard otherwise."

Quentin laughed. "I've no reason to attack you or your daughter. And if I did, this conversation wouldn't be taking place."

When César didn't respond, he said in a serious tone, "Let's do business, César, and I'll see what I can do."

César waited a few seconds. "Thursday."

With bonhomie in his voice, Quentin said, "Ah! Looking forward to it, my friend."

Without a word, César hung up and stared at a point in the middle distance. *On my list of jackals that could be coming after us, Quentin, one name is at the top.*

Yours.

CHAPTER 16
Not Over

———

"Where's Luc?" César was obviously irritated and impatient.

Jacqueline stood with him by the Maserati and shook her head. "I haven't seen him today."

Vianne was just coming out of the house, dressed in slim jeans and a coral-colored blouse.

"Damn it," said César. "I told him yesterday I wanted him to drive me to the airport this morning. Why isn't he here?"

Vianne heard the conversation from a distance and walked up to him.

"I'll drive you," she whispered.

César looked at her, and his dark mood brightened. "All right. I'd like that."

Vianne smiled, held her hand out for the car key, and whispered, "Let's go."

The low-slung sedan moved quickly out of the valley and down the snaking N193 through the hilly Corsican countryside of Sarrola-Carcopino.

Vianne's driving impressed César. She drove fast but not carelessly. He watched the light touch of her hands on the leather-covered wheel, and the way her eyes were everywhere, never missing anything.

They spoke softly about some of César's plans as the car flashed past a long series of stone arches in a field, the ancient remains of the Aqueduc de Mezzana.

"What was that man's name?" Vianne whispered.

"Quentin Maillot. The head of La Chose."

She was thoughtful for a moment. "He's the one trying to kill us?"

César kept his eyes on the hills to either side. "Maybe not he himself. But my gut says if he isn't, he knows who is. For certain."

"Why?" A soft breath.

César shook his head and said, "By now Maillot suspects that it was us who sent that animal Zorzo to hell." He smiled grimly.

Vianne eyes shone, her mind working as she pushed the Maserati to eighty miles per hour. "You're not afraid?"

César glanced at her and shook his head. "Not at all. He needs me, and his cover story about smuggling gold is just that—a cover. I'm meeting with him in Marseille face-to-face. He'll tell me what he really wants, and I'll find out who's after us."

The sound of the car's powerful engine thrummed its insistent backdrop to the scenery flying by.

"But what if—" Vianne's whisper stopped short.

She thought she saw something shiny from the corner of her eye, and a fast streak of smoke arrowed from the far woods.

Before she could react, the world exploded.

She opened her eyes.

Down was up, up was down.

Whatever had just happened had flipped the Maserati over, and the hurtling car had loudly scraped its way down the roadway on its roof. Its windows, shattering one after the other like timed firecrackers, spewed shards of glass to either side of the screeching, sliding, upside-down car. The entire machine from the back of the seats to the rear bumper was mangled and twisted.

Her chin was tucked down on her chest, and the suede lining of the sedan's ceiling pressed into the top of her head. She looked to her right to see César in a similar plight, but blood was seeping from a cut in his scalp somewhere under his hair. She reached over immediately and shook him, but his eyes remained closed.

She twisted painfully in the driver's seat. Her slim frame had probably saved her life in the now warped and cramped space—a heavier person would have been mortally compacted.

She contorted herself into an easier position, pushed hard, and was able to get the door open. She half angled, half sprawled out onto the pavement. Her body ached in a few spots, but she knew immediately that nothing was broken. Looking at the road behind the car, she saw a tremendous black-and-brown skid mark where the car had slid a hundred feet on its roof before coming to a stop. At the start of the trail of paint and glass and metal bits she could just make out a small crater with smoldering streaks of ash radiating out in a starburst pattern.

Something had exploded under the moving car.

She ran to the other side of the wreck and pulled with all her might on the inverted passenger-side door. It grudgingly opened as the upper edge of the window frame screeched on the pavement. She got on her knees and looked into the car.

César was either dead or unconscious, and she tried to get her arms around his chest to pull him from the smashed sedan, but he seemed solidly jammed behind the crumpled dashboard. *Allez,* pleaded her inner voice, come on. She tried to find any angle from which she could pull the man free or at least dislodge him enough to get a better hold.

Then she saw him come awake.

The steel-gray eyes slowly focused and settled on the girl's frightened face. He shook his head once and said in a hoarse voice, "Are you all right?"

She nodded in a soaring relief that confirmed how deeply entangled their relationship had become. But in the next second she saw the expression on his face change. He was looking past Vianne to a point behind her and to the side, and he began to desperately try to free his arms.

In frustration he said, "Do you have it on you, Vianne?"

She put one hand behind her and smoothly pulled her Beretta 3032 Tomcat from its belt holster at the small of her back. She looked once at César, but his face told her there was no time, not even for words.

She twisted around on her knees with the gun in both hands, and saw two men running. They had been hidden in the cover of the nearby trees and were sprinting straight at her and César across the grassy, rock-strewn meadow. They were three or four dozen yards from the car, both with guns out.

She pulled one leg up and forward to steady herself, held the gun tightly in two hands, and fired.

The .32 caliber Beretta didn't have the brute power of a .45 or a 9 mm, but the deadly hollow-point rounds that she had loaded in the clip tore into the center of the first man's chest. The man's feet left the ground from the punching force, and slammed into a ditch on the side of the road. The gun in the dead man's twitching hand went off like a bomb, but its bullet hit nothing, and its echo ricocheted from the near mountains.

From behind her, she heard César's voice. "Again, Vianne," but she needed no prompting.

Ten yards from the car, the second man had stopped running, frozen in temporary shock by the fast death of his partner. Getting a grip on his surprise, he aimed his gun at Vianne and knew that he wouldn't miss. But the confidence of the hired killer vanished, and he suddenly, savagely grinned in a rictus of confused panic.

Vianne's first round went a bit wide and high. The second pulverized the man's collarbone, and in a sudden mist of blood his whole right arm swung free from his shoulder. Her next round hit him low in the torso, blasting a kidney, his liver, and a portion of his entrails out through his back.

Unlike his compatriot, it took him almost an entire minute to die.

Vianne stood in the road, bracketed by the innocent scenery and the echoes of echoes. *Wait,* said her inner voice. *Not over.*

She narrowed her eyes, shielding them with one hand, and nervously scanned the near mountains and their steep forests, but saw nothing. *Why isn't it over?* she asked herself in sickening, adrenaline-charged desperation.

Nothing moved.

When she was finally comfortable that the sounds of her immediate surroundings had settled back to normal, she turned and bent again to the pavement and to the task of pulling César to safety.

Now he was moving, and with her help started to painfully extract himself from the prison of the crushed car. In a minute or two, he was standing on the pavement, leaning hard on the slim, gasping woman.

The two stood there for a minute, holding each other up, he in his burned and dirty Brioni suit, she in her road-soiled jeans and torn blouse. They both scanned the area intensely to see if they might catch a glimpse of anyone else in the vicinity, anything moving or out of place.

Vianne held the Beretta in front of her at arm's length and tracked it left and right. After another minute, she lowered the gun and slowly replaced it in its belt holster.

For a brief moment César looked at her face with unalloyed admiration and gratitude—and respect for her impressive resolve and almost otherworldly presence of mind that had saved both their lives.

A few drops of blood dribbled from the deep cut on his head. He wiped them off his face and realized that he was not in very good shape at all.

A delivery van came around the curve a few hundred feet behind them, and when the driver saw the blasted car, the disheveled girl, and the bleeding man, he came to a fast stop.

Vianne and César walked shakily to the driver's window. After a brief talk and the passing of a wad of bills to the man behind the wheel, they went around to the passenger side and got in.

The driver, a local handyman who knew Duval by reputation, put the van in gear, guided the vehicle around the smoking wreck of the Maserati, and wondered how he would spend the money that the bleeding man had just handed him. The money that ensured that he hadn't seen the two massacred corpses lying in the grass, if he were ever asked.

In less than a minute the van was gone and heading back toward the Duval estate, three miles away.

In the seat next to Vianne, César felt the dull sledgehammer of shock, his eyes rolled up in their sockets, and he passed out.

Quiet.

Nothing moved.

The car, almost blasted in half, lay upside down in the center of the deserted road, its engine ticking cool. The two dead bodies sprawled nearby in the grass.

A few birds sang.

Concealed in the trees up the side of the mountain, the shooter's eye had watched through the crosshaired sight of a shoulder-mounted rocket launcher as the faraway van disappeared around a curve.

While the dark-haired girl with the gun had been blowing apart the two men with impressive efficiency, the professional had quickly reloaded the heavy mechanism to finish off the targets. But a mounting ring had snapped on the metal tube, and it was impossible to fire a second deadly rocket-propelled grenade.

Watching through the launcher's sight, the shooter's mind was on the future—the two incompetent backup hitters lying dead in the grass already forgotten.

Well.

Doesn't César Duval have unbelievable luck?

And doesn't Vianne?

Perhaps the girl brought that luck with her from Marseille. But there seems to be much more to it—she has the grace under pressure of an ice-cold assassin. Yet she's so ridiculously young.

Who is she really?

Whoever or whatever she is, it's not likely that Duval will let his guard down for another single second, and I won't take any more risks at the moment. By sunset, he'll have every dangerous ally he can bribe on high alert.

A chilling cocktail of adrenaline, dread, and anticipation ran up the shooter's spine.

Until now, I believed César to be on the wrong track, clueless about me. But what if I'm wrong? If—when—he figures this all out, he'll certainly become the hunter and I the prey.

Well. That would be interesting.

The killer's brow furrowed.

This is the last time I squander my valuable talents on bad equipment and incompetent, no-talent help. That girl's a professional killer, no doubt about it.

Next time I'll make sure she's looking me in the eye when I twist my knife into her heart.

The shooter began to pack the rocket launcher in its special case.

No more screw-ups. Time to relieve the world of Vianne.

A smile formed on the assassin's lips.
Besides. I owe it to myself.
And to a ghost.

The van had barely come to a stop when Vianne was out and sprinting to the main house to get help. She altered course before reaching the front door when she saw Bernard coming around the side of the building with the dogs.

Without a word she grabbed his sleeve and pulled him toward the van.

It took Bernard less than a second to react. When he saw his unconscious father, he reached into the van, worked the man out, and slung him over his shoulder. In less than a minute he had brought César into the house and settled him gently on the long couch in the living room.

Jacqueline, hearing the commotion, came into the living room, took one look at César, and ran to him. Kneeling at his side, she ran one of her hands over his face.

César grunted and coughed and opened his eyes.

"Oh, God, César. What happened?" Jacqueline's face was a study in frightened concern. She looked around for Vianne, who was nowhere to be seen.

Bernard stood behind Jacqueline and let out a long, relieved breath when he saw his father blink and try to focus his eyes. Bernard knew that movement meant life, and his worry quickly evaporated.

César put a hand up to his blood-soaked hair, cringed with pain, and said, "Where's Vianne?"

A moment later Vianne ran into the room from the kitchen, a hand towel and a quart of Beefeater in her hands. Marta was right behind her with more towels and gauze bandages.

César began to sit up and started to say something. But the words became a yell when Vianne put a hand around the back of his neck and carefully poured some of the 100-proof gin on his wound.

"*Merde*! What the hell!" He put his hands to his soaking hair and felt as if he would pass out again from the pain.

Bernard held back a laugh and looked at his stepsister. "*Brava*, Vianne."

But her face was a study in concentration, her thoughts focused on what had just happened on the road and what might happen next.

At first she thought that one of the two men with guns had thrown a bomb or a grenade at the car. But a second before the explosion, she had seen a shining streak at the corner of her eye as she was driving. It had flashed out of the forest on one of the hillsides.

Whoever had launched the missile was still out there, still alive, and, most likely, still determined to kill.

"*Merde sainte*!" Luc stood frozen in the door to the living room, his face incredulous at the sight of his father sprawled on the couch bleeding.

Vianne was rock still, every nerve in her body tense.

César's face turned to granite, and his eyes bored daggers into Luc's. He said nothing, but the question was everywhere in the room: *where were you, Luc?*

"I … I was up in the villa," Luc stammered. "Sleeping off a binge. I know you wanted me to drive you, but I figured Eduard or Jacqueline would be here and—"

"Or me." It was Vianne's whisper.

Luc turned to his stepsister.

She stood with her hands at her sides, fists bunched, still as stone. "Rocket," she finally whispered. "I saw it."

César looked at his eldest son for a long minute, and the silence in the room was treacle. Finally his voice broke the tension. "I'll speak with you later, Luc. For now we have a big problem."

Luc was almost cross-eyed with shock. "Who?"

César looked suddenly exhausted. "La Chose. Quentin Maillot."

Luc started to ask questions, but Vianne didn't hear them. Her mind had gone elsewhere.

Something is going to happen, she thought, *and very soon. Everything is wrong. Everything is—*

And then, for the second time that day, she heard her inner voice finish her thought:

Not over.

CHAPTER 17

Plane Ride

———

"You must take me."

César watched her from a few feet away. "I *must* do nothing, Vianne."

"I know Marseille. Better than you." The whisper had an intensity that bordered on desperation.

It had been two days since the attack, and everyone's nerves were raw.

"That's not a factor," he said, his voice flat.

"It's *my* life at stake." The muted anger lit up Vianne's eyes. "*Our* lives."

"You've seen what can happen." César patted the bandage on his head, his eyes level. "The answer is no."

"*Fous-toi!*" She pivoted on her heels and fired three fast rounds into the target at the far end of the warehouse. The shots were as haphazard as her emotions, and the cracking blasts of the gun seemed amplified by her fury.

César looked down the long room at the untouched target. "Lousy shooting. Worse language."

She hurled the Beretta onto the small table at her side, loudly scattering the neat lines of waiting ammo. Then she took a single fast step up to César, and without warning slapped his face hard.

He grabbed both her hands in his and forced them down against her sides. His eyes were fires. "Don't you ever—"

"You put me into this," she breathed between clenched teeth, her body writhing, trying to break her arms out of the iron grip of his fists. "So I'll finish it for us."

Their faces were inches apart, and she shook her head wildly from side to side, her hair a shining black cyclone. From the whirlwind came a last desperate whisper. "You gave me your word!"

He took a deep breath and waited for the storm to pass. After a few seconds he saw that the worst was over, and he let her go.

They stood in the empty warehouse, eyeing each other in silence.

Her lips pursed tightly, and her eyes danced with anger and unmistakable resolve.

"You gave me your word," she repeated, almost beneath the threshold of human hearing. "And I gave you mine."

His heart hurt as he looked at Vianne. The situation had spun out of control. There were too many dangers, too many mistakes begging to be made.

But she had a point. He *had* put her into it, and she *had* saved them both. Now the call was hers.

"Marseille," she breathed. "I must go."

He said nothing, realizing that there were more facets to her urgency than met the eye. After a thawing fifteen seconds, his face showed that he had allowed her to win.

Seeing that everything had suddenly changed, she backed up a few steps and swept her Beretta up off the table. Slipping it into her belt at the small of her back, she walked toward the door.

She didn't look at César as she passed him, but he heard her whisper, "*Merci.*"

"Why aren't I going with you?" Luc's face was dark, but César's mind was made up. He had already acquiesced to one request that grated against his better judgment, and he was ready for his son's question.

"I need you here, Luc. We're at war now," he said distractedly. He was in the process of carefully and quickly packing the clothes he would need. "While I'm away, I want you to stay here in the house, not at your beach apartment. Here and alert and ready to travel. And to oversee the estate while I'm away." He looked at his son with an even expression, but inside his brain was racing. "If anything changes, I'll let you know."

"But what if—"

César interrupted him. "Just be here. And don't oversleep." The sarcasm dripped like syrup.

"Sorry," Luc said with little conviction. "What difference did it make that I slept while Vianne drove you? You both lived, thank God."

Their eyes locked for a moment in the classic mutual standoff of a father and a son, and then César said, "Be careful."

He had a sudden odd need to placate Luc. "My trust is in you. As always." He patted his son's rough cheek, the one with the faded scar. Then he opened the door and strode out.

Luc walked behind him through the house and out into the bright sunshine.

Eduard was waiting by the Mercedes along with Matteo, a reliable bodyguard who had also worked for César for years. They were talking to Bernard, who was, as always, cheerful.

Jacqueline and Vianne were speaking softly with each other, half sitting against the open trunk of the Mercedes.

"Be careful, Vianne." Jacqueline had only a sketchy idea of the purpose of the trip, and was developing a bad feeling about it. "Please listen to César. Carefully."

Vianne saw the misgivings in Jacqueline's eyes and touched the older woman's hand. "I'll take care of César," she whispered with a sly smile. "I won't allow his eyes to wander."

"*Zut*, Vianne, and what about *my* eyes when he's gone, eh?"

Their quiet laughter calmed the nervousness that had wrapped itself around Vianne's heart. She whispered to Jacqueline, "He loves you, Jacqui."

Jacqueline looked at the ground for a moment and smiled faintly, but said nothing.

Luc placed the luggage in the trunk and said a quick goodbye to his father. Then he turned to Vianne.

"Be alert," Luc said. After a few odd seconds he leaned over and kissed Vianne's cheek. Then he walked back to the house, feeling the girl's eyes on his back.

César took Jacqueline aside and whispered something to her. She whispered something back, and kissed him.

"Bon voyage," Bernard said, bear-hugging his father and then his stepsister in turn.

In his powerful embrace, Vianne whispered, "We'll be back in just a few days. Easy."

"Easy," repeated Bernard as he released her and kissed her on both cheeks. He stood back and rocked on his feet.

Vianne couldn't help but wonder what was going on inside Bernard's head. *It must be calm and light in there all the time.*

César and Vianne got into the back of the car, and with the two bodyguards in the front seats, the Mercedes left the estate for the airport.

Luc stood at the living room window, watching the retreating car.

I should have noticed this coming over the past three years. I'm smart enough to see the handwriting on the wall: Father is starting to groom Vianne, allowing her to dive deep into the family business. I don't care how young she is, how honest and true she may show herself to be. I know what Father's up to.

In the future he wants to skip over me again, like he would have with Bernard and even Isabelle.

It's possible that Father may be incautious or delusional enough to give her the reins, let her take over. She's smart and icy cool, and she knows what she's doing.

And for all I know, she's been planning something like this from the first day she showed up here.

His eyes narrowed, and the corners of his mouth turned down. The scar on his cheek ached slightly.

"Vianne is only passing through," he muttered to no one. *She may have ingratiated herself with everyone here over the last few years, but she hasn't fooled me.*

One day now, very soon, the perfect, beautiful, wonderful Vianne may be no more.

Vianne's face was glued to the small window as the engines scrolled up to speed and the fifty-passenger regional jet moved into position on the runway.

She had never been on a plane, and unconsciously moved her hand to César's.

He wore a dark gray Brooks Brothers suit with a subdued tie over a cream shirt.

She had on a simple wine-colored dress by Yves St. Laurent, matching pumps, and large sunglasses. They had the look of a successful international businessman and his discreet, expensive escort.

César looked over his shoulder at Eduard and Matteo, both sitting in the row behind them. The two men seemed emotionless behind their dark glasses, but Eduard lifted his head a fraction of an inch in acknowledgment that he was focused and vigilant.

César turned back to see Vianne's three-quarter profile framed in the sunlight that was pouring in through the small window. He admired the mature determination in her face, and was surprised at the small thrill that rushed through her hand into his as the plane accelerated and roared east and out over the sparkling blue Mediterranean Sea. An image of Isabelle pulsed in his heart.

Sensing he was looking at her, Vianne turned to him and breathed, "You think we're being followed now?"

He nodded.

She saw the storm brewing behind César's gray eyes and turned to gaze out the window again.

He chuckled to himself in wonder at how she rarely seemed to show fear, and how she never wasted a single soft word. Anyone else would have asked more questions about the trip, the plan. But Vianne seemed to calmly understand that whatever she needed to know, César would tell her in good time.

And time had suddenly become precious. He touched her hand, and she looked at him. "Quentin Maillot may want us to smuggle something out of France, probably gold," he said.

"Will we do that?"

He looked at her and said, "What do you think?"

She smiled and turned to the window. She whispered to the bright sky outside, "Better run, Quentin."

César's brows involuntarily furrowed a millimeter or two. *This woman,* he said to himself, *is constantly evolving. Now she's become something completely unexpected, someone very different from the person I thought Isabelle would grow to be.*

An hour later, as the jet came into sight of land, it made a half turn north and began its descent. Vianne watched through the small window as the city of Marseille grew closer. She was shocked at the tableau spread below her in the morning sunshine.

In the clear light, the place where she was born looked huge, sprawling, and unfamiliar. She saw the busy port clogged with boats and freighters as the plane flew over the Château d'If, the castle-like fortress on a small island a mile offshore. Her eyes were wide, and she thought she could make out the tight district of streets around the docks where she grew up.

Mother and I lived in just a small part of this city, she realized with a sour feeling. *And from what I can see from this height, it was the worst part.*

She suppressed a shudder.

The plane continued north over land, and a couple of minutes later made a right turn over Martigues and out over the Ètang de Berre, the five-mile-long lagoon north of Marseille.

The jet turned into its final approach to the Aéroport de Marseille Provence, and it seemed to Vianne to speed up as its distance above the water rapidly decreased. At what seemed the last minute before crashing into the sea, a runway on a long man-made spit of land was suddenly flashing beneath the plane.

There was a bump and then a smaller bump and then the sound of the jets reversing. She squeezed César's hand as they leaned forward along with the other passengers under the strong and insistent deceleration.

Two minutes later the jet pulled up to a spot a hundred feet from the terminal. A rolling staircase was wheeled up to the plane, and the exit door hissed open on its track.

César and Vianne filed out the door in the queue of passengers.

At the top of the stairs, Vianne stopped for a fraction of a second, her eyes narrow and cautious in the bright morning light. She looked to the left and right, and smelled the air carefully.

Marseille.

Back to where I started.

In spite of the warm sunshine, a chill crept into her heart, and she felt eyes watching her. Her inner voice said, *Careful.*

She walked down the metal steps and out onto the tarmac.

CHAPTER 18

A Familiar Place

QUENTIN MAILLOT STOOD AT THE glass-and-steel railing and took a drag on his Dunhill gold-tip cigarette.

The drug lord owned the entire top floor of the newest, most desirable building in the Carré d'Or district of Marseille. But the magnificent view of the harbor and the blue Mediterranean from his well-guarded penthouse pool deck was lost on him.

The disaster of Kemal Zorzo had been in the forefront of his mind. Quentin had suffered a paranoiac fit when he heard the news of the man's suspicious death, but so far had been unable to find out who had set up the clever and dangerous Turk.

The fact that the man had been taken out in Corsica was disturbing.

And that fact was eclipsed by the stark, existential threat that the death of the Turkish criminal had suddenly presented to Quentin and his gang, La Chose.

Somehow, I have to retrieve what's mine, he said to himself for the hundredth time. *And without being destroyed—which is quite likely if I'm not careful.*

A blond woman lay on her back on a lounge chair, working on her tan. She wore a tiny bikini bottom and a pair of Ray-Ban sunglasses. On the small drink table by her side, a phone rang.

Quentin turned at the sound and saw the woman reaching for the phone. "Don't touch it."

The woman shrugged and started to turn over on her stomach when Quentin said, "Go inside." The woman shrugged again, picked up her tube of Bain de Soleil, stood up, and disappeared into the penthouse.

Quentin sat down on the vacated lounge chair, ran a hand through his thick hair, picked up the phone, and said, "*Oui.*"

A familiar voice said, "Duval has arrived, along with two of his attack dogs and the girl."

"Where are they now?"

"Le Petit Nice-Passédat."

Quentin was familiar with the tony, expensive hotel on its rocky perch above the water on the exclusive Anse de Maldormé. *The Corsican has style, I'll give him that.*

He hung up, put his elbows on his knees, and steepled his fingers in front of his lips in deep thought.

The key to my survival has just arrived in Marseille. And as a bonus, he brought that girl along with him.

That interesting girl.

He picked up a half-empty martini glass on the small table next to him and downed its contents in two gulps. Then he started making a series of phone calls.

César had booked three rooms at Le Petit Nice-Passédat—one for himself, one for Vianne, and one for the two bodyguards.

That night Vianne couldn't sleep.

She stood by the elegant room's open window, the light breeze off the water moving her hair. Before her lay the dark Mediterranean, a full ivory moon slowly rising from its distant edge. Boats rocked gently in the lunar light. *I'm back,* she thought with a shudder for the hundredth time.

It was almost three in the morning when Vianne got into bed and fell into a fitful sleep.

"I'll be back in the afternoon," she whispered.

She and César were sitting at a small, outdoor table in the hotel's restaurant, overlooking the sparkling morning sea.

César eyed her from behind his sunglasses. He had little to say, and was relieved that she wouldn't be around him today, in case something went wrong with Maillot. He had suspicions about what Vianne had in mind, and they troubled him. No matter what, he would make sure she was protected.

"Fine," he said.

She looked at him quizzically. *Fine? That's it?* her eyes asked, surprised by his quick, uncharacteristic acquiescence.

César looked over her shoulder at the table in the corner where the two bodyguards sat.

"*Non,*" Vianne whispered in anger, watching where his eyes went, realizing why he was so calm and assured. "*Non,* I need to be alone."

César smiled.

Eduard drove carefully.

The car was a forest-green Renault, supplied by the hotel from a rental firm. Eduard was familiar with the large city, had been in Marseille before. Vianne sat next to him and offered him little in the way of driving directions. Her annoyance with Eduard's forced presence was almost palpable.

It was only when they approached the densely packed area that radiated out for several miles from the busy port that she realized that the surroundings were familiar, and started to give him quiet, exact directions. The expression on her face remained cold—her eyes watched everything.

She directed Eduard to a cobble-paved street and had him pull the car to the curb across from the little *poissonnerie.* She sat still and looked up at the single window on the floor above the fish store—the small window that let the light into the room where she had spent her childhood and her mother had been murdered.

Vianne sat in the passenger seat in silence. She put a hand on Eduard's sleeve. He saw angry tears in the girl's eyes and knew enough not to say anything.

After a few minutes she wiped a hand across her face and whispered, "*Bon,*" and told him where she wanted to go next.

Twenty minutes later Eduard pulled the Renault to a stop in front of the large tan stone structure that was the Benedictine convent on the rue Edmond Rostand.

"Wait here," Vianne whispered as she opened her door.

The man was about to get out of the car, but her face stopped him. He knew most of the story of what had happened to the girl in this building, and when her eyes bore into his and told him not to dare come with her, he nodded and sat still.

Eduard watched through his wraparound sunglasses as the woman walked up the stone steps of the nunnery, pulled open one of the massive wooden doors, and disappeared inside.

It had been three years since Vianne had walked out of the convent doors with Zelda Latour and nearly been killed by Benito.

Now she walked straight through the large high-ceiling room at the front of the building and made for the hallway at its end that led to the Mother Superior's private office. Vianne was a study in black: simple black dress cut six inches above her knees, shiny black pumps, ferociously black gleaming hair. The only counterpoints were the sparking diamond *V* on her chest and the minuscule splinters of glittering light in her dark eyes.

She looked neither right nor left, and in the sanctuary of the nunnery the sounds of her heels were staccato gunshots on the marble floors. She passed a couple of Sisters who looked at her with surprise, but she paid them no heed.

She came to the door she was looking for, opened it without knocking, and strode inside. She swung the door closed behind her with one hand, and stood still.

Mother Odette was sitting at her desk, phone receiver in one hand, rosary strand in the other. A large Bible lay closed on her desk, a long stainless-steel letter opener as a placeholder. The gold crucifix at its end stuck out from between the thick book's pages.

The nun looked up quickly and saw the girl. Her eyes widened, and she skipped a breath or two and slowly replaced the phone's receiver in its cradle while the party on the other end was still talking.

She cleared her throat and started to get up from her chair. "You …" she began.

Vianne interrupted her. "Sit down." The hissed whisper unquestionably a command.

Odette slowly lowered herself back into the chair and stared at the familiar face. *This girl is no longer just pretty,* she thought. *Now, three years later, she's startlingly beautiful. And moreover—* incredibly—*she's still breathing.*

The nun let her gaze travel up and down the young woman.

"You're alive," the Mother Superior finally rasped softly. Her calm demeanor masked her inner tension. Frantically trying to put some order into the situation, she smiled crookedly and said, "What a pleasant surprise."

Vianne stood still—no movement, no words.

Odette picked up the rosary beads from her desk and fiddled with them. She leaned forward in her chair and said, "I thought you were dead." The beads clicked in the still air. "We all did, here at the convent. Many prayers were said for your immortal soul." She smiled. "Isn't that ironic?"

Raw energy seemed to radiate from Vianne's eyes, and the silence could have been cut with a knife.

"Zelda Latour," Vianne finally whispered.

Odette began to shake under her habit. "What … Zelda? What about her?"

A single whispered word: "Address."

"I don't know it, I can't, she—"

"Now." Vianne breathed, and shifted her body, bending one knee a fraction of an inch, letting her arms move slightly away from her sides. Something in the odd gesture made Mother Odette cringe.

Vianne leaned over the desk. One hand rested on Mother Odette's Bible and the sharp, crucifix-tipped letter opener.

After a few seconds the nun pulled her eyes off Vianne, opened a desk drawer, and drew out a small leather-bound book. She flipped through a few pages, then took up a pencil and wrote the Rainbow Madam's address on a scrap of paper. She held the small page out to Vianne.

Taking the paper, Vianne lifted her head and whispered, "Adèle. Is she here?"

"Adèle? Adèle Dupuy?"

Vianne nodded once and was about to whisper, *Yes, Adèle the novitiate. The shy, fair girl with the wine-stain birthmark on her neck. My only friend in this dreadful place.*

But before she could whisper it, Vianne's heart almost stopped as she saw the Mother Superior's face go stark white and the old nun's hands start shaking.

Oh no, Vianne thought as the sickening realization hit home. She reached down across the desk, and with both hands grabbed the front of Odette's habit, pulling the woman forward hard.

"When?" Vianne whispered.

Mother Odette stared up into the girl's eyes and thought she saw the tiny flames of hell. She mumbled, and Vianne quickly slapped her face, hard.

"*When?*" the low word hissed again from between Vianne's gritted teeth.

Odette tried to get up, but the young woman held her forcefully in the chair. The nun seemed to collapse in on herself, and sat still. Then she looked up at Vianne with a leering grin that dripped venom.

"A few months ago, *Vivienne,*" she slurred. "*Je suis désolée.* Sorry, but you are too late. Certainly your friend Adèle has made Madame Latour richer by now, and by a hefty profit margin, I'm sure."

Vianne slowly let go of the nun and stood up straight. She breathed deeply and remained staring at the Mother Superior.

The air in the room was thick, and Odette continued, "If she's still alive, that is." She looked Vianne up and down from her chair. "She was certainly nothing like you."

As the long, tense seconds ticked by, the nun's composure visibly evaporated. "You piece of gutter *merde,*" she finally spat at Vianne, abandoning her Kabuki of civility. "What are you going to do now, you filthy little *chatte,* kill me? Kill the Mother Superior of a convent, the kind and loving caretaker of orphans?"

Mother Odette smoothed the front of her habit and glared at Vianne. "I'm certain your mother would not have approved, eh?"

Vianne blinked.

Odette sat back in her chair and narrowed her eyes in triumph at the deadly, beautiful woman in the black dress—at the sparkling diamond *V,* at the glittering darkness in the now-hesitant eyes.

"Ha!" Odette said archly, her unassailable logic and her sharp insight into the human condition wiping away her fears. "I didn't think so."

Vianne waited a few more silent seconds and decided what her mother would really have wanted. She lifted one hand, and without taking her eyes from the woman who had sold her three years earlier, slowly made the sign of the cross in the still, calm air.

Her other hand went to the Bible and to the sharp, gleaming letter opener.

Five minutes later Eduard saw Vianne coming down the steps of the convent.

She walked quickly, her eyes scanning left and right. She reached the Renault, immediately got into the passenger seat, and slammed the door closed.

He said to her, "Are you all right?

Vianne nodded. "Take me back to the hotel," she whispered.

CHAPTER 19

Over Coffee

"*Bonjour, mon ami.*"

César knew the man was there. He had spotted him getting out of a dark BMW sedan with two other men half a block away.

He decided to study his cup of coffee as the man approached through the loose crowd. When he sensed that he was close enough, César looked up from his small table at the busy outdoor café in the Vieux Port district of the city. A clock on a nearby street lamp said 1:00 p.m.

Quentin Maillot stood before him. The man wore expensive jeans and a light suede ecru sport jacket over an open white shirt. A tiny comb hung against the center of his shaved chest on a link chain.

César spotted the man's backup—two heavily muscled youths with hard faces and obvious bulges in the pockets of their sweatpants. The musclemen scanned the area once or twice with dead eyes, and then sat down at a nearby table, adjusting their chairs to give them an unobstructed view.

A few yards behind them, Matteo sat at a third table, watching everything through his dark glasses.

"Quentin," César said without getting up, automatically filing away everyone's position in his mind.

Maillot ran the tiny gold comb through his black mustache. "Sorry we couldn't meet in a more intimate venue, César, but I do enjoy being out in the open air this lovely time of year."

He pulled out the other chair and sat down opposite César. "I was happy to hear your voice this morning. And so pleased you're in Marseille."

César eyed Quentin across the table and saw that he hadn't changed in the half-dozen years since he had last laid eyes on him. He didn't have to remind himself that the man's insipid small talk was a blind, a distraction.

Quentin Maillot was extremely clever and had the morals of a hyena. His brutality was legend in the French underworld. It was rumored that he had murdered his own brother during a fight over drug turf and then shipped the dismembered pieces of the body to various politicians in France, Italy, Germany, and Spain.

The man raised a finger for a waiter, and ordered coffee. Then he gazed down his nose at César and said, "Help me with something, my dear friend. I need your expertise, your Midas touch."

The waiter set a cup of coffee in front of Quentin. He picked it up and took a short, tentative sip. He saw César's eyes sweep their surroundings again, checking the two toughs behind Quentin, and his own man Matteo. Quentin shrugged inside. This elaborate caution was actually mundane—an everyday practice in both men's lives—like breathing. But it cautioned him that Duval's train of survival ran on tracks parallel to his.

When César said nothing, Quentin sat back in his chair and said, "Kemal Zorzo's little enterprise is on the block, César. It will go to the highest bidder, who will be me."

"Bidder?"

Maillot showed a line of small, straight teeth and gave his head an odd shake as if he were trying to find the right words.

He sighed. "All right, it will go to the fastest, the most connected, the most—"

"—the one with the most firepower. Is that what you're trying to say?" It was César's turn to take a sip of coffee.

Quentin shrugged. "What does it matter what the means are, eh? Suffice it to say that within a week or two, Zorzo's entire network and all his treasure will be in the control of La Chose. And that's where you come in."

"I will come in only when you hand over the source of my troubles."

"Ah, the man who was running Benito Scapalone's brother." Quentin scrunched up his face into a mask of distaste. "Could it be the same fool who tried to blow you up on the road to the airport last week?" He looked up at the sky and sighed.

César waited and thought, *Suicidal to underestimate Maillot. Showing he had knowledge of the rocket attack isn't just braggadocio. It may have been Quentin or his lackeys behind the rocket or it may not have been. He's strutting his knowledge of events to muddy the waters, at best. Was La Chose actually behind the attacks? Now I'm not as certain as I was.*

And something's not right. Something's stirring behind Quentin's arrogant demeanor. César took another sip of coffee and realized what it was.

Something's scaring the man.

Maillot settled a now-serious gaze on César. "Are you aware of how your reputation has been, how do you say, *tarnished* with this fixation on that girl of yours? Everyone who is anyone believes that you may have gone over the edge. Not necessarily gone soft. Just over the edge."

"Just get me whoever's responsible for the attack, Quentin. It's become a family matter."

Quentin waved a hand in the air. Light glinted off a diamond pinkie ring. "You sound like a Mafia criminal, César. Or should I say Unione Corse? Tsk, tsk."

César's face was hard. "Yes or no, Quentin."

Maillot let out a long breath. "I told you once, César. It was Giuseppe Randazzo."

"Then persuade Randazzo to hand over the piece of *merde.*"

"Even *I* may not be able to do such a thing, César. By this time you've obviously tried the same thing and failed." He put a finger to his face and tapped his lips in thought. Then he made a moue with his mouth and said, "For you, César, I will give it a shot. But only if ..."

César crossed his arms in front of his chest and waited.

"*Only* if you do one small thing for me, César, and I'll help you. I swear I will."

César's face showed what he thought of Quentin's oath.

"I need your assistance, my good friend," the drug lord continued. "I need you to get me something."

César was silent. His face was stone.

"It will be easy for you, my friend." Quentin's eyes showed the opposite.

Finally César said, "Well? What is it that is so easy that you can't do it yourself, Quentin? What do you want in exchange for what should be given to me for free?"

Quentin took a sip of his coffee, dabbed his mustache with a napkin, and leaned over the table until his face was close to César's.

Then the head of La Chose said, "I need Zorzo's boat, César."

"What?" César wasn't sure he had heard Quentin right.

"I need the *Crescent Rose*."

CHAPTER 20

The Rainbow Madam

AT THE HOTEL VIANNE TOLD Eduard she would be staying in her room and asked if he could please leave her alone.

"I'm tired," she whispered to the bodyguard. "I think I'll sleep."

It took her a few minutes to wash, fix her hair, and gather some things she needed in a shoulder purse. Then she walked out of the room, relieved that Eduard was nowhere in sight.

Being very cautious, she was able to get a taxi near the hotel without running into the bodyguard. Through a pair of fashionable Gucci sunglasses she watched the neighborhoods and streets from the backseat of the cab. She had put her hair into a heavy ponytail with a thick rubber band—a small but surprisingly effective attempt at changing her looks.

A half hour later the taxi let her off a few blocks from the address on the scrap of paper the Mother Superior had given her.

She walked slowly toward the small, low apartment building in the 14th Arrondissement. This part of the city consisted of many such structures—moderately priced, somewhat seedy housing for the general working population of Marseilles.

Zelda Latour owned the entire three-story building, renting half of its thirty apartments and using the others on the top floor for her busy prostitution business. It was rumored that Zelda also housed her priceless collection of crystal and glass art sculptures somewhere on the premises.

Two or three hard-looking men lounged on the sidewalk in front of the building, and a few loitered across the street. From time to time, equally hard young women came in and out of the lobby door. At one point a well-dressed older man with slicked-back silver hair strode into the building.

A preferred customer, Vianne thought. She took a few deep breaths, hefted the black leather shoulder bag that she had brought with her from the hotel, and adjusted her sunglasses.

She walked straight up to the building, ignoring the stares of the young hookers and the men hanging around, all obviously in Zelda's employ. In the small and surprisingly clean lobby, a rail-thin young girl leaned against the wall smoking a cigarette. Vianne asked her if Zelda was around.

"Why are you whispering?" the dyed-blond girl asked. The insides of her arms sported ornate, flowery tattoos—a cover for clusters of needle marks—and her vacant eyes confirmed the story of serious drugs.

Vianne was saddened but not shocked. She had grown up around hopeless women who were at similar rock bottoms in their lives. But this girl was really young, she thought—not more than fourteen—and a river of anger coursed through Vianne.

"I was careless," Vianne cautioned in a whisper, and pantomimed cutting her vocal cords out.

The girl merely nodded and said, "Zelda's in her parlor. You know, on the third floor."

Vianne gave her a small smile and walked toward the staircase at the back of the lobby. She took one more look at the doomed girl, then turned and went to find the Rainbow Madam.

Vianne didn't have to wonder which room was Zelda's "parlor." A huge, muscular man with a shaved head, dressed completely in black, stood at one of the doors in the otherwise empty corridor on the third floor and stared hard as she walked toward him.

Benito's replacement.

As she approached the giant, her soaring adrenaline levels made her skin tingle, and she breathed deeply to gather a bit of control. She looked up at the man's face and whispered, "Madame Latour, *s'il vous plaît.*"

The man was all business, and his body language showed barely controlled violence. "Who are you?"

"Quentin Maillot sent me," she whispered in Marseille French, betting her life that the large bald man knew the drug king's name and reputation. She lowered her sunglasses for a moment so the man could see her eyes. Then she opened the black leather shoulder bag to display what was inside. It was stuffed to the top with money.

"I'll give it to her," the man said, reaching for the bag, but Vianne took a step back.

"Only me," she whispered. "Don't make my owner mad."

The man studied her face carefully. "Stay," he said, and disappeared into the room.

A minute later he returned and said to Vianne, "Go in."

Vianne nodded, went through the door, and heard it close behind her.

She blinked, and for a long moment she didn't understand her surroundings.

The large room was crowded almost floor to ceiling with glass pedestals, glass tables, and glass shelves displaying a thick, virtual forest of crystal statues, transparent figurines, and translucent objets d'art. There were a few wine-red satin chairs, and a large maroon settee faced the room, its back to a large picture window. Light from the window streamed through the glass menagerie, splashing an explosive kaleidoscope of a thousand tiny refracted rainbows on the walls, the ceiling—on everything and everyone in the room.

Including Vianne.

In front of the window Zelda Latour sat in the center of the settee, a thick ledger in her lap. A pair of muscular young men flanked her on either side. They both wore tank tops that showed off their oiled shoulders and biceps. An ornate phone sat on a glass coffee table in front of the trio in the midst of fifty or sixty glass statuettes and paperweights.

"The rules," the octogenarian madam said without looking up. "For each piece of glass you break, you spend an hour with Danté. You met him out in the hall."

Vianne stood amidst the startling collection of glittering objects saying nothing, prisms of light playing on her face, her body.

After a minute, Zelda looked up and inspected Vianne over the top of her thick glasses. "I'm honored. Monsieur Maillot must be in need of something." Her eyes zeroed in on Vianne's shoulder bag. "And he wants to prepay, as I understand from Danté. Well, he can … he can count on …"

Her voice came to a slow halt. Her small eyes squinted hard. "Do I know you?"

Vianne shook her head, her heart racing. Her eyes flashed behind the large sunglasses, and she reached into the shoulder bag.

The two men on either side of Zelda immediately began to get up, but relaxed when a bushel of money landed on the book on Zelda's lap.

Vianne saw the old woman eye the pile of cash. It looked to be at least ten thousand dollars in US currency.

"Ah!" Zelda smiled with honest delight. "The good monsieur is obviously in need of high-quality product, superior companionship."

She looked carefully at the woman standing on the other side of the glass coffee table for another few seconds. "How can I help Monsieur Maillot? What does he want?"

The two muscular men were enraptured by the conversation.

Vianne took a deep breath. "Adèle Dupuy," she whispered.

"*Eh?*"

"He wants to buy Adèle Dupuy," Vianne repeated in a low breath.

Vianne saw Zelda's mind at work.

After a few seconds, the old woman said, "I have so much wonderful inventory, so many better, younger girls. Why her?" An odd look suddenly came into Zelda's face, and she said, "How does he know about—?"

"Only her," Vianne whispered.

One of the men on the settee leaned toward Zelda and showed his perfect white teeth. "The man must be interested in a nun, eh?" he said with a chuckle. "He's gotten religion, *non*?"

Zelda's head turned a few millimeters to the side, but her eyes bored into Vianne's. "What you ask is not possible. I sold that redheaded piece from the convent three months ago, and I can't ..."

Vianne tensed as she heard Zelda's voice trail off, and she saw a sudden, panicked light of comprehension come into the old pimp's eyes.

"Sold to whom?" Vianne whispered, but she realized with sickening certainty that the game had changed.

Zelda's eyes widened and she hissed, "*Ouah,* I *do* know you! I watched you die in the street!"

The old woman's mouth spluttered with anger, and with her veined fists she punched the two men sitting on either side of her. "Take her. Hold her down," she hissed.

The two men started to rise off the settee.

"Where's Adèle?" Vianne whispered one final time, but she knew that the chance had passed. It was too late.

Now the two men were standing, and only the clear glass coffee table separated them from Vianne.

Prisms of light played across the room, and Zelda growled like an animal from the settee.

Vianne reached quickly into her shoulder bag, and her hand came back into view with the gun she had placed there under the money.

The two men came at her, but not fast enough, and she pointed the Beretta at the first one's chest and fired. From the distance of less than a yard it blew a hole in his chest, and the sound of the shot was immense in the room.

Delicate glass objects exploded from the sound, the trajectories of crystal shards crisscrossing through the air. The first man's body fell sprawling into the glass coffee table in a smashing, glittering crash.

Vianne breathed deep, turned slightly, and fired again twice while rainbow chips zipped around her.

The second man tripped sideways, blood exploding from his face, and he stumbled into a dozen tall glass statues amid the screeching smashing of crystal and the stunning, loud obscenities of the gunshots. Light exploded and danced in darting spectrums while glass chips—misted red with blood drops from the bullet wounds and from the scores of cuts on the man's falling body— filled the violent air.

In the tornado of crashing, breaking, flying glass Vianne knelt quickly on one knee and pivoted to face the door, her short dress riding up her thighs.

The huge bald Danté barged in from the hallway like a mad bull, gun in hand, and the sight of Vianne's long legs naked up to her exposed black panties made his trigger finger pause for one second too long.

Vianne didn't breathe, and without pause shot three rounds at the charging Danté as he barreled into the room.

Blood snowballed from his chest and neck as his pistol roared. The sound of his 9 mm automatic going off was impossibly loud as his momentum launched him into the forest of glass and rainbows and sprays of blood.

Non! Vianne turned her eyes with wrenching disbelief to the sudden fire on her shoulder.

As the bulky giant fell headlong into what was still standing of the red-sprayed glass forest, it all but detonated, and the crashing crystal maelstrom was everywhere.

The slug from Danté's gun had sizzled past Vianne, leaving a vicious red seam in her shoulder, and slammed straight through Zelda and the settee before violently exploding the picture window behind the Rainbow Madam. The booming echoes of the guns and the dying hollers of the men and the crashing of the glass caromed back and forth in the swirling gun smoke and the jittering flying rainbows.

Mon Dieu, Vianne screamed in her mind, but she kept her lips tightly shut.

Beretta clasped in her two fists, she slid back down into a sitting position on the floor, blood-splattered legs wide apart. With one hand she gingerly touched the charred streak on her shoulder. It had begun to ooze blood through the shredded clothing, and she thanked the stars that the bullet hadn't been an inch or two lower.

Keep going, her inner voice urged, and Vianne nodded. She took a deep breath, stood up, and turned shaking to face Madame Latour.

Zelda seemed to have been pushed by a giant hand into the plush settee, a spreading scarlet stain covering the front of her body. Vianne stepped over one man's twitching body and through the piles of broken glass. She bent over Zelda and saw that the old woman's chest was still moving.

"Adèle," she whispered urgently into the woman's ear. "Where is she?"

Zelda's eyes opened slowly, and her gaze slid to Vianne's face. "Why should I tell you?" she croaked, and a thin rivulet of blood poured from her lips.

Vianne bent low and took off her sunglasses to let Zelda see her eyes. "It will count," she whispered. A tiny reflected rainbow glowed on Vianne's cheek.

Zelda laughed weakly and coughed up more blood. Her eyes turned upward, her body shook once, and it seemed to Vianne that she had expired. But a moment later the woman's lips moved and she purred as if in a reverie, "He gave me half a million francs for her, you know."

"Who, who bought her?"

Zelda opened her mouth, and what came out was a long, barely comprehensible, gurgling belch.

Vianne shook Zelda's shoulder hard, but the old woman was gone.

As Vianne stood up, she heard the approaching sounds of running feet out in the hallway.

In the hallway, two men, guns at the ready, crouched on either side of the door.

Signaling to each other with their hands, they moved crab-like into the room and gaped at the devastation that was the parlor of the Rainbow Madam. What they saw brought them to a stunned stop. The entire room was calf-deep in shining, glinting shards of glass, most tinged a pinkish scarlet with blood. Three bodies, one of them the fearsome Danté, lay in varying states of mortal damage and deconstruction among the glass.

Zelda sat upright in the center of the settee, unquestionably dead.

The two men were still, pointing their weapons to the left and right in the dissipating smoke.

Only death was there.

One of the men, nerves on fire, stood up and carefully crunched his way across the glass-strewn floor. He looked out through the picture window's now-empty frame. Directly below, the building's fire escape zigzagged down to the street.

A young woman was rushing down the last few steps.

Before the man could react, he saw her reach the sidewalk, sprint across the street, and disappear between two buildings.

"Are you insane!"

"Don't blame Eduard," she whispered.

César looked as if he would explode. "I'll blame whomever I damn please! What the hell were you thinking?"

Vianne cringed intermittently as César stood behind her and swiped at her cut shoulder with a clean hotel hand towel soaked in vodka from the minibar. He used as much gentleness as he could muster, considering his state of mind.

She was wrapped in a hotel robe with one shoulder pulled down so César could tend to it. She had been showering awkwardly, trying to keep the water spray off her aching shoulder, when César had burst into her hotel room.

She had dried off as best she could, slipped into a robe, and come out of the bathroom. When she had showed him the wound, he thought he would have a heart attack. But her quiet words about what had transpired in Zelda's parlor left César dumbfounded.

"*Mnn!*" Her whisper was harsh, and she scowled at César over her shoulder as he pressed the vodka-soaked towel against the wound for what seemed the hundredth time. Her eyes shot daggers, and she smelled of hotel soap and vodka and frustration.

César had stationed Eduard outside the door of the hotel room, the man fearing for his life. Matteo was ordered down to the hotel's lobby and told to stay on high alert.

"If I had known this would happen, I would never have allowed you to come to France with me." He touched the wound with the towel.

"*Mnn!*"

"We have to get out of Marseilles. Right now."

Vianne narrowed her eyes.

He stood back a step, his body language obvious and dangerous. "I'll concede that you did society a favor by killing Zelda, but what you did was impossibly risky, completely stupid ..." He stopped speaking, trying to control his anger.

Vianne was suddenly shaky, and she almost stumbled. César swept her up in his arms and dropped her gently onto the bed.

She shook her head, and after a few seconds propped herself up on one elbow.

"I failed," she whispered, fatigue starting to take over. "*I* did. Don't blame Eduard."

"Eduard let you slip by him," César said without emotion. "He's finished."

"Please, no."

César sighed inside, and softened his tone. "He's getting older, Vianne. He's a good man and a loyal employee. I won't do anything bad to him."

Vianne let her eyes stay on César's for a few extra seconds and then nodded a *merci*.

César sat down on the edge of the bed. *She's had the kind of day that would have brought grown men to their knees,* he thought. *There's something inside her that I still can't see clearly, some kind of inner force that drives her like a caged cheetah.*

"I'll make the arrangements now. We're going back home."

He saw a wave of strained relief and resignation cross Vianne's face. Isabelle had that same way of melting his anger, he recalled. And this ... this *cheetah* was still coming of age as a woman, he thought, a woman with sharp claws and a secret heart.

"I'm sorry about your friend, Vianne," he said. "About Adèle." He touched her hand. "I don't have to tell you about how life is. You know it for yourself. We do our best, but sometimes things happen that we just can't fix, no matter how hard we try."

Her eyes softened.

"Rest a little. I'll be back soon, and then we'll go home." He stood up, gave her a tight smile, and left.

She nodded, now utterly spent, and let her head fall lightly onto the pillow. A moment later she fell into a deep, dreamless sleep.

CHAPTER 21

The Crescent Rose

———

VIANNE WALKED UP TO WITHIN a yard of Luc, looked away for a second, then slapped his face hard.

The man shook his head a time or two, put a hand to his cheek, and was about to say something when she launched another hit at him, this time with a fist that nearly broke the skin.

The man stumbled back in disbelief.

Jacqueline started to say something, and Bernard quickly put his arms around Vianne's slim waist from the back, lifting her off the ground. He had a hard time—it was like trying to hold back a bobcat.

Vianne struggled, arms flailing, legs kicking, murder in her eyes.

A few feet in front of her, Luc composed himself as well as he could and rubbed his aching jaw. He shook his head again and said to Vianne, "What the hell? Are you crazy, you little—"

Jacqueline held a hand up. "Enough!" she said, a rare anger in her usually modulated voice. "Both of you."

Vianne's lips were pressed into an angry slash, but she stopped moving and whispered over her shoulder, "Put. Me. Down."

Bernard smiled and gently lowered her to the floor.

Jacqueline saw that Vianne was about to go for her older step-brother again, and put a hand on her upper arm. "Don't."

Luc glared at Vianne. He had just come out of the house with Jacqueline and Bernard when the Mercedes had driven up from the airport.

César was at the car giving Eduard and Matteo instructions when he heard the ruckus behind him. He walked over and sur-veyed the ongoing drama.

He looked at Luc, a dark bruise already forming on his chin. "You. Luc. What's going on here?"

"I don't know. I came to welcome you and Vianne back, to kiss her cheek, and she just went off the deep end."

Vianne balled her fists, and her eyes sent two lightning bolts at Luc. She spit on the ground in front of him.

César looked at her. "What's with you?"

She took a few deep breaths. Finally she took her eyes off Luc and whispered to César, "Nothing."

As she brushed past Luc, she made a classic rude gesture at him with her hand.

Jacqueline gave Luc a look and followed Vianne into the house.

Luc glared at her back as she disappeared through the door. He rubbed his sore chin and turned to his father. "Hormones?" he ventured.

"No, that's not it."

Luc threw his hands in the air and stalked off toward the warehouse.

"What *is* it?" asked Bernard.

César put his arm around his younger son's shoulder, and they walked toward the house. "I'll explain later," he said.

"What happened in Marseille, Vianne?" Jacqueline stood in the doorway to Vianne's room. "And why the sudden hate on Luc?"

Vianne threw her shoulder bag with the Beretta onto her bed and turned to face Jacqueline. She saw the look of concern on the older woman's face and searched for the few right words to describe what had happened.

Finally, she whispered, "Luc's whores."

"What?" Jacqueline walked across the room and leaned against the sill of the open window. "What do you mean, Vianne?"

Vianne's body slumped a bit, and she immediately felt the dull pain in her injured shoulder. She sat down on the side of the bed. "It's a problem, Jacqui," she whispered.

Jacqueline listened carefully as Vianne outlined what she knew of Adèle's fate in a few soft sentences. She finished with a quiet condemnation of Luc's addiction to prostitutes—an addiction that added fuel to the fire of sex slavery.

"Prostitution is legal here, Vianne," Jacqueline said. "You know that."

Vianne shook her head. "Selling girls against their will," she whispered. "*Méprisable.*" Despicable. She felt like bunching her fists.

Jacqueline was well aware of what had happened to Vianne when she was sixteen—how close the orphan had come to being sold into sex slavery. But she was still suspicious of the ferocity of Vianne's attack on Luc. "I see," Jacqueline said carefully.

As if reading Jacqueline's thoughts, Vianne whispered, "I have a bad feeling about Luc now. It'll pass."

Jacqueline stepped closer, sat down on the bed next to Vianne, and turned to face her. "I've been with César seven years now, Vianne. When I first arrived, Bernard welcomed me immediately, but it took Luc years to get used to it."

Vianne watched her face intently.

Jacqueline looked away, remembering. "Luc thought his father had betrayed his mother, that I was an opportunist who had taken advantage of a vulnerable man going through a tragic time. But that couldn't be further from the truth. César was just being César—being a real man who knows who he is."

She touched Vianne's hand and said, "That's why he saved you."

"He never thought I was Isabelle?" Vianne whispered.

Jacqueline laughed softly and shook her head. "Maybe when the monster Benito had his gun to your head, but not after that. Not after he discovered who you were in that hospital. He knew you weren't Isabelle then, but he took you in anyway, damning the consequences that might have followed."

Vianne knew it was true, had known it for a long time.

She squeezed Jacqueline's hand as she would that of a sister. Then she silently thanked her stars for the good fortune that the Duval family had showered on her, and for the help she would need from them in the future.

The very near future.

"Maillot wants us to sail the *Crescent Rose* ten miles out and away from Ajaccio, free from police interference." César took a bite of pasta and watched the faces of the other three people at the kitchen table. "At that point he'll have his own Sea Ray Forty-Five waiting with men to board the *Rose* and take her the rest of the way to Marseilles. We will trade boats, and then we'll return to Ajaccio in the Sea Ray."

"That's a very expensive boat," Luc said. "We're getting it for nothing."

"No, we are performing a service. Maillot is trading his forty-five-foot boat for the dead Zorzo's seventy-five-footer. The Sea Ray is merely our fee for making the trade."

Luc was skeptical. "Surely Mignone has torn the boat apart looking for more heroin. He wouldn't stop at the hundred kilos, and Maillot knows that heroin is gone. What makes that yacht so special?"

"I don't know," César said, a shadow coming into his face.

"And what will stop him and his men from just taking the boat from us by force? He isn't a choir boy, you know."

"No, Quentin needs us. They all need us. He just wants that boat, and he won't risk mucking up the deal. He knows that I'll come after him too fast and too hard to make a double cross worthwhile."

Luc shrugged, scorn in his eyes.

César ignored the look. "But something just isn't right. Quentin isn't interested in the *Crescent Rose* just for its value, though that value is high. Something else is on it—something vital to him, hidden somewhere that I'll bet even the police couldn't find."

He looked at his younger son. "What do you think, Bernard? Any ideas?"

Luc rolled his eyes at his father's kind indulgence of his brother's damaged mind, but Vianne watched and listened carefully.

Bernard smiled, happy to be asked his opinion. "Get me on the boat, Papa. I'll know what to do if only—"

Luc cut in rudely. "Sure, Bern, whatever you say. Now, what I—"

Vianne shot a look at Luc and hissed, "*Ferme!*" She glared at him for an extra second, and then turned to Bernard and breathed, "Go on, Bernard."

Luc seemed ready to jump across the small table and grab Vianne's throat, but César gave a warning cough fraught with impatience. *Rather than dissipating, the bad blood between my oldest son and my stepdaughter seems to be deepening to a bright scarlet.*

But Bernard seemed oblivious to the interplay. "If I get on the boat, I will find what you're looking for."

"We're not even sure what that is," César said.

"How, Bernard?" Vianne whispered. "How will you find it?" Her inner voice said, *Listen carefully.*

"Papa knows."

All three looked at César.

César stared at Bernard for an affirming minute. He knew that ever since the head wound, his son seemed to have developed an odd sixth sense. *That's why he's such a good hunter,* César thought. *He knows where an animal will be before the animal does, and he senses what the next moments will bring before they happen. He sees things. And he finds things.*

And my other son has been too busy with his own interests to recognize his brother's subtle gifts. But I've seen them.

César's eyes slid to Vianne. *So has she.*

Then he said, "This is an opportunity for us to move forward."

Luc felt as if he had to say something. "How will doing the bidding of La Chose and putting everything in danger move us forward? Won't we be putting a bullet in our own heads in the long run if not sooner?"

"Not if we're careful," César said. "Not if we're smart." He scowled and looked from face to face. "Unless we make a big change in the game, we won't survive."

There was silence at the table.

Vianne took in a long breath, let her eyes move to Bernard for a moment, and whispered, "The *Rose* is the key."

"I can't do that."

Gustave Mignone stood next to César on the pier in the shadow of the *Crescent Rose.* The yacht was parked stern-first in a slip flanked on either side by similar boats owned by wealthy foreigners, most of them visiting from Cannes or Monte Carlo. César's own nameless Hatteras was berthed on the next pier over.

The two men stood inside a sagging cordon of yellow-and-black police tape. A seagull slept with its head under its wing on one of the boat's railings.

"Of course you can." César seemed relaxed, confident. "You're in charge."

"How did you know about Zorzo, César? How were you so well informed about his being on this boat that night? And his hundred kilos of heroin?"

César shrugged, adjusting his sunglasses. "I was just one step ahead of you, I guess. Did you find anything else on her, on the *Crescent Rose*?"

Mignone gave César a look. "We turned this yacht inside out, César. I had divers inspect the hull underwater. Even ripped out all the interior bulkheads."

"All of them, on the whole ship?" César's eyebrows jumped over the top of his sunglasses.

"The whole ship."

César watched the inspector's face carefully. "What did you find?"

Mignone looked at him with frank transparency. "Nothing. Just a few caches of guns, an extra kilo of White, some expensive furnishings, some halfway decent art, and a big saltwater fish tank in the master suite with a small shark swimming around in it."

César was about to say something, but Mignone beat him to it. "We smashed it and searched it. The fish we released unharmed into the sea." He made a sarcastic smile. "You can tell your daughter that no sharks were injured in the police search."

"Let me borrow the boat, Gustave." César's voice was suddenly cold. "You made a deal, remember?"

Mignone snorted. "No, César. My deal with your daughter was to be a bit more circumspect concerning your affairs. It didn't include handing over a piece of million-dollar police property."

"I just want to borrow it, Gustave. I'll return it." César took off his sunglasses to display his sincerity to the inspector.

"Why?"

"Family outing."

Mignone took a step closer. He was a good five inches shorter than César. "This boat is registered in Malta to a dummy corporation, which is owned by another dummy corporation and so forth down the line. If it isn't in Zorzo's personal inventory, it belongs to equally repugnant scum." He paused for a moment. "Perhaps the real owner will come to claim it one day."

"I can help you there, Gustave."

"Oh, you can?" The shorter man squinted up at César. "Well, then, who owns the *Crescent Rose*?"

"I'll tell you right now, but I just need to use it for a few hours. I'll bring it back."

Mignone shook his head. "I'm sorry, César. In light of everything that this boat brings with it, it's impossible."

César put his sunglasses back on. "Then why did you agree to meet me, eh?"

Mignone drawled, "I'm the chief inspector of this city. I owe it to my constituency to be on top of everything."

The two men stood looking out past the small forest of boats. Finally Mignone turned to César. "All right. Who's the owner?"

César smiled and said in a low voice, "La Chose. Quentin Maillot."

Mignone nearly choked. But before he could say anything, César said, "I'll pick up the boat tomorrow night. I'll bring it back the following morning."

"This had better be to my benefit, César."

César raised his chin an inch. "Or what, Gustave?"

"Or you'll never see the light of day again."

César smiled. "That might happen anyway."

From the top of a low building a half block away, a pair of eyes watched through binoculars. The tiny figures of César and Inspector Mignone walked off the pier between the large boats.

The eyes followed César until he reached his Mercedes, and watched as he got into the car next to Eduard and the two drove off.

Things are coming to a head, César. Let's see how you're going to handle them. I hope, truly hope that you come through this alive. I need you alive. I need to show you where you've gone wrong—and make my point, my grand statement.

I need you to suffer, César, as I've made you suffer before. And the best way I know to do that is to blow precious Vianne to smithereens before your eyes.

Then, and only then, will I let you die.

A gibbous moon had pulled itself out of the edge of the calm dark sea, and the *Crescent Rose* rocked quietly in her slip.

Belowdecks, Vianne and Bernard made their way slowly through the cabins. They had little need to say anything to each other, preferring to use the signs and body language they shared when they hunted together in the forest.

Large sections of the walls and floorboards of the luxurious cabins had been pried off. Furniture had been left in disarray, with the stuffing pulled out by the police searchers. A smorgasbord of damaged objects of all sorts littered the floors of each room.

The two made their way quietly into the large master suite that took up half the ship's area below the main deck. They stood in the doorway and swept their flashlights around the large cabin.

The bed had been moved across the room, and the panel in the floor that had concealed the hundred kilos of China White gaped empty. The walls had been torn apart, and the bed's mattress had been shredded in search of more drugs, its downy filler crammed in a heap in a corner of the room.

Where a giant fish tank had once been positioned, there was now a large, messy heap of gravel, sea plants, and broken glass covering half the room's teak floor.

Bernard and Vianne walked into the cabin and stopped in its center, their flashlights making slow ghosts across the jumbled clutter, their feet crunching through the reeking gravel and glass. This was the last place on the boat they were searching, and they had run out of places to look. The hope that Bernard would somehow find what the police had missed had waned, and after a few more frustrating minutes Vianne turned to leave.

"Wait," said Bernard.

Vianne stopped in the doorway and turned to look at the bulky, reassuring form of her stepbrother.

Bernard was in the middle of the room, slowly turning in place. It almost looked as if he were feeling something in the air of the quiet space. Finally he stopped, facing the window.

"Vianne," he said, a soft excitement rising in his voice. "Those police, they missed it. I found what Papa's looking for. It's still here."

She watched as his features formed a calm smile of triumph revealing a deep, hidden, almost supernatural intuition. She touched his arm, her face confused, as the beam of her flashlight played over the shambles of the stateroom.

He turned to her and with dead certainty in his voice said, "Come with me, Vianne. I need some help."

The next afternoon Jacqueline stood in the living room of the estate, arms crossed in front of her chest, eyes wet with anger and fear. "Don't do this."

César walked up to her and said, "There's nothing to worry about. Nothing will go wrong. I've protected us all so far, and I've made very careful arrangements for tonight."

"To hell with your arrangements, César," she almost spat, and walked around him. She got to the bedroom door and turned to face him. "Things are getting too dangerous. Too out of control."

César stood calmly, but his face showed his concern for the woman. He knew that Jacqueline would see this through as she always had, but he understood that it was a lot for anyone to endure. But too much had happened to stop now. Tonight he would set in motion a change that had long been coming. And if the stars were properly aligned, they would finally reveal the face of his mortal enemy.

The killer of his daughter, Isabelle.

He didn't touch Jacqueline to reassure her, sensing it was the wrong thing to do at the moment. Instead he just smiled and said, "No turning back now, my love. All I need is your blessing."

Her face said she wanted to stamp her feet, but after a minute she walked over to him and reluctantly took his hand in hers.

"I'll wait for you here," she said, turning her face away when he tried to kiss her.

Without another word, she left the room.

That night the *Crescent Rose* pulled away from its slip and made its way out into the harbor.

It motored south, then made a slow turn to the east past the lights of the dozens of boats clustered at Port Tino Rossi, and headed out into the Mediterranean.

Ten miles out, a boat running with no lights came dimly into view.

The *Crescent Rose* came to a slow stop, and a sleek forty-five-foot Sea Ray pulled up a few yards off the starboard side of the yacht. A voice cut through the soft sounds of the night sea.

"César. Are you there?"

"Ready," the reply floated over the short distance.

Quentin Maillot chuckled. "I'm so glad you've kept to your word, *mon ami*." Quentin stood at the stern of the Sea Ray. He wore a bulky pea coat, beneath which was hidden an Uzi submachine gun. Eight men with assault rifles were hidden strategically in his boat.

"Pull closer," came the voice from the *Crescent Rose*.

Quentin was suddenly off balance. *Something isn't right,* he thought. *César sounds very relaxed, almost* too *in control.* He signaled the man at the wheel to keep the Sea Ray steady where it was.

"César!" he shouted, a false bonhomie masking the uncertainty in his voice. "Show yourself!"

A man appeared at the rail of the *Crescent Rose,* dressed elegantly in a pearl-gray Brioni business suit. He stared across the short distance at Quentin. "Deal's off," he said.

Quentin's heart missed a beat, and he thought it would stop altogether. "What do you mean, 'deal's off'? No one reneges on—"

"I know who the killer is." The tone was mocking.

"Why, you fuck," Quentin said between gritted teeth as he frantically wrestled the Uzi from its place inside his coat. "What—"

But he never finished the sentence. The man in the suit stepped aside, and two figures appeared from behind him. They were dressed in black from head to toe, and between them they hefted a dark, heavy duffel bag. They aimed quickly and carefully and heaved the object across the twenty feet that separated the two boats and onto the Sea Ray's deck. It bounced heavily once and stopped at Quentin's feet.

The head of La Chose jumped aside and stared at the large, heavy black satchel on the deck in front of him. After two tense seconds he snapped his head back to look at the man at the rail on the *Crescent Rose.*

The man's cuff links winked in the moonlight. In one hand he held a small, plastic box with a single red button on it.

"*Ciao,* Quentin," the familiar voice came from across the water. Then he moved back a few steps, making sure his body was out of range, and pressed the red button.

The stern of the Sea Ray, along with Quentin Maillot, exploded in an earsplitting thunderclap. The sea lit up in a fireball as zooming pieces of the powerboat blasted out in all directions from the center of a hideously loud chrysanthemum of white fire. A whirlwind of hurtling projectiles crashed into the side of the nearby *Crescent Rose,* puncturing a galaxy of small holes above the waterline as other flaming chunks of the Sea Ray rocketed out over the water like blazing mortar shells.

The front half of the Sea Ray, vomiting roaring flames and body parts, was flung into the air from the force of the explosion. It crashed down and sank within seconds, the water around it an angry yellow-orange cauldron of flaming fuel. In less than a minute, the noxious stew had burned itself out, leaving a low black cloud hovering above the water's surface.

The sea around the *Crescent Rose* settled—putrid with the smell of gasoline and roasted meat.

The man in the pearl-gray suit came back to the rail and studied the glowing oil slick that marked the grave of the head of La Chose. He hawked loudly and spat over the side, and then turned to eye the man behind him.

"Let's go," he said, and his underling gave a short nod and walked quickly to the wheelhouse.

Then Giuseppe Randazzo turned his head for one last look at the midnight sea, loosened his tie, and went belowdecks. He tried to make himself as comfortable as he could.

It was a long way to Sicily.

CHAPTER 22

The Name

"I KEPT UP MY END, Giuseppe. Now it's your turn," César said into the phone.

"In good time, Duval. I know who you're looking for, and I'll tell you." Randazzo was in his den at his well-fortified palazzo in Palermo. He felt comfortable, triumphant.

César knew that Randazzo wouldn't cross him. He waited patiently, phone in hand, letting the Mafia don pontificate a bit more.

"I'll admit that I do like my new yacht, César. Thank you for that. I'm having it sent to the Benetti works in Viareggio for a refurbish. They're going to paint it black. And I'm changing the name to *Santa Rosalia.* How does that sound?"

"Heavenly."

"Ha, César!" *Sì,* heavenly ...

When César had returned from his meeting with Quentin in Marseille, the first thing he had done was call Randazzo and offer him a trade. The old mafioso was automatically skeptical, but César was certain he would rise to the bait. It was very tasty bait.

Once he was satisfied with Giuseppe's commitment to his plan, he had allowed Vianne and Bernard to sneak onto the *Crescent Rose* the night before Randazzo and his crew took it to sea. He had garnered a slim hope that somehow his son and step-daughter could discover Quentin's true motive for trying to retrieve the boat.

They had.

The following night César had stood in the shadows on the dock and watched Giuseppe and his hit team steam away on the *Rose,* certain that the rules of the game he was working on were about to change.

Giuseppe had understood the importance of what César wanted in trade. César needed the name of the shadowy enemy who had been dogging him, his family—his stepdaughter. Randazzo knew that César would have a case of perpetual *agita* until that foe was put down. *How clever that I never told him that name until now,* the mafioso had thought contentedly as he stood at the rail of the boat. *So much has been gained by being quiet, professing ignorance, and holding back.*

Now I can trade that one little inconsequential name for so much: the crippling of my mortal enemy La Chose, and a chance to push my way into their very profitable business.

He had gazed out at the midnight sea and thoughtfully rubbed his hand on the teak railing. *And I get this nice boat in the bargain.*

The outcome was a foregone conclusion. Quentin Maillot had to be put down. He was ruthless, vicious—*un animale.*

But I'm worse ...

César knew that from this point forward the Randazzos would be occupied with fighting the remains of La Chose for turf and power, leaving him breathing room to exact his revenge on his unknown tormentor and protect his family into the future without having to look over his shoulder.

"Well, Giuseppe?" César said into the phone. "The name, please."

"*Un minuto.*"

Randazzo looked at the two men lounging on the heavy furniture in his darkened office—one was his chief bodyguard, the other his nephew Antonio. He motioned for them to leave.

When he was alone, he rubbed the back of his neck for a moment and made a face. *Perhaps I should lie to César again or just let this whole thing fester for a while longer.*

But something told him that this time he should go through with it.

"All right, César," he said into the phone, and told him the name.

"Who is that?" César said, suddenly concerned that he had never heard the name before.

Giuseppe cleared his throat. "Do you remember our old friend Miguel Muñoz?"

"Yes. So?"

"Well, your dedicated enemy was a close friend of Muñoz." The mafioso gave a lewd chuckle. "Very close, if you know what I mean."

Silence between the two men.

Then it all came to César Duval in a blinding instant of understanding. He involuntarily gripped the phone hard, and his eyes closed tightly. After half a minute he spoke in a raw tone, "You're certain?"

"*Non c'è dubbio.*" No doubt whatsoever.

For a moment he thought César had hung up. Then he heard the man say, "We're both paid up now, Giuseppe. Even. Let's keep it that way."

The old don would normally have said a few more words, but he decided to wait until César hung up. When he heard the click at the other end, he pushed himself out of his chair and went to the window to open the shade and let a bit of Sicilian light into the room.

"*Buona fortuna,* César," he said to the glaring sunshine, and shook his head slowly. Good luck.

You're going to need it.

Luc was up at the villa on the mountainside when the phone rang. It was his father asking him to come down to the warehouse. He needed his oldest son's presence for a meeting of the family.

Luc sensed something was wrong as he approached the long, low building behind the wheel of one of the four-wheelers. Matteo watched Luc as he drove through the overhead door, and Luc saw the tightness in the bodyguard's eyes and in his body language.

When he got off the machine, he knew the problem was larger still when he saw Eduard standing at almost military guard near one of the walls, a black assault rifle in hand. The man nodded to Luc and walked to the overhead door and closed it.

César, Bernard, Jacqueline, and Vianne were in a far corner of the capacious room, gathered around a single bright lamp that hung from the ceiling. On the floor directly below the lamp yawned the open circular mouth of a black fifty-five-gallon drum. As Luc approached the three-foot-tall metal cylinder, he saw that there was something inside.

"Thanks for finally making it here, Luc," César said sarcastically. He gestured at the drum, then walked to Bernard and put a hand on his shoulder.

Bernard smiled broadly, Jacqueline was thoughtfully attentive as if hiding an inner secret, and Vianne's face was a dusky veil—unreadable.

Luc wrinkled his nose. "What's that stench?" He eyed the metal drum. "A body?"

"You tell me," César said, and pointed at the drum with his eyes.

Luc got closer, but all he could see was what looked like a rough stew of glass and gravel, shot through here and there with rotting seaweed. "What is this?" he asked.

"The Turk's fish tank, Luc," Bernard said in a happy voice. "Minus the fish …"

Bernard had somehow seen it, had figured it out, though he himself didn't know precisely how or why.

He was unable to analyze his own thought process that led to his revelation, but he had developed an odd awareness that his brain had been changed in his brush with death those years back. He had never thought of his head as damaged—just altered. Where he was once calculating and brilliant, he was now intuitive and prescient.

Over time it had turned out to be a good trade.

"Come with me, Vianne," he had said, standing in the dim center of the yacht's damaged stateroom. "I need some help."

The two had gone up on deck and found a large drum used to store rope. They had brought it down to the master suite and spent the next quarter hour transferring the odious remains of the smashed fish tank and its contents into the drum. They had made certain not to miss a single piece of the repellent mess. Finally they had filled the container almost to the top, secured its lid, and then managed to get it up on deck and manhandle it off the yacht.

Now it was here in the warehouse.

"Luc," César said. "Tell me what you see."

Luc looked from his father to Jacqueline and Bernard, and then his gaze stopped on Vianne's face. She raised her chin and looked down her nose at him, and her eyes said, *Go ahead, Luc. Get a little dirty.*

He carefully put a hand down into the roughage and gingerly pulled up some gravel and seaweed and small hunks of broken glass. He looked at the contents of his palm in mild disgust. Then he turned his face to his father with an expression that said, *So what?*

Jacqueline surprised Luc by stepping in front of him and lifting one of the slimy pebbles of gravel from his palm with a thumb and forefinger. He stared at her as she wiped the rock carefully with a small handkerchief and held it up to the single harsh light.

Her deep brown eyes glowed in concentration as she turned the rough translucent cube this way and that in her fingers.

Vianne watched in fascination.

"How big do you think it is, Jacqui?" César asked nonchalantly.

The statuesque, auburn-haired woman seemed to be calculating carefully. After a few seconds she said, "Ten or twelve, maybe more."

"What should it yield?"

Luc dropped the rest of the messy goulash back into the drum and watched his father's girlfriend carefully. Over the last half-dozen years he had had little to do with Jacqueline Murat, but suddenly he felt that he might have been making a mistake.

Jacqueline took her time and finally said, "At least one three-carater, round. Two one-carat pear shapes, and maybe a half-dozen smalls and some melee." She looked up and held the inch-long rock out to Vianne.

Vianne took the rough cube in silence and hefted it in her palm as she gazed at Jacqueline with frank admiration at the woman's secret knowledge.

But Luc's face couldn't betray his accelerating excitement. He looked at his brother. "How many do you think are in here,

Bern?" he said, tapping the side of the large drum. His eyes were wide with the enormity of what was sitting in front of him.

"Thousands," Bernard said. "Most are about the size of the one Vianne is holding. Some of them are larger."

"Zorzo had them mixed into a thick layer of glass and gravel at the bottom of his giant fish tank," César said. "They fooled everyone except Bernard." He looked at Vianne, who was turning the small, dull cube in her hand, a puzzled expression on her face.

Jacqueline saw the questions in Vianne's eyes and chuckled lightly. "In their rough form, diamond crystals look like worthless gravel, even at close inspection. They have to be cut and polished. That brings out their beauty and multiplies their value." She paused thoughtfully. "In this case, great value."

Bernard laughed. "The Turk even had a shark swimming around, guarding them."

Vianne finally let a smile play on her lips as she watched the older woman. *How well Jacqueline kept her knowledge of diamonds secret,* she thought in silent admiration. *Another reason César loves her. Certainement.*

Jacqueline had acquired some very useful knowledge before she had met César. During her four years in prison for stealing a painting from the Uffizi Gallery in Florence, her cellmate, Allegra, had introduced her to the world of diamonds.

Allegra had been convicted of smuggling and fencing diamonds for the Caltabiano mob in Turin and was oddly fatalistic about her inevitable capture and incarceration. She found Jacqueline a quiet and easy friend who was in a somewhat similar circumstance.

By the time Jacqueline had been released from prison, she knew her way around the darker side of diamonds. And when César had learned that his lover had that valuable knowledge, he offered to send her to Antwerp, the diamond-cutting capital of Europe, to meet some people and get some hands-on experience with diamonds themselves. Jacqueline agreed immediately. She had fallen deeply in love with César and wanted at all costs to be useful to him, to his family.

She had lived in Antwerp for a few months, receiving a world-class education in diamonds from a business associate of César's. The man ran a diamond-smuggling operation that doubled as an "importing" business, and Jacqueline returned to Corsica with the right connections and a strong knowledge of diamonds that was sine qua non for the Duvals' own smuggling interests.

Jacqueline looked over at the dull, uncut diamond in Vianne's hand and said to her, "That one stone will cut out into around twenty-five thousand US dollars' worth of polished diamonds. Probably more."

Vianne did a quick mental calculation. If that were the case, the slimy, fish-smelling gravel filling the drum was worth tens, maybe hundreds of millions of dollars on the black market. And she sensed it would bring multiples of that if the stones could be cut and then brought to market through legitimate channels.

Jacqueline looked over at César, who glanced at her with a knowing mixture of love and secrets shared. She smiled modestly.

Then César suddenly turned a hard face to Luc.

"What?" Luc said, flustered.

César let half a minute of silence go by while he studied his son. Finally he waved a hand at the drum. "This is what Quentin Maillot was after, Luc. I think I know what this is—the major part of his fortune and those of the top dogs in the French Connection."

"Why was it on Zorzo's boat?"

"Zorzo was insane—imagined himself a god or a devil. He saw himself dominating the Levant and the Middle East as its potentate of heroin. But in spite of all that—maybe *because* of all that—he was trusted by the worst of the worst. When it came to diamonds, he was the bank for drug kings like Quentin Maillot and La Chose."

Vianne looked at César, gestured at the drum, and whispered, "Did you know this was on the yacht?"

"No, I only knew about the China White." He glanced at the drum, shook his head, and made a small shrug. "But I'm not surprised."

"Aren't the other owners of these diamonds going to come looking for them?" Luc asked.

César's face swiveled to his. "Probably. They may be stopped by the publicity that Mignone has garnered for himself from the seizure of the drugs and his killing of Zorzo, and conclude that Corsican police have found their cache of diamonds from the fish tank. But if they persist, and try to locate the boat, they won't find it in Corsica. They'll have to get it in Sicily—take it from the Mafia, from the Randazzos." He made an ironic face. "That would probably be suicidal."

He looked at his silent stepdaughter. "The trail would lead to Sicily—not here to us."

Vianne's eyes held César's for a few seconds. She gently placed the rough diamond on the top of the pile in the drum, stepped back a pace, and whispered, "So now we're safe?"

César looked from Vianne to Bernard to Jacqueline and turned his thoughts to the name that Giuseppe Randazzo had given to him—the person who wouldn't stop coming at him or his family no matter what. "Safe? No, we're not."

He looked at Bernard and said, "Close it up, son," waving his hand at the drum's lid.

Then he called to Eduard, who was standing near the other end of the warehouse. "Secure the building."

As the Duval family walked back to the main house, César said to Luc, "I want to talk to you in my office."

Luc looked as if he was about to say something, but César stopped him cold with the single word, "Alone."

"For what I have in mind, the diamonds need to be polished, finished."

"That's crazy," said Luc. "We can't throw thousands of stones into the diamond market for polishing at once. It will send up a hundred red flags. Ask Jacqueline: I'm sure she'll tell you the same."

César just glared at him and didn't say another word.

They were alone in César's office off the living room. The long silences were becoming oppressive, and Luc started fidgeting. Finally he could take no more.

"What's wrong?" he said to his father. "What is it?"

César studied his older son's face, his eyes. They were the same color as his but lacked the backlight of cunning and the flintiness of a lifelong fight for survival. An odd thought flickered in the back of César's mind: *Those attributes, which are missing in my son Luc, Vianne has in abundance.*

"I'm taking Jacqueline to Zürich. We're going to be making arrangements with contacts concerning the diamonds. I'm leaving you in charge to take care of things here."

"You're taking Vianne with you as well?"

César gave his son a cold look.

"What about the murderers of La Chose?" Luc asked, pivoting off the topic. "What if they were waiting for Maillot to return and when he doesn't, they come after us?"

César shook his head. "Without Maillot, La Chose is in disarray—a pack of hungry jackals who will eat each other. That's not my main concern, Luc."

He stopped speaking as if weighing his words. Finally he said, "I now know the name of our shadowy enemy."

Luc was about to say something but stopped when he saw the look in his father's narrowed eyes.

"Where were you the day Vianne and I were attacked on the road?" César asked.

Luc's face blanched. "I told you, I was up in the villa sleeping off a party the night before in Ajaccio." For a brief instant a vision of the tattooed prostitute he had slept with that night came to his mind, but he pushed it away.

His voice rose in indignation. "You don't think that I—that I had anything to do with—"

César lightly slapped Luc's face. "Would I, Luc? *Should* I, Luc?"

The two men stared at each other in silence.

Finally César said, "Of course you didn't have anything to do with it."

"Then why the slap?"

"Because I *needed* you that day on the road. Because there were other times that I've needed you, and you were off drinking and screwing every girl in Corsica." He gritted his teeth. "Because you have to straighten out your life and fast, for your own sake and for the sake of this family."

He pulled his hand back as if to slap him again. "If words won't do it, I'll just keep using this method until I have your attention."

Luc's composure began to waver. "All right," he said in a tone of clear resignation.

César suddenly felt tired. His eldest son had always been difficult, but for all their differences, he knew Luc would never harm, never betray his family. *Not even Vianne?* he pondered with a tempered hope. *No. Luc may resent her, maybe even hate her, but I don't think he would harm her even if he had thought of doing so. It would be the same as harming me, and in the final analysis, that he would never do.*

"I need you and Bernard—need all of the family to help me now, Luc. We have to get rid of the animal that's stalking us once and for all. Together."

Luc felt his heart calm down, and he looked at his father. "You can count on me. You always can."

Then he surprised César when he said, "And don't worry about Vianne. I'll watch out for her." He smiled. "She was right anyway."

César raised his head an inch and looked down his nose at his son. "About what?"

"About things, about my whoring around with women. It was something Isabelle would have thought was wrong as well. I'm certain of that."

César nodded and believed he saw a flicker of truth in his son's face. *I've made many, many mistakes,* he thought, *but I don't think my children are among them.*

"Stay here," he said as if making up his mind about it all, and opened the door. Jacqueline, Bernard, and Vianne had been speaking with one another in the living room, and they turned as one at the sound. They saw César beckon to them.

When they were all in the office, he looked at each member of his family in turn. Then he took a deep breath and furrowed his brow, and Vianne immediately read his eyes. He was remembering something or someone he would rather have forgotten.

"Who is our enemy?" she whispered.

He looked straight at her, and with an unwanted flash of dreadful premonition, saw her as a distant silhouette in the cross-hairs of a killer's riflescope.

"She calls herself Mistral."

Part Three

We should die of that roar which
lies on the other side of silence.

—GEORGE ELIOT

Mistral

———

THE MISTRAL IS A COLD, dry, northwest wind that is born in the French Alps and barrels down the valleys of the Rhone and Durance in late winter or early spring. It is fast and strong and insistent as it scours Provence and Marseille, sometimes reaching wind speeds of fifty miles per hour until it finally dissipates out in the Mediterranean.

Once in ten or twelve years it clashes with another wind, the sirocco, which sweeps into southern France from North Africa.

In the rare instance when a mistral and a sirocco meet, a ferocious storm rages until both winds have savagely destroyed each other's power.

Then they both inevitably die …

The woman stood in the dawn light coming through the window.

Her feet were bare, and the slate floor was cold. She wore only a black satin robe, snugged with a sash at her narrow waist. One hand held a porcelain cup of coffee, and quick traces of its sharp aroma played tag in the still-cool air pushing gently through the open window.

She was tall—five feet ten in her bare feet.

Thick, platinum-blond hair swept heavily across her brow at a diagonal, covering one eye, and fell straight down both sides of her face. The rakish coiffure was cut at an angle that followed her jawline—its arcing, pointed ends curving forward in the front, almost meeting under her chin.

Her lips were a red slash, her cheekbones well defined. Her skin was olive, and her eyes were dark and heavy lidded and radiated a smoky mixture of accusation and dismissiveness.

She put the cup of coffee on the windowsill, shrugged out of her robe, and stood in front of the window, the city spread out in front of her under the blue Spanish sky.

The tail of a gold-and-indigo cobra began between her shoulder blades, ran down her spine, then curved around her waist. The snake's head terminated two inches below her navel, and glowing venom dripped from its wide-open jaws into the carefully shaped dark tangle that confirmed the artifice behind her gleaming blond pageboy.

The best tattoo artist in Barcelona had created the serpent, and the threatening position of its realistic fangs had a disconcerting effect on her lovers, both male and female.

She didn't care if anyone saw her naked in her window. The apartment was on the top floor of a prewar apartment building in the Gothic Quarter of the city. She liked the quirky style of this section of Barcelona, and her window afforded her an almost unobstructed view of the zucchini-shaped spires of the Basilica de la Sagrada Família.

She idly stroked one of her breasts, and a quick memory surfaced of how once a certain someone's hand had touched her there. César Duval's hand …

She had been born thirty-six years earlier, and the name on her birth certificate from the Miami hospital was Angelina de la Cruz.

Angelina had grown up in a barrio section of Miami called Liberty City through a dysfunctional, bitterly disappointing childhood and violence-splattered teen years. Her mother was a refugee from Cuba with no education and few prospects who had run through a series of useless men-friends for most of her adult life. Angelina never knew who her father was, and never cared.

As she grew through a hard, angry life on the hard, angry streets, an understandable obsession with violence and the satisfying revenge it offered had slowly blossomed inside her. Unlike other young adults living on the fringe of civilized society who turned to lives of crime to finance drug dependencies, Angelina's addictions were more complex. She wanted to somehow become someone she wasn't—someone perfect, beautiful, powerful. For that she needed money to escape her dead-end life and money for all the trappings necessary to refine her obsessive goal of narcissistic, physical perfection in every way.

But her goal seemed forever out of reach as her progression through life became a steepening slope of snowballing theft, petty crime, and prostitution. Finally, after entering into an intimate liaison with the head of a powerful Miami gang, she gravitated to the most logical and lucrative method by which to advance her life: she became a killer for money.

A good one.

Her fluent Spanish was a necessity in her burgeoning and profitable career in South Florida. But she was getting too good at what she did. Her dark reputation grew, not only within the gangs, but with the police as well. After one close call where she was nearly caught, she decided that it was becoming too dangerous for her to remain in Florida, too risky to live in the United States any longer.

It was then that she decided to erase her past as best she could. Angelina de la Cruz's given name—Angel of the Cross—was the polar opposite of the woman she had become. She came to a decision and discarded it, and never looked back.

She became *Mistral*.

Resourceful, smart, and with a carefully accumulated bankroll of blood money, she flew to Spain with $100,000 in small bills in her luggage and a promise to herself to lie low and find a better life, a *different* life.

But she was still young and ambitious and a quintessential outsider to the mainstream of civil living, and it wasn't long before she was yearning to be back in her old line of work. And her search for employment led her to a man named Miguel Muñoz.

Miguel was in his late thirties, a dozen years older than Mistral. He was the type of man that Mistral could actually admire, actually *love*: a brutal, hard man—half wild animal—whose every breath dripped machismo.

And love him she did. Completely.

He was the kingpin in a preeminent Spanish narcotics syndicate, and she was delighted. They understood each other—loved each other. He gave her a gold ring with her initials engraved inside the shank. "*Mi amor por ti es para siempre,*" he had said, his black eyes flashing with the gravity and importance of the gift.

And she calculated that as he got to know and trust her, he would find her invaluable as his personal *asesina,* the occupation at which she was an accomplished expert.

As the years went by, her reputation and status in the underbelly of Spanish crime grew quickly, but in 1973, when she was thirty years old, everything changed abruptly. In the summer of that year a vicious surprise attack smashed Miguel's syndicate irreparably.

A man named César Duval orchestrated the assault. He and a group of his Corsican henchmen demolished the operation and effectively took over Muñoz's lucrative drug pipelines. In a matter of days, hundreds of kilos of heroin went missing, and authorities assumed they had been diverted and were now in the control of Duval's heavily shielded and seemingly impregnable operation on Corsica.

But that assumption was never proven, and the hijacking of the drugs from one criminal enterprise to another had an odd twist to it. César Duval had seen to it that the drugs wound up harmless and destroyed on the bottom of the Mediterranean, fifty miles off the coast of Spain.

One of the casualties of the mob war was Mistral, who was injured when three dark men stormed Miguel's apartment. She and Miguel were both nude and caught completely by surprise. Muñoz was able to grab a gun secreted in the bed and fired wildly at the men. All three opened fire on him at once, and he was killed instantly in a hail of bullets.

Mistral, who tried to attack the men with her fists, was caught in the crossfire. A bullet punched through the side of her abdomen. Another missed her face by a hair, branding a scarlet crease above one eye. She stumbled to the floor in pain, certain that she was done for. She spat curses at the three attackers in gutter Spanish and dared them to kill her, hoping they would do just that, reasoning that she wanted to be dead first if they were planning to rape her.

But the gunmen cast warning looks at one another, and a minute later, the largest of the three slung Mistral's body over his shoulder and they all left the room.

As her upper body hung limp and bleeding against the man's back, she closed her eyes and cursed at what was happening and whoever was behind it, vowing that if she lived, she would avenge Miguel Muñoz. Somehow.

But the pain was exquisite, overpowering, and in a few seconds she was unconscious.

When she opened her eyes, she was in the small cabin of a tossing boat with a single window in one wall. The bed she was in was narrow but clean.

Her forehead was bound and covered in gauze. She had been bandaged around her waist, and a thick wad of cotton, the size of a small pillow, was secured in place against her left side. Luckily, the bullet that had passed through her body had done little internal damage. But the scar on her forehead from the near miss would never disappear completely, and she would forever keep her hair cut at a diagonal, covering the blemish.

A silent, stern-faced older woman sat by her bed, and from time to time administered to the bandages. When Mistral tried to ask her questions, she merely ignored them in silence. Finally, as the sun began to set outside the porthole, a man strode into the small cabin.

He whispered to the older woman, who immediately left the room.

His stormy gray eyes settled on Mistral, who lay suspicious and alert in the bed, a sheet pulled up to her chin. Her intuition told her immediately who he was. He was the man who had quickly and viscously ripped Miguel's drug operation to shreds and then sent her lover to Hades.

He was César Duval.

Her dark eyes went wide when Duval produced an automatic pistol from his inside jacket pocket and pointed it at her.

"Who are you?" he said in badly accented Spanish.

Mistral deemed it wise to act terrified. It wasn't much of an act at all—Duval's dark reputation preceded him.

"I—I'm Angelina." She hadn't uttered the name in years, and it seemed strange in her mouth. "What's—?"

The man took a step closer to the bed and put the muzzle of the gun to the center of her bandaged forehead. "Only the truth will save you. Where are the rest of Muñoz's partners?"

César was fairly certain of where they all were—nourishing crabs two hundred feet under the boat—but he had to know if there were any loose ends that might have been overlooked. The woman seemed to be the only one left alive unaccounted for—the only unfamiliar face in the bunch.

This phony platinum blonde might be innocent, he had reasoned when her unconscious body was brought aboard his boat. *If so, I won't hurt her, won't have her blood on my hands. But I have to know for sure. If she's involved in any way with the moving of the drugs, beyond being a prostitute or clueless girlfriend, I'll drag her ashore and leave her to the local police.*

Her eyes tried to read his face, and she inferred that pleading ignorance would most likely be taken for the lie that it was and he'd kill her on the spot. She said, "I know Miguel is, *was,* in a dirty business. But I know only him, no others."

She waited as he stared at her. Finally, unsettled by the long silence, she said, "My business is sex, *señor.* Sex for money, and Miguel had a lot of money." She paused for a moment. "And a lot of *yeyo,* cocaine."

"What else?" César said, the stony expression on his face unchanging. She felt a small lessening of the pressure of the gun barrel on her forehead.

Mistral's street nose almost smelled the heady scent of survival. *This man might actually let me go if I play him right,* she thought with cautious relief. Her confidence flooded back. She painfully pulled herself up on the pillow, allowing the sheet to slip down to her bandaged waist. "I need *yeyo, señor,*" she said plainly, not surprised that his eyes flicked down to her naked breasts.

The man was immobile for a long half minute, his face still an unreadable mask. Finally he put the gun back inside his jacket pocket and stood silently at the bedside.

He made up his mind. "The wounds will heal."

She looked down at her breasts. "I *need* it," she repeated. Then her eyes went back to his, and she let her mouth stay open half an inch.

He frowned. "Sleep now. In the morning you will be let off the boat."

She reached out and took one of his hands and placed it on her breast. "You are sleeping here as well? In this bed with me?" She kept her hand over his. "I hope it's true." *I do hope it's true, so I can somehow find a knife and kill you in your sleep. So I can cut off your prick and jam it into your screaming mouth in payment for what you did to Miguel.*

César narrowed his eyes for a moment, and took his hand back. Then he walked to the door and turned to face her.

"*Adiós,*" he said. A moment later he was gone.

She shrugged painfully, and her eyes narrowed in a suppressed fury that seemed to strangely invigorate her. She stared at the end of the bed for a while. At the spot where the murderer of the only man she would ever love in her life had stood and mocked her. She burned his image into her mind.

One day I will hunt you down and hurt you, Señor Duval, as you have hurt me.

No, that's not true.

I will hurt you much, much more.

She turned from the window with its panorama of the Barcelona morning and walked slowly into the bathroom. She ran a shower, waited until the water was hot, then stepped under the scalding spray. In the shifting steam around her she imagined she saw that face from her past, the face with the stormy gray eyes.

It was good killing Isabelle, César—satisfying to know that your daughter bled to death in your arms. Your life was altered forever from that minute on, as was mine when you murdered Miguel.

And as for Luc—well, I'm still working on him. How many times in the last few years he slept with me in Ajaccio, all the while believing I was only a clueless hooker with a snake tattoo, while I was using him to carefully keep my eye on you.

I even gave him that small brand, that little scar on his cheek during some rough sex. I was tempted to do much worse to him, but I like the idea of you seeing my handiwork, my message, whenever you look at your son.

And as for the bullet that nearly ended Bernard's life? Me again, César.

She distractedly soaped her body as her mind swept through her obsessions. She looked down at her hand in mild surprise.

She had unconsciously squeezed the bar of fragrant soap into a shapeless hunk.

CHAPTER 24

Damp Whispers

———

It was almost ten p.m., and the streets were quiet around police headquarters. The pavement was still wet from a brief shower, but the clouds had already ceded the sky to a few brave stars.

Inspector Gustave Mignone was on his way to his car when he was suddenly surprised by the sound of a soft, muffled cough. He whirled to see César Duval's stepdaughter standing in the light of a street lamp a few feet away.

She wore a summer raincoat, its collar turned up, framing her face and hair. The glint of a diamond on her chest was the only spark of light in the darkness.

His eyes traveled down her body. He saw that she wore plain, hard-soled black pumps, and wondered why he hadn't heard her coming up behind him on the pavement. But then he reminded himself that this girl was, by her odd nature, very quiet—quiet in her whispers, quiet in her movements.

Quiet in every way, I'll wager, he snorted to himself. He tried to decrease their six-inch difference in height without her noticing by pushing himself up slowly on his toes. He felt like lighting a cigarette, but refrained.

"Hello, Vianne."

Her eyes seemed to gleam in the light of the street lamp. "Can we talk?" she whispered, and merely stood where she was.

"*Talk*? That's ironic. Where's César?"

She ignored the question.

Mignone looked up and down the street. With the exception of a few police officers walking to or from the station on the next block, they were alone.

"He sent you, César did?" He stepped toward her until he was close enough to have to look up to see into her face. "That last deal of yours cost me a valuable piece of police property. On top of that, my entire force is now on high alert for drug pushers from France, mafiosi from Sicily, and God knows whom else."

Vianne looked down at the short man in silence. She was well aware that the inspector's professional reputation had skyrocketed across Europe with his extermination of Kemal Zorzo and his seizure of two million dollars' worth of China White.

She chuckled to herself. *After that coup, losing the yacht was just a collateral cost of dealing with the Duvals, Monsieur Mignone.*

Gustave could smell Vianne's natural pheromones in the cool night air. *What is that—hyacinth, sandalwood? Is she wearing that scent or is it just* her?

It *was* her, and he moved back a step—being this close to the woman was too visceral, too distracting. To quell his sudden and unbidden reaction to the girl, he said, "I suppose César sent you to offer me another outlandish trade?"

"I'm here for me," she whispered.

"I doubt it. Certainly César has sent you to—"

"He's out of the country," she interrupted softly, and touched the sleeve of his jacket. "Just me."

He raised his chin and surprised himself by saying, "Very well. What do you want, Vianne?"

"Mistral," she whispered, and she saw instantly from his face that the man had heard the name before.

"No one knows who Mistral is, Vianne," the inspector said with transparent unease. "He or she is said to be a freelance assassin responsible for murders across Europe and even farther."

She quickly threw him a look that said, *You know it's a "she."*

Vianne tightened her grip on Gustave's sleeve and moved an inch closer. He was suddenly oddly uncomfortable.

She leaned her head toward his and whispered, "Get me to her, and I will give her to you." Her breath was mint.

He almost smirked. "How?"

She smiled slightly, and he noticed the perfection of her white teeth even in the shadows of the night.

Gustave Mignone couldn't remember a woman having such an electric effect on him. Not even his wife, not even his mistress. *And she's so damned young,* he fretted. He stared up into her eyes, at a temporary loss for words—cursing his diminished height, cursing the inexorability of time.

When she said nothing—just stood looking at him, *breathing* at him—he finally said, "What did you want me to do?"

He felt her other hand on his other sleeve. "A few phone calls," she whispered.

Seeing his look of intrigued confusion, she put her mouth near his ear. "Interpol." She saw Mignone's eyes narrow at the mention of the international police organization. "Tell them you're tracking César Duval while he's in London."

He pulled away a few inches and looked at her eyes. "Tracking him? In London?"

Her eyes were suddenly unreadable.

"That's it?" he asked. "Just a few phone calls?"

She shook her head and leaned a final time to put her lips at his ear. "One more thing," she whispered. He felt her breath, felt her hands on his arms, felt other things he didn't want to feel.

"Say I'm not with him, not with César," the lips whispered even more softly.

"Where should I tell them you are, Vianne?" As he said it, he realized that she could have no other name.

"Here. In Corsica …"

Her last word was almost silent, but rang loud in Gustave's head:

"… alone."

Without another word, she let go of his arms, turned on her heels, and walked away down the wet sidewalk. Mignone watched her and finally remembered to breathe.

A half block away, a figure stood still in the shadows, fists bunched, eyes ablaze.

Giuseppe Randazzo couldn't sleep.

In the painting on the wall above the headboard of his huge bed, Santa Rosalia, the patron saint of the Sicilian city of Palermo, turned her eyes to heaven in beatific peace.

He looked to his left. A woman was asleep and had moved herself as far away from Giuseppe as she could without falling off her side of the bed.

Giuseppe snorted again, but didn't move. She was a third his age, and he liked that, and the fact that she found him physically revolting mattered not a bit to him. A man at this stage of a hard life deserved whatever he could take.

But this girl meant little to him. Another one did, however—one with a cobra tattoo.

Perhaps I shouldn't have given Mistral to César Duval after all, he thought, his heavy brow furrowing. *I'm not worried about her somehow coming after me. That would be suicide, and that* puta *wants to live very badly.*

But she is good at what she does, and now I may have bitten off my own nose to spite my face. There is too much going on now to have any unnecessary distractions.

Over the last few years, Mistral had contracted a couple of assassinations for the Randazzo clan—one in Spain, one in Morocco. She had never been to Sicily, nor had she met Giuseppe face-to-face, but she had proven to be a stone cold murderer—efficient and tidy. And being a woman was an extra plus in a heavily male-dominated profession. It was excellent cover.

What am I missing here? Giuseppe thought. *Maybe it* is *the fact that she is a woman and might act crazy. Don't they all? But how far would craziness get her?*

He turned in the bed and smiled into the darkness.

CHAPTER 25

Vault

———

CÉSAR AND JACQUELINE STOOD IN the cool, quiet, well-appointed anteroom, facing the three men.

César wore a steel-gray Bond Street sharkskin suit and black open-collared shirt.

Jacqueline was silent in her tailored ecru jacket and knee-length skirt. Maroon high-heeled pumps matched her silk blouse, and her auburn hair was gathered in a stylish chignon. Her deep brown eyes took in everything from behind large, lightly tinted Fiorucci sunglasses.

Two of the men were uniformed armed guards who stood carefully watching the couple, and a tall, middle-aged man in a sober pinstriped three-piece suit stood between them. He had a bland expression permanently and professionally imprinted on his face below a high forehead and thinning, sandy hair.

His name was Edgar Schnellen, and he considered himself the standard by which all other Swiss bankers should be measured: wise, quiet, observant, and discreet. Over the course of his career, he had become emotionally immune, even welcoming, to the steady influx of corrupt politicians, rapacious military men, money launderers, contraband dealers, and tax cheats of every stripe who found their way to Switzerland and its serious and civilized respect for *schwarzes gelt,* black money.

And their journey inevitably led to this edifice, the Zürcher SuisseBank.

Inset in one wall of the room, an immense, round, carbon-steel door yawned open. Eight feet in diameter, it offered a peek into the walk-in safe deposit vault.

A table with five or six gleaming steel boxes of different sizes was positioned between the three bank employees and the couple from Corsica. César pointed to the largest box, a sharp-cornered metal coffin a foot wide and high and two feet deep. "Is this the largest you have?"

"*Oui. Le plus large.*" Edgar Schnellen's French was halting and harshly accented, and Jacqueline thought it almost comical. She had no desire to tell anyone that she spoke passable German, relying on that secret to try to catch anything important that might be said.

"I will need two of them." César's face was bland, his tone almost impatient.

Schnellen cleared his throat. "You realize that no drugs or weapons are allowed in these boxes." His eyes traveled up and down the couple, a jealously etched wrinkle in his brow.

César Duval had been a customer of the bank for ten years, and Edgar knew him as well as a Swiss banker could know any of his furtive clientele. The banker had also met the beautiful Jacqueline Murat on more than one occasion, and was pleased that she had accompanied her mobster lover on this trip. He had wondered what she would be like in bed, but he had a mistress already who was well paid, and if Jacqueline was of that bent, he probably could not afford her anyway.

But none of these emotions showed on his blandly smiling face.

César ignored Schnellen's admonition and said, "The two boxes will have to be close to each other and next to my existing box."

Edgar wrung his hands and moved his head around a bit to convey the difficulty of such a request, but Jacqueline raised her chin a fraction of an inch and said, "The Julius Bär Bank a few blocks away had as many boxes as we wanted, Monsieur Schnellen." She saw him pale a tiny bit, and she cast a baleful eye at the large, round vault door. "Their vault is larger, as well."

Edgar gave up on his transparent show of difficulty, which had been aimed at getting them to pay a higher box-rental fee, and said, "*Ach,* Frau Murat, for you and Herr Duval nothing is impossible. I will effect some shuffling of boxes. We have done so before."

He looked at César, who stood detached and impatient, and continued. "*Ja,* come. I will show you where your new boxes will be—right next to your existing one."

"I need to access mine now, Edgar." A small key appeared in César's hand.

The banker pulled a master key from his pinstriped vest pocket, and the three entered the vault. The fronts of the boxes ranged from floor to ceiling, taking up three walls of the room.

César walked determinedly to the far wall that was reserved for the largest of them.

Schnellen came up beside César, tapped the front of one of the boxes, and with a flourish, waved his other hand at two more to its immediate left. "*Voilà*! Your existing box and its new vault mates." He inserted his key into one of the two locks on César's box.

César followed suit with his key, opened the square brass door, and pulled his box out of its position in the wall. Then he eyed Schnellen. "We will just be a moment."

Edgar straightened up and nodded. He left the room and closed a barred gate over the circular opening to the vault. César and Jacqueline were alone.

They walked into one of the small private rooms off the vault, locking the door behind them, and César placed the box on the table set up against one of the walls. He lifted the lid and peered cautiously inside. He had a grudging trust of the pompous Swiss banker, but one never knew. He motioned to Jacqueline, who came over and looked into the box.

Fully half the safe deposit box was occupied with rubber-banded stacks of money—US dollars, French and Swiss francs, deutsche marks. Ten one-kilo bars of gold lay banded in a short stack, gleaming in the light. Two Colt .45 caliber pistols rested in their oily cloth bags.

Recalling the volume of the contents of the drum back in the warehouse in Corsica, Jacqueline said, "We will certainly need the other two boxes when we bring the rest of the diamonds here to Switzerland."

"Your pocketbook," César said quietly.

She put her large Fendi purse on the table next to the box and pulled out two chamois bags the size of grapefruits stuffed with uncut diamonds. She placed them in the metal box, nestled between the stacks of money.

They both stared at the crowded box for half a minute.

Finally César said, "Yes. We'll need more room." Then he looked at Jacqueline and said, "Let's go for a walk."

The Bahnhofstrasse is Zürich's main downtown boulevard and the most famous street in Switzerland. It is a center for finance and business as well as one of the world's most exclusive shopping avenues and the third-most expensive street for retail properties in the world.

The wide boulevard, flanked by five- and six-story classical-style buildings, is ruled by pedestrians—the street allows little automobile traffic, and modern electric trams glide with obsessive Swiss punctuality on gleaming tracks inset in the pavement.

A bit over a mile long, the Bahnhofstrasse starts at the Hauptbanhof, the main train station, and passes Rennweg, Augustingasse, and Paradeplatz, finally ending at the Bürkliplatz on Lake Zürich.

César and Jacqueline strolled arm in arm through the lunchtime crowds of tourists and businesspeople as small, multicolored flags on the buildings fluttered in the cool, clean air. Their eyes occasionally went to the windows of famous-name retail shops, but Jacqueline could see that César's mind was on other things.

Eduard walked a couple dozen yards behind them, taking in everything and everyone from behind his sunglasses. He had waited for César and Jacqueline outside the bank, and was instructed to hang back as far as was reasonable. Switzerland was one of the few places that César felt he could let down his guard a little bit.

Jacqueline loved the city of Zürich, where people seemed calm and stable. The Swiss understand civility and security and order, she thought, and their underlying obsession with money was a perfect means by which to maintain that happy state of affairs.

At the next corner César stopped and said to Jacqueline, "Look." He pointed with his chin at a five-story building across the street. It was solidly built of large, gray brick, and its first floor sported two or three high-end retail stores. A few investment companies and a private bank occupied the upper floors of the building.

Seeing the question on Jacqueline's face, César said, "That's ours. That building."

"What are you talking about?"

"I bought it two years ago." He looked casually to the left and right at the people, the trams, and the linden trees planted in orderly procession along the sidewalk. Then he looked at her and smiled.

"I had come up with the beginning of a plan, a plan that I think you'll like to hear about. And now the diamonds have changed everything, made everything possible."

Her face was an open question, and he smiled at her.

"Now we have to change our lives, and our selves as well."

In his lover's deep brown eyes he saw confusion, but also a silent approval.

"Let's go back to the hotel. I'll explain on the way."

She answered the phone on the sixth ring, and waited in silence.

"He is in London," came the man's voice, distorted by the distance. "Went there on some kind of business."

"How do you know?"

"The usual way. I hear all calls going in and out of Mignone's office. This one was to Interpol. It's as safe as gold."

"César is alone in London?" asked Mistral.

"His sons and Jacqueline Murat are with him, and a bodyguard as well."

"What about the girl, Philip? What about Vianne?"

Detective Philip Jouet looked nervously out the door of his small office. "Duval didn't take her with him. She's here in Corsica, at her stepfather's estate."

Mistral stared ahead, eyes unfocused.

"When do I get my money?" The man looked around nervously. A few uniformed officers walked by in the hall. He had checked three times to make sure his boss, Inspector Mignone, had not come into the building yet.

There was a long silence on the phone that screamed, *Tread lightly.*

Then Mistral said, "When I learn you're not lying, I will pay you." Her voice had taken on a low animal quality, clearly indicating what she was capable of if the caller *was* lying.

"My money, please," repeated the thin, nervous policeman.

Mistral breathed evenly, and her eyes seemed to fix on a point in the air a few feet in front of her. Then she said, "I have something to attend to first," and hung up.

CHAPTER 26

Something to Attend To

———————

CÉSAR PHONED FROM SWITZERLAND TO let his sons and step-daughter know that he and Jacqueline would be leaving Zürich the next afternoon.

"Is everything all right at home, Bernard?" he asked, caution heavy in his voice.

Bernard smiled. "Of course. It's just me and Vianne here."

Marta was in Calvi visiting her nieces, and Eduard was with César and Jacqueline in Zürich.

"Where's Luc? Is he there?"

Bernard shrugged. "No. I don't know where he went. You know Luc." He smiled at Vianne, who was sitting at the kitchen table.

César's voice was level. "Be watchful, son," he said, and hung up.

Vianne was nervous. For the last day or so, restlessness had crept into her soul—a sly dread that bad things were coming. She studied Bernard and held up an empty cup for him to see. "Out of coffee," she whispered.

Bernard threw her one of his unending smiles. "I'll go into town and get some. We need a few more things as well." He was the stand-in family cook while Marta was gone.

He walked to Vianne and bent over and kissed her cheek. A moment later he had gone out the door, heading for the warehouse to get one of the cars.

She sat still, feeling a silent sub-audible keening in the still air of the kitchen. Something awful was about to happen.

Her inner voice was silent.

Vianne got up and walked into the living room. The feeling of unease was huge, and after thinking for a minute, she got down on her knees and reached under the long couch. Her hand came back clutching a matte black semi-automatic AK-47 assault rifle. It was one of several weapons hidden around the large house for use in case of an emergency. Her hand went back under a second time and brought out two loaded, curved clips.

She tossed the gun and the clips onto the couch, frowned, and walked to the large window. As she stood staring gloomily out across the lawn, she saw Luc drive up in his white Alfa Romeo convertible. Her eyes narrowed when she saw him lurch out of the car, obviously still drunk from whatever the night had offered him.

A minute later he staggered into the living room, spotted Vianne, and walked up to her. He reeked of alcohol.

She stepped back a pace and whispered, "Go away."

Luc hated the almost inaudible words. "Why were you talking to that cop prick last night, Vianne? What are you doing to us?"

Vianne's heart skipped a beat, and she froze. *He followed me? How could I have missed him?* Her eyes turned violent. "Go back to Ajaccio," she breathed.

"What's your damn plan, Vianne, you little traitor? You can't trust Mignone. Or are you plotting something with him? And who the hell are you to tell me what to do?" The resentment that he normally kept under control bloomed in his chest like a dark flower nourished by too many stiff drinks.

She said nothing—just looked at him with angry, glittering eyes.

He felt his muscles tighten, felt violence bubble to the surface, a long-repressed impulse to finish off this dangerous, meddling bitch once and for all.

But first I'll have her …

"Leave," was all she whispered.

"Oh, I should leave?" The fabric of his self-control was fraying. *How about I stay and I take something for* me, *Vianne?*

Without a breath in between, he was on her, surprised her, pushed her with his arms and with his body up against the living room wall. His hand came out of nowhere, his strong fingers closing like iron on her throat. With his other hand he grabbed her left arm and twisted hard.

He pushed his face so close to hers that their noses almost touched. "My father's far away, Vianne," he growled. "And you're finished in this family."

She tried to kick him, but he was very fit and very fast in spite of his inebriation, and he weighed at least a hundred pounds more than she. She saw tiny red veins in the whites of his eyes, and the alcohol was a harsh, almost overpowering presence. His body shook, and she was suddenly unsure of what she could do—the man was out of control.

Before she could react, he swung her around quickly and put her into a painful headlock. He dragged her across the room and tossed her onto the long couch on top of the black rifle. She quickly grabbed it from beneath her and tried to swing the gun like a club, but Luc was on her, and he easily grabbed the gun and tossed it over the back of the couch.

She struggled and kicked, but he had the strength of whiskey-saturated fury in him and crushed his mouth onto hers.

She bit down hard, and blood from his lip seeped between their faces.

He managed to slap her face, and with an animal power he grabbed the front of her blouse in one fist and ripped it.

She wasn't wearing a bra, and the sight and feel of her naked beneath him strengthened his drunken resolve to finally complete the forbidden act that had lain percolating in his subconscious for almost four years.

She knew what was in his mind—had seen a mirror of it those years ago when she had had to kill Marcel before he killed her mother—and knew she was now in serious trouble. If she somehow had to kill Luc to save herself, that was what she would do.

But he was a wild man, sensing through an undulating veil of alcohol that there was no turning back. He grabbed at the waist of Vianne's jeans and with a powerful, one-armed tug, pulled them painfully down until they were bunched around her calves.

He slapped her face again, and though she fought hard with all she had, he was just too strong.

Her heart ached mightily with the knowledge that no matter what, her whole world was unraveling at this, its most perilous moment. She was suddenly certain that someone in the police station had contacted Mistral. Vianne sensed that the murderer was coming. Sensed that she was close, very close.

But now *this*.

His hand moved and roughly tore her panties from her and tossed them like a soft black leaf over the back of the couch. They fluttered down onto the assault rifle. His bloodshot eyes traveled her body. "Finally," he breathed.

Then he looked at César's diamond *V* mocking him from between her breasts, and then into her hating eyes, and rasped, "It will be easier if you're sleeping through this." He balled his fist and pulled his arm back to swing a final knockout punch at her head.

Vianne spit hard into Luc's close face, hating him to the last, but before he could land the punch—and before she could even think—the man seemed to float up and away, surge off her, yelling and bellowing her name.

She watched in astonishment as Luc's body twisted in the air five feet above her, and she saw the two thick, powerful arms that were holding him as a strong man would hold up a snarling dog. Then Luc soared, screaming across the room, and crashed through one of the glass French doors.

Vianne turned her head.

Bernard was standing there, arms out from his side, panting like an animal, his normally happy eyes now indescribable in their fury. He was here, in the house, hadn't left. His car's battery had died and he hadn't driven to town after all, but had been in the warehouse trying to start it, to no avail.

She didn't know what to do, what to say.

He saw the blood on Vianne's bruised face, and his whole body seemed to cringe. In a single movement he picked up one of the wool throws that decorated the couch and gently covered her. His breathing was loud in the room. "I'll be back in a minute," he said, in a voice hoarse with murderous intent.

Bernard crossed the room in three strides. He didn't hear Vianne whispering from behind him, pleading for him to stop, and his large body disappeared through the broken door frame.

A moment later she heard Luc yelling and cursing in a high-pitched voice from outside the house, and the sound of thumping blows, and then one final grunt and a moan, and then silence.

A few seconds later, Bernard stepped back into the living room.

He stood still, rubbing his sore fists and staring at his step-sister, who was now standing, her hands shakily pulling her jeans up. She turned her naked back to him.

"Don't," she whispered, and Bernard immediately looked away.

A minute later Vianne had slipped her torn blouse back on. She walked carefully to Bernard and tapped his shoulder. When he turned and saw her bruised face, he put a fist to his mouth in anger at what his brother had done, what Luc had tried to do.

Vianne looked at her powerful stepbrother carefully, her heart jumbled with intersecting emotions. "*Merci,*" she finally whispered, and leaned forward toward him. She put her head against his broad chest and, hearing the faint beat of his racing heart, began to calm down. Then she looked up at his face and was thankful for this powerful, simple, and loyal man.

She was about to whisper something else when her attention snapped to an odd sound. It sounded like a fly.

An insistent, buzzing fly.

Bernard heard it too.

They looked into each other's eyes and somehow realized that what was about to happen was a confirmation, a culmination of the danger and inevitability of their lives—of all the Duval lives.

They broke from each other and sprinted for the door.

Vianne was the first to see it, and she caught her breath.

Without wasting another second she whispered, "Hurry. Bring Luc."

Bernard ran to retrieve his unconscious brother as Vianne whirled and ran back into the house.

CHAPTER 27

Toggle Switch

THE BLACK TWIN-ENGINE CESSNA T310R was a whining insect, a loudly buzzing fly in the crystal-blue distance as it raced a hundred feet above the valley floor. In less than a minute it flashed over the estate. The pilot confirmed that the large house was indeed César's, the plane accelerated upward, and then it veered away over the valley.

The sleek turboprop, its engines straining, circled back, and the pilot settled the plane into a straight-line course toward its target.

As the plane approached, something detached from its undercarriage and zoomed toward the house, leaving a thin white vapor trail. The black Cessna heeled over in a sharp turn and rapidly accelerated out of range.

For a second nothing happened.

Then the front of the Duval estate exploded in a yellow, orange, and white fireball of thundering, rocketing hunks of concrete, wood, metal, and glass.

The detonation blasted furiously upward and outward, tearing apart half the house's walls, showering the grass, the nearby warehouse bunker, and the lakeshore in flaming ash. What had been a solid structure seconds earlier was now a violent, twisted hailstorm of tumbling bits and pieces swirling in the roaring echoes of the huge blast.

The contorted and collapsing skeleton of the front of the structure burned with the fury of a giant blast furnace, and in less than a minute it collapsed in on itself with a heavy *thump.*

Smoke climbed thickly into the sky from the burning devastation, turning its bright Mediterranean blue to dark, ugly gray.

Out of the thick cloud of roiling smoke, from around the back of the house, the white Alfa Romeo convertible appeared, accelerated past the burning inferno as it kicked up a trail of dust, and made for the main road. The top was down, and next to Bernard, who was bent over the wheel in concentration, Vianne's hair whipped urgently in the wind. Luc's unconscious body was wedged into the cramped space behind the seats.

Far off down the valley, the Cessna completed a wide turn and headed back for one more pass over the estate. As it flashed through the smoke belching from the destruction, the pilot, eyes narrow in concentration, spotted the Alfa, a swift white fox sprinting below on the curving road. The plane blasted over the car at a terrifyingly close height and heeled over into another turn.

This is going to be easy, the pilot thought. *I have three more rockets and there's no place for them to hide.*

In the passenger seat, Vianne wrestled a clip into the assault rifle that she had scooped up from the floor behind the couch before the living room was destroyed. As the car flashed down the N193, she kept one eye on the Cessna as she pushed herself as far back in the leather seat as she could.

From behind her she heard a moan, and she turned her head quickly to see Luc starting to stir.

Bernard heard it too, and he reached back between the seats with one hand and slapped his brother's face. "Don't move, and shut up," he said loudly over the sound of the car's straining motor.

Luc opened his eyes, but they wouldn't focus, and he lay still, trying to understand what was going on.

Before anyone could say anything, the black Cessna came up from behind and roared so low over the Alfa that the sports car was buffeted sideways in the air draft, and Bernard had to grip the wheel to keep the car under control.

Vianne felt the car slowing down, and she grasped Bernard's arm. He looked at her and she pointed urgently ahead, her whole body telling him to speed up, keep going.

She looked to the right and left and then to the rear, but couldn't spot the plane, though she knew it was just a matter of a few seconds until it was on them again.

A precious half minute ticked by as they hurtled down the road, passing a few slower cars and a pickup truck.

Finally, through the windshield, Vianne made out the tiny speck of the Cessna in the distant sky straight ahead, lining itself up to make a head-on run on the car. She leaned to her left, put her mouth near Bernard's ear, and whispered, "Don't slow down."

Before Bernard could say anything, she had grabbed the top of the windshield frame and pulled herself up until she was standing. The wind was fierce, and she had to hold tight with her left hand to keep from being blown back into the seat, or worse: out and over the back of the speeding car.

With her right hand she hefted the AK-47 and settled its butt against her shoulder. She tilted her head to the right, saw the plane up ahead growing fast, and sighted down the rifle with both eyes narrowed.

The wind whipped her hair in a black fury, her torn white blouse fluttered violently in the rushing air, the car flashed full bore down the road, and the inner voice that lived in Vianne's heart was clear: *Don't miss.*

In the Cessna's cockpit, an arm reached forward, putting a slim finger on the toggle switch that would launch one of the rockets from under the fuselage. A gold ring gleamed on the finger, a tiny dividend from a thousand drug deals and a thousand deaths. Through the windshield, the pilot was satisfied that the Alfa had reached an arrow-straight section of the road and was on a perfect collision course.

A grim, professional smile curled the pilot's lips, her finger ready on the button.

Vianne's eyes began to water in the wind, and she knew that from a distance of more than four hundred meters the rifle would be useless, the rounds would have no effect—if they made contact at all. She had to let the plane get dangerously closer if she and Bernard and Luc were to have any chance.

Don't miss, her inner voice repeated.

As the zooming plane and the approaching car closed in on each other, she took in a deep breath, and through the wind and the speed and the tumult and the hopelessness of the hurtling madness she suddenly heard her mother's voice. *There will be a future.*

Bam! The first shot. Her mother's voice spoke of a safe, calm life far from despair.

Bam! Bam! Bam! Three more shots, all wide and off the mark. It would be a bright life where Vianne could be anything she wanted.

Bam! Bam! A life where she would finally be in control.

Bam! Bam! Bam! Bam! A life where the decisions would be hers and hers alone.

Vianne blinked as the last final, furious seconds imploded on themselves, and she held her breath as she saw the plane closing in, untouched and rock steady on its deadly course.

It comes to *right now*—it comes to *this*—

Bam!

The finger on the plane's dashboard jerked the toggle switch, sending the rocket on its way. That one tiny motion did its damage, but it was just a small spasm of an already dead body, and had happened a millisecond too late.

Vianne's last and final round had blasted through the windshield, through the pilot's skull and out the back of the plane, and had rendered any more body movements of the dead woman in the pilot seat mere random traumatic muscle contractions.

Through the bright afternoon air, the rocket arrowed toward the car, trailing a line of gray smoke. As Vianne fell back down into her seat, it screamed straight over her head, veered downward, and exploded in an ear-shattering fireball fifty yards behind the car.

In the next fraction of a heartbeat, the plane itself roared a few feet over the Alfa and then gained altitude. Vianne turned in her seat and watched as the black Cessna receded into the distance high over the valley, climbing into the blue sky.

In the blood-splattered cockpit, the pilot's dead body was slumped over the controls.

A quarter mile past the car at an altitude of around a thousand feet, the twin-engine plane slowly, almost gracefully, heeled over and, spinning on its axis, its wings milling, headed straight down. It augured into a rocky hillside, and its double gas tanks and the two remaining rockets exploded violently. The roar was muffled by the distance, and the searing yellow-and-white fireball was a grim, blossoming funeral pyre.

Bernard pulled the Alfa to the side of the road, turned off the engine, and hesitantly glanced at Vianne.

In the sudden quiet she turned and looked back at the roiling cloud rising from the atomized wreck of the plane. Then she slowly stood and stepped up onto the passenger seat to get a better view. Her black hair was an unruly, lank avalanche, her blouse was in sweaty tatters, and the AK-47 was still gripped in her right hand. Her heart was pounding, and as she studied the scene, glimmering splinters of light flashed in the irises of her eyes.

She took in a long breath—savoring, loving the clean air of life. In a low bush by the side of the road a bird sang.

Vianne glanced down at Luc, who was groggily coming to, and felt like aiming the rifle at him. Then she looked at Bernard, his white-knuckled hands still gripping the steering wheel.

She whispered, "It's over."

Bernard's nervousness gave way to relief, and he motioned for Vianne to sit down.

She leaned back into her seat, wondering if all the hate, all the violence, all the fear was really over at all.

It's up to you now, said her inner voice.

Then Bernard started the car and made a tight turn, and they sped back toward what was left of their home.

CHAPTER 28

Last Chance

———

VIANNE WATCHED THE SMOKE RISING from the flattened rubble that was once the front half of the Duval estate as they drove around the wreckage toward the warehouse.

Bernard parked the car on the grass, and he and Vianne extricated Luc from the cramped space behind the two seats. Luc's face was puffy and bleeding. He was coherent, but too shaky to stand on his own. Bernard and Vianne supported him from under his arms and guided him into the warehouse.

They hefted him onto one of the low hay bales that they used for target practice, and Luc lay dazed, staring at the metal ceiling above him.

Bernard watched as Vianne strode purposefully out of the building. She returned a minute later from the Alfa with the AK-47 in her hands, and walked to the far end of the long room to stand in the spot where she usually practiced shooting.

She waited in silence, and after a minute Luc sat up on the hay bale. His eyes focused, and he saw Vianne at the end of the long room.

She raised the rifle to her shoulder in one fluid movement and fired a single loud shot. A blossom of hay puffed outward from between Luc's spread legs.

"W-wait!" Luc held up a shaky hand and looked at Bernard, who was standing against the wall. "Stop her, Bernard!"

Bernard looked at his brother for a moment, then over at Vianne. The large man merely shrugged.

Bam! Another shot, and more hay exploded around Luc. The round missed his body by mere inches.

"Vianne! Vianne, please!" Luc's voice was hoarse with fear.

Bernard looked back at his brother, his face stony. "She means it, Luc. What you did to her. It was bad."

"I—I was drunk, Bernard. I didn't know what—"

Bam! This time Luc felt the bullet whiz by his left ear like a huge, angry hornet and smash into the concrete wall behind him, knocking some small, stony chunks into the hay. He stared at the slim figure at the other end of the room and yelled, "For God's sake, Vianne, you can't do this!"

He started to get off the hay bale, but another *bam!* and another hornet stopped him cold, this time so close to his upper arm that he felt its burning slash as it rocketed past at two thousand feet per second. Luc froze and closed his mouth, unsure of how his stepsister would end this. Even from a distance he could see that the events of the last hour had turned her into someone or something unknowable, unstoppable.

Now no outcome was off the table. He sensed that his luck had run out, and understood with icy clarity that the woman had become a killing machine.

Odd, he thought to himself through his fear. *This is the first time I've thought of her as a woman, not a girl—not a* chienne, *a bitch. She's a woman abused, a woman hurt. What have I done?* He slowly put his hands up in front of his face in prayer, a gesture he hoped she would see from the far end of the room.

With a short sweep of the rifle, Vianne motioned for Bernard to come to her, then aimed it back at Luc.

Bernard walked the length of the warehouse and came close to his stepsister.

Still training the rifle at Luc, she leaned to Bernard and whispered in his ear, "I have the right."

Bernard looked into her face and said simply, "He's my brother." The words were calm. "And he's César's son."

Vianne sighted down the rifle again and saw Luc trembling. Even from a distance she was able to make out a spreading area of wetness on the crotch of his pants. She held back a satisfied smile.

"He would kill me," she whispered to Bernard without looking at him.

Bernard made a thoughtful face. He shrugged again and said, "I'll talk to him."

Vianne watched the man walk down the long room. She saw him approach Luc and start speaking. From a distance, she saw Luc's nervously attentive face, his body as still as a rock.

Finally, Bernard finished talking to Luc and stepped back.

Luc stared at his brother for a few more seconds, and then his eyes went to Vianne. He took in a deep breath and nodded at her.

Vianne waited half a minute and then slowly lowered the rifle to her side. She walked down the room toward Luc, her eyes ablaze with cautious attention, the bruise from the slaps an angry red smudge under her left cheekbone. Finally she stopped in front of the two men and the hay bales.

No one said anything, but Luc reached a hand out to Vianne.

Ignoring the hand, she whispered, "You pissed your pants. *Quel porc.*"

"Forgive me?" Luc managed to say, his face sincere. "Please."

The surrounding quiet was redolent with the smell of gun smoke and urine.

Her next whisper was almost below the threshold of hearing. "Next time I'll kill you."

Then Vianne let her eyes relax and she turned to Bernard.

"Come with me," she whispered.

They walked out together, leaving Luc in the warehouse to nurse his wounds, the remainder of his hangover, and whatever scraps he could dredge up of his conscience.

But instead of walking toward the part of the house that had not been destroyed, Vianne led Bernard down to the shore of the lake. Its sapphire-blue water sparkled in the sun. They stood side by side in silence for a few minutes, and finally Bernard turned to Vianne.

"What happens now?" he asked.

Vianne kept looking out over the lake as she whispered, "I'll be back in a day or two."

"Where are you going?"

Vianne didn't answer, her eyes locked on the lake and the mountains behind it.

Bernard's brow creased. "Do you want me to come with you?"

She shook her head.

"Where, Vianne? Where are you going?"

Vianne's hand tightened on the AK-47 that she was still holding, and her inner voice said, *It all must end now.*

Then she turned to look at her stepbrother, and as the smoke rose behind her from the wreck of her home, she whispered, *"Je t'aime,* Bernard."

CHAPTER 29

A Promise Deferred

THE FOLLOWING MORNING CÉSAR AND Jacqueline met with a certain Herr Schiesmann, one of Kanton Zürich's most influential politicians. Many things were said in the sanctuary of the man's private office, and many things were agreed upon.

The couple spent the rest of the day searching properties in Küsnacht, an exclusive suburb of the city. By the time they returned to the Baur au Lac Hotel, they were exhausted, and they had a late dinner on their suite's balcony overlooking the Zürichsee, its waters dark under the stars.

They spoke in soft voices, certain of who they were and of their place in each other's lives.

"You're sure?" Jacqueline finally said quietly, watching the lights on the boats out on the lake. She took a small sip of coffee and looked at César.

He nodded. "Positive. The family will be safe here. And I won't be changing my mind."

He reached a hand across the table. "Besides, this beautiful scenery is a perfect setting for a wedding, eh?" He motioned with his head. "Maybe out there on a large pleasure boat on that lake?"

She took his hand in hers.

The next morning they took the first flight to Corsica.

When Eduard brought the car into view of the remnants of the house, he automatically slowed down.

In the backseat, Jacqueline gasped and César gritted his teeth.

The entire front half of the house was a field of rubble, with the interior of some of the still-standing rooms now open to view. Eduard parked in front of the wreckage, and the three got out of the car and stood immobile, paralyzed by their raging emotions. They heard the sound of activity from within the undamaged part of the building, and were partially relieved when Solomon and Sheba ran to them, barking a greeting.

The spell broken by the noise and the dogs, César made his way through the wreckage and nearly crashed into Bernard, who was dressed in worker's clothes and covered with dust.

César gripped his son's shoulders in relief. "What happened? Where's—?"

"A bomb. From a plane."

César turned to see Luc standing in a half-demolished doorway, equally coated with grime and flush from exertion. The two brothers had obviously been trying to create at least a bit of order from the chaos.

César's eyes narrowed to angry slits. "A plane? We were bombed from a plane?"

"We tried to call you in Switzerland, but by the time we discovered where you were staying, you had left." Luc tossed the hammer he had been working with to the floor and wiped his palms on the side of his work shirt. "And we couldn't very well call the police, could we?"

César noticed that something was different about his son. Luc seemed completely sober, and sounded in control. Was it this catastrophe that had straightened him out? Or something else? "Who was hurt? Was anyone—?"

"Where's Vianne?" Jacqueline, visibly shaken, had made her way through the detritus to stand behind César. "Is she all right?"

Luc nodded. "She took care of the plane."

César's face was a study in shock. "Eh?"

"Blew it out of the sky," Bernard said with a smile.

"Who was in the plane?" César asked in a low voice, his mind racing to get a firmer understanding of what had happened.

Bernard laughed. "Papa, there was nothing left of it, just a giant hole in the ground."

Mistral, César knew. *The murderous bitch wanted me to see this, see the death of my sons, see the death of—*

"Where's Vianne now?"

Luc and Bernard exchanged looks.

"She left a while ago," Luc said, shaking his head. "She wouldn't say where she was going, and insisted we not hold her here or follow her."

"Why did you let her go?" César began to growl, but Jacqueline touched his arm.

Luc sighed in frustration, and added, "She went up to the villa for an hour or so, then came back down the mountain, got into the Alfa, and drove off." He looked at Bernard. "We both tried to stop her, but you know Vianne."

Bernard looked at his father. "Where do you think she went?"

César let his eyes roam over the devastation that was once his home.

He had no idea.

CHAPTER 30

Trade

———

GIUSEPPE RANDAZZO RARELY WENT INTO Palermo anymore.

But it was such a beautiful day that he had decided to take one of his nephews and a bodyguard and visit his favorite restaurant for lunch, the Focacceria San Pietro on the Via Alessandro Paternostro.

He brought along the girl who slept with him as well. "She is too pale," he said in a sideways voice to his nephew, who couldn't have cared less. "Needs a little sun."

The four sat at an outdoor table that afforded a clear view not only of the sparkling Mediterranean, but also of anyone coming down the street from either direction. The round table with its white tablecloth was crowded with dishes of pasta, baskets of hard bread, two bottles of wine, and plates of cheese and olives.

Giuseppe and his nephew Antonio were busy at their food, and the bodyguard kept careful watch of the surroundings as he too methodically consumed mouthfuls of linguine. The slim, pale girl ate almost nothing, her eyes glassy, her soul beaten—her heart emptied of emotion.

Giuseppe looked up idly from his plate of pasta and prosciutto, squinted in the noon sun, and stared at something up the block.

From a distance, a slim young woman walked at an even pace toward the restaurant. She wore a short, black skirt with low-heeled black pumps. Her skin had what seemed a deep exotic tan, and her thick hair gleamed. She wore sunglasses, and her only jewelry was a diamond *V* glinting in the sun between the open top folds of her black silk blouse.

She looks familiar, Giuseppe said to himself. *Where do I know her from?*

His feral survival instinct suddenly gripped his gut. He almost choked on his mouthful of linguine in a rare moment of uncertainty, and an even rarer moment of fear.

"*Che succede?*" he sneered out loud. What's going on?

He swallowed, sat still, and gestured for the others at the table to stand up. *Now.* Both Antonio and the bodyguard rose quickly and felt for the guns under their jackets. The pale woman got up with them and backed away in confused fear.

The girl in black approached to within a few yards of the table and stopped, arms at her sides. She carried no purse, and her hands were empty.

She said nothing.

The thirty-year-old Antonio and the bodyguard were stunned by this foolhardy *bellezza,* this beauty. They glanced at each other. What on earth had the old man seen in her to trigger this sudden and unusual reaction? She was obviously unarmed, certainly harmless and outnumbered. And besides—she was just a girl.

Giuseppe's pale *concubina* stared at the girl from the shadow of the restaurant's awning, shaking and in awe, praying that what was about to transpire would not involve blood. Or death.

But the young woman in black just stood on the hot sidewalk, legs slightly apart, looking down at the old but dangerous mafioso and his plate of pasta.

No one moved. No one spoke.

Finally Giuseppe Randazzo said, "*Buongiorno,* Vianne."

She was still and silent.

"*Prego,*" Giuseppe said, making a motion with his hand. "Please. Sit. Have a glass of this good wine, and tell this old man what you are doing in Palermo on this pleasant day."

Vianne looked over to Antonio and then to the bodyguard. Her eyes settled on the frightened young whore for a moment, and then went back to Giuseppe. With deliberate slowness, she sat at the table opposite the old man.

Giuseppe snapped his fingers and made a pouring motion with his hand. A waiter, who was standing in readiness near the restaurant door, hustled up with a clean glass and poured wine for Vianne.

She took a small sip and slowly removed her sunglasses. The irises of her midnight eyes immediately caught the Sicilian sunshine and gleamed with tiny sparks.

Antonio and the bodyguard were nonplussed, and they openly stared at the odd tableau as they stood a few feet away. Who was this young *volpe* who held such sway over the great scion of the house of Randazzo? Who or what were they watching?

Vianne leaned forward across the table. The diamond *V* rocked slightly on its thin chain like a glittering pendulum between her half-concealed breasts.

César, you are an animal, thought the old man, appreciating the girl's beauty, but he kept his mouth closed.

Vianne whispered, "Do you own Mistral?"

Giuseppe burped a laugh. *Where is this* bambolina *going with that?* he wondered. *Why in the world would César send her here? Is he with her? No, that would never happen. He would never put a woman, let alone his precious stepdaughter, in my path, here in the center of my sanctuary.*

No. She's come to Sicily under her own counsel.

Ignoring her question he asked, "How is my good friend César, eh?" He looked with exaggerated pantomime to the right and left. "Where is he? Is he here?"

Vianne merely shook her head but said nothing.

The old man's face darkened. "No, *signorina,* I do not own Mistral. No one does."

Vianne's eyes bored into his and she whispered, "She's dead."

Giuseppe's head moved a fraction of an inch, and he pushed out his lower lip. "This I did not know," he said, and Vianne saw in his face that it was the truth.

Her breath was like the wind. "I killed her."

Giuseppe shrugged and lifted a forkful of pasta to his mouth. *Well, if that's so,* he thought, *it's quite an accomplishment.* He chewed for a few seconds and said, "So?"

"Trade with me," she whispered, and leaned back in her chair. Her eyes never left his.

He put down his fork, and caution veiled his eyes. "Trade? What kind of trade does César want to make?"

Vianne shook her head. "Me. Not him." The words were annoyingly soft, but Giuseppe knew the ring of truth when he heard it.

"What could you offer me that I would be interested in?"

"Diamonds," she whispered.

"Eh?"

"Uncut. No trace," she whispered. "Half a million dollars' worth." She looked over at the two men standing in the shadow of the awning, then back at Giuseppe. The old man signaled to the bodyguard to stay where he was.

Vianne reached down with one hand and extracted a wad of tissue from a fold in her skirt. She dropped it near Giuseppe's plate of pasta.

The mafioso reached with both gnarled hands and un-wrapped its contents. Inside the tissue was a rough cube the size of a golf ball, obviously an uncut diamond, obviously very valuable.

"Fifty thousand dollars," Vianne whispered. "There are nine more."

Giuseppe lifted his gaze from the stone. "What would stop me from just taking this, eh?" though he knew full well that if anything befell this young woman, he would likely not survive César's wrath.

She ignored the question and whispered, "The other stones are here in Palermo, waiting for you."

"Hmph. You've been a busy little girl, haven't you?"

Vianne just stared at him.

Giuseppe nodded. "I haven't all day, and my lunch is getting cold. What do you want in trade?"

Vianne waited a few more seconds and then her eyes slid over to the pale, shaking girl half hidden behind Antonio and the bodyguard.

"Her," she whispered …

The giant fist of the gunshot had pushed Zelda Latour deep into the cushion of the plush settee, a crimson stain quickly spreading and covering her chest.

Vianne, her shoulder burning, her clothes and legs splattered with blood, stepped over one man's twitching body and through the gun smoke and the deep pile of broken glass and crystal. She bent over Zelda and saw that the old woman was still breathing.

"My friend Adèle," Vianne whispered urgently into the woman's ear. "Where is she?"

Zelda's eyes opened, and her gaze slid to Vianne's face. "Why should I tell you?" she croaked, and blood spilled from her lips.

Vianne bent low and took off her sunglasses to let Zelda see her eyes. "It will count," she whispered. A tiny reflected rainbow glowed on Vianne's cheek.

Zelda coughed up more blood. Her eyes turned upward, her body shook once, and it seemed to Vianne that she had expired.

But a moment later the dying pimp's lips moved and she purred as if in a reverie, "He gave me half a million francs for her, you know."

"Who?" hissed Vianne in desperation. "Who did you sell Adèle to?"

Zelda opened her mouth, and what came out was a long, barely comprehensible, gurgling belch. "Giu-giu-seppe Ran-da-da-zzo-o."

Vianne's eyes went wide and her heart skipped a beat. With one hand she shook Zelda hard, but the old woman was gone.

As Vianne stood up, she heard the approaching sounds of running feet out in the hallway.

Giuseppe fingered the diamond cube, hefted himself around in his chair, and studied Adèle, whose eyes were wide with fear. She was visibly shaking. For a few long moments he eyed the pale novitiate that he had bought from the Parisian pimp. Finally he swiveled back to face Vianne.

"*This* girl?" he asked Vianne, pointing to Adèle, uncomfortable with his inability to see any clear point to the request.

Vianne sat still and nodded once.

"Why?"

Vianne stood up, put her two hands on the table in front of her, and leaned down until her face was three inches from the old man's. She wanted him to get a close look at her eyes.

"She's my friend," came the whisper as the bodyguard and the nephew automatically stepped close to her. Antonio grabbed one of her arms as if to pull her back, but Giuseppe waved him off.

The old man leaned back in his chair, tilted his head to the side, and studied Vianne. "You came here alone, to Sicily, to barter uncut diamonds with me. Me, Giuseppe Randazzo." He snorted. "All to rescue your friend?"

Vianne waited a few seconds and nodded once.

Giuseppe looked over at Adèle and spoke to her for the first time. He pointed a finger at Vianne and said, "You know her?"

Adèle nervously fingered the tiny five-pointed star pendant on her chest and looked as if she was about to pass out from fear. She murmured, "From the convent."

Giuseppe let out a sigh. "From the convent." He looked at Vianne. "You are also a nun?"

Vianne breathed, "Is it a deal?"

Giuseppe got up slowly from the table and stood in front of Adèle, who looked about to faint. Without taking his eyes off the pale woman he said in a loud voice, "No."

The waiter, who had been watching the drama from the doorway, slowly backed away into the restaurant. The only other thing that moved was the bodyguard, who shifted his stance to one of readiness.

Giuseppe closed a hand around Adèle's wrist and pulled the girl over to the table to position her next to Vianne. He let go of Adèle's arm, sat back down heavily in his chair, and stared up at Vianne.

"No deal." He picked up a hunk of hard bread, dipped it in the remains of the marinara sauce, and took a bite. As he chewed, he cast a baleful eye up at the two women.

Vianne raised her head slightly and moved in front of Adèle. She was about to whisper something to her when the old man let out a sudden laugh accented by a few flying bread crumbs.

"Go, Vianne," he said, making a dismissive wave with one hand. "Go back to Corsica and take the whore, I mean, the *Sister*, with you. Her charm as a virginal nun long ago lost its luster." He took a sip of wine. "And here …"

He picked up the rough diamond and held it out in front of him. "There's no trade. Adèle is my *gift* to you, for which you will one day owe me. I have too much going on now to have to think about César Duval's stepdaughter holding a grudge, or César himself, for that matter."

Vianne hesitated for a few seconds, then took the diamond and closed her hand around it.

"But you can tell César that all our business is done. Now that Mistral is dead, we can both go about our separate lives in our separate worlds with one less distraction." He popped another piece of bread into his mouth and watched Vianne carefully as he chewed.

Vianne looked over at Antonio and the bodyguard, whose faces had turned to stone. Then she nodded once, gently took Adèle's arm, and began to walk away.

"Vianne."

She stopped at the sound and turned her head to look over her shoulder at the old man.

"Vianne," Giuseppe Randazzo said in a low voice made dark with a lifetime of menace. "Unless I feel the need to call in this favor, I don't want to have anything to do with you. Ever again. Don't forget that."

Their eyes locked for a last few seconds.

She held her fist out at arm's length, opened it, and let the diamond fall into the gutter. It clattered once and came to rest near a dead rat.

Then she turned and, putting an arm around Adèle's quaking shoulders, guided her friend away down the sun-drenched Sicilian street.

CHAPTER 31

A Walk on the Beach

ON THE PLANE BACK TO Corsica from Sicily, Adèle held tightly to Vianne's arm with a grip that was augmented by both fear and hope.

"You're breaking it," Vianne whispered, looking down at her arm.

"*Je suis désolée.*" Adèle almost burst into tears. "Oh, *merci*, Vianne, *mille mercis.*"

Vianne turned away and looked out the small window at the sky.

"What will happen when we get to Corsica?" Adèle asked timidly when she had composed herself. "I've nowhere to go."

"*T'inquiète pas,*" Vianne whispered. Don't worry.

"But—" Adèle began.

Vianne patted her hand. "I'll think of something."

"Where's the body?" César Duval's voice was cold ice chips coming through the phone.

Inspector Gustave Mignone grunted with irony and said, "Everywhere. The explosion of Mistral's plane was so complete that we were lucky to find even some blood and bits of bone. But it was her. We found her ring."

"What?"

"In the crater blasted by the plane. A gold finger ring engraved on the inside in Spanish, '*Por A. de la C. con amor.*'"

"A. de la C.?"

"Do your homework, César," Mignone said. "Mistral's real name was Angelina de la Cruz. I surmise the ring was a gift—most likely from Miguel Muñoz. Now she's joined him for a long hot eternity together."

César was quiet for a few seconds. Finally he asked, "Who was the rat?"

Mignone pressed his lips together, and then said, "Someone here. I don't yet know who, but I have some idea. I will ferret him out, you can be assured."

"You will tell me when you have." It was an order, not a question.

The inspector let out a bitter laugh. "Better still, I'll tell your stepdaughter."

César's voice lowered to an icy rasp. "You will never tell her anything again. Not without me present."

"I suggest you rein the girl in, *Monsieur* Duval. Though it appears that with Vianne you've let a dangerous genie out of a lamp."

César was about to say something when Mignone growled, "You may be Corsican, my friend, but you don't own the whole country, and especially not its police force."

"Depends, Gustave," César said, ending the conversation.

As he hung up the phone, he thought, *Mignone is more or less right in everything he said. About Corsica, about me—about Vianne.*

Now it's time to go.

César had been both furious over the attack on his family and the destruction of his house, and relieved that by some miracle no one was hurt or killed.

And when Vianne returned from Sicily and told him where she had been and what had transpired, he flew into a rage.

He began to excoriate her in gutter Corsican for the outlandish risk she had taken in Palermo. When she shrugged with mock incomprehension at the words, he switched to French, and his yelling and threatening was so severe that he looked to be on the verge of physically assaulting her.

But Vianne merely turned her back on him in silence, crossed her arms on her chest, and waited for the tantrum to subside.

"What the hell do you think you were doing? You don't know Giuseppe Randazzo, what he is capable of, how your life means nothing to him. He would kill you as soon as look at you!"

She kept her back turned.

"You risked your life for this friend of yours, this Adèle. What were you thinking?"

Vianne finally turned and stepped close until their faces were a few inches apart. Her whisper was even softer than usual. "Rescuing an orphan in trouble. Sound familiar?"

"It's different," he said, raising his chin with the hauteur of someone who was never questioned and was always obeyed. But

Vianne saw that he couldn't mask the sudden, unbidden rush of affection that had bloomed in his face, had crept into his eyes.

"It's exactly the same," came the whisper, and she kissed his cheek once, turned on her heels, and went out the door.

Jacqueline and César stood in the living room of the villa far up the side of the mountain. Down in the valley, the partially wrecked estate looked like a dollhouse, half of which had been stepped on by a giant. Luc and Bernard were tiny figures far below, overseeing some equally tiny local workers who were charged with cleaning up the destruction and securing the part of the estate that wasn't destroyed. At least the kitchen and a few of the bedrooms remained intact.

When Luc had asked when the rebuilding would start, César had surprised him by being vague and noncommittal.

"You don't want it repaired?" Luc had said to his father.

"Maybe we build a whole new one," Bernard had offered, always ready for work.

"Maybe," César had said to his sons, and left it at that.

"This girl," he said quietly to Jacqueline. "This Adèle. What are we going to do with her?"

Jacqueline's face was taut, and her eyes had taken on a defeated look. Her reaction to the reality of the attack on the estate was profound, almost as if she had been physically assaulted. Over the years she had become used to the "inside" life with César, but this had shaken her. If there had been any hesitation left in her mind about leaving Corsica, it had evaporated when she laid eyes on the devastation that had been her home.

"You're asking the wrong person. I'm quite sure Vianne already has some ideas on that topic."

"Yes," César said, confronted by yet another inevitability. "I'm certain she does."

Philip Jouet carefully packed his uniform and the rest of his clothes.

He had known that one day it might end like this, and now he was leaving—leaving the force, leaving Ajaccio, leaving Corsica. And fast.

He smirked. *Well, I have enough detailed information on Gustave Mignone to protect myself for the rest of my life. I have ample proof of the inspector's secret deals with Duval and a host of others, his trading of police information for favors and money.*

But things have taken a turn and won't reverse themselves.

Mistral was supposed to pay me, but she's dead, so that's lost. And what's worse is that I've no idea if she left evidence of my agreement with her.

So I must run.

But there was one thing Philip Jouet had to do first—one person who had to be neutralized. That person had been the pivot point, the single individual who had put this disaster in motion, who had pushed him to flee in fear from his job, his career—his life.

That girl. Vianne.

He knew where Vianne was. And he knew what he had to do.

He touched the butt of his .45 caliber automatic to make sure it was holstered beneath his jacket, and finished packing.

"Zürich?" Luc asked. "Switzerland?"

César nodded. "Switzerland is unique, special. The whole country is like a well-guarded vault, and it defends its people. And its patrons."

They were in the kitchen, which had escaped the explosion that had leveled the front of the house. Jacqueline and Bernard sat with them at the woodblock table. The dogs slept near their feet.

Vianne stood leaning against the stove, arms crossed in front of her chest, silent, watching, listening carefully. She had asked Eduard to walk with Adèle around the lake while the family had this meeting.

César continued, "It's more than past the time I should have done this. For all of our sakes we are getting out now—out of our business, out of danger. Regardless of what happens, even with our enemies either dead or distracted, things will not be improving in Corsica—or in France, for that matter—for many years. And besides …" He looked to each of their faces in turn. "No more taking chances with our family."

Bernard clasped both hands to his heart. "I like it."

Luc winced. "We don't speak German."

The bruises on his handsome face were dark, which made the scar on his cheek seem more pronounced, and when his father asked him what had occurred, Bernard had cut in to say they had had a fight, brother to brother, a private matter, and it was settled now.

When César had looked questioningly at Vianne, she had merely nodded and turned away. She had made certain that Luc knew where he stood with her. There would be no more trouble.

"Zürich is an international financial center, and although German is mainly spoken in that city, French is pervasive and is the primary language in half the country." César leaned back in his chair. "More important, they understand the language of money with crystal clarity."

"I will teach you," Jacqueline said to Luc. "*Gern geschehen.* My pleasure."

Bernard smiled broadly at the strange-sounding language. "*Ja!*" he said, the only German word he knew.

César looked at his stepdaughter, but she was silent, and her face betrayed nothing. "Well, Vianne," he said. "Any thoughts?"

She shifted her body but remained leaning on the stove, gazing at the floor. She thought of her mother, of her nighttime stories so long ago of a safe and bright future. *Well, Switzerland certainly sounds safe, and César's retreat from our violent world may be what was in the stars all the time.*

Finally she looked up and whispered, "Adèle?"

César was about to say something, but Jacqueline interjected. "You rescued her, Vianne. Traditions say you are responsible for her now." She gave César a hard look, but it wasn't necessary.

"She can come with us," César said. "I was already making the arrangements."

He looked sideways at Jacqueline and then said to Vianne, "Your friend will have to change her name for safety's sake. Ask her to pick one out, the sooner the better."

"When do we leave?" Vianne whispered, and everyone looked at César.

"Within a week," he said, his face set in familiar determination. "Maybe ten days."

Philip Jouet spent almost three days in the woods surrounding the Duval estate. He was waiting, stalking in a professional, efficient manner, and finally on this day his chance had presented itself. Through his binoculars he watched as the woman hefted a few bundles of what looked like clothing into the passenger seat of a white Alfa Romeo. Then she got behind the wheel and drove off.

Alone.

Philip was able to get to his car and follow her. *Today settles all scores,* he thought to himself. *I will kill her quickly and I will run. Duval will think that somehow Mistral still lives and has exacted her revenge. I know how to survive, and I will.*

Though he was thin and wiry, he felt sweat begin to accumulate in his armpits as he kept a safe distance behind the white sports car.

The girl drove into the city alone, parking on the street in front of the Paroisse Saint Roch Catholic Church on the Cours Napoleon.

Jouet watched from a half block away as she took the bundles of clothes inside to the donation box. He laughed to himself for the precautions he had taken to remain out of sight. *Why am I being so cautious? She doesn't know me, or have an inkling of my role here at the very end of her life.*

In less than five minutes she came out of the church into the sun, settled behind the wheel of the Alfa, and drove off down the coast road.

Though it was late in the afternoon, it was still hot.

Jouet had the windows of his Fiat open. When his target turned the Alfa off the road to park near one of the almost deserted public beaches, he was overjoyed with expectation and excitement.

Now, he thought happily. *Now is the time. Now the tango will come to its inevitable end, and only one of us will leave the dance floor alive. And of course, that will be me.* He watched as the solitary girl walked slowly toward the ocean.

She wore a short, loosely fitting dress, its sheer folds of silk almost translucent in the light. She disappeared behind a thick clump of trees, and police detective Philip Jouet, determination and murder coagulating in his heart like a dark red mud, got out of his car and walked across the street and down toward the beach.

The low, hot Mediterranean sun burned his eyes, but he didn't care. In a few minutes it would all be over.

He warily approached the trees but didn't see her, and he started off down the sand. He walked quickly, and his shirt soon stuck to him—soaked through from an equal measure of the summer heat and from a nagging realization that his target had momentarily eluded him.

The sun was low, and the last of the sunbathers had left the beach hours earlier.

After a hundred yards he slowed down to scan his surroundings, nervous that he had lost his quarry. *Not good—not good at all.*

He plodded on, ignoring the sweat and the gritty distraction of the sand accumulating in his shoes.

Once again he looked back, and this time his steps faltered. He came to a stop and rubbed his eyes with the back of a hand. *There she is. Back there.*

In the distance, in line with the lowering sun, a hazy female figure jogged at a slight angle to the shoreline. Her body moved in silent deliberation. On a low dune a few yards from the water's edge, she slowed to a walk, the brilliant ball behind her imperceptibly but inexorably closing the short gap between itself, her silhouette, and the sea.

It occurred to him that somehow their roles might have reversed. *Is* she *following* me *now?*

Jouet's eyes narrowed at the vision of the slim, young woman—a distant wraith against the bloated Mediterranean sun. His nerves thrummed with caution, though he was certain she was unarmed, harmless. *She's got nothing.*

The figure came to a stop near a scattering of almost-buried rocks, and then stood still—a monochrome ghost against the sun's violent orange.

Some of the sheer folds of her silk dress floated around her—shimmering coronas in the hot breeze. A few sparks of reflected light winked from the edges of her hair.

The two were the only ones on the deserted stretch of beach. Now she was *his,* and she had taken on a fantasy persona in his mind—an insistent erotic image that stirred him. A thought sparked in the back of his mind:

A pity I must kill this particular girl at this particular moment. But I will.

He pulled an automatic from its belt holster at the small of his back, cocked the slide, and started walking toward her through the sand. He was confident that she had no means to either attack him or defend herself. But he was cautious nevertheless, and didn't take his eyes off the ghostly figure in the distance.

Down the beach, the hints of silk swirled around the silhouette.

He walked a dozen more steps—close enough to be in killing range—and realized that now she was facing him, watching him.

He narrowed his eyes to slits. *Damn this glare.*

She placed a foot on a low beach rock, and his eyes were drawn to a point between the silhouette's thighs. The intense light of the sun behind the woman was almost too bright to endure. A single harsh ray shot through the gap where her legs met, and it burned his eyes—as if her sex were aiming a laser into his brain and somehow mocking him.

His breaths became shorter.

His endorphin levels soared.

The far-off intersections of light and dark coalesced, and he shook his head in a double take as he saw her smoothly, quickly, bend at the waist and run her hands down to the sand. He lifted his free hand to shade his eyes.

She brought the Beretta up in a single sweep from its hiding place in the rocks and shot at him three times in quick, measured succession.

Before he could fire his own pistol, the rounds slammed into him. One of them skewered his heart, another a lung. The third scorched through his stomach and smashed into his spine so violently that two vertebrae split apart.

He was dead before his body hit the sand.

The sweltering hush that followed the gun blasts held only a single, far-off cry of a seabird and the rhythmic *shh* of tiny waves at the water's flat edge.

The light dress whispered gently against her smooth skin. She slowly lowered the gun and studied her would-be killer's dead body from afar. The bright flecks in the irises of her eyes glinted in the day's fading light.

She didn't approach the corpse, preferring to stand in silence several feet from the water's edge, listening, waiting, and after a few seconds her inner voice whispered, *Time to go.*

Her hands absently smoothed her billowy dress as she cast a final, confirming look at the lifeless clump in the distance: it had already become dusted with a powdering of blown sand. She took in a long breath of sea air and reflected for a moment about who she was, why she had survived up to now, and the inevitability of her destiny.

The moment passed, and a small smile came unbidden to her lips.

A few more silent seconds ticked by, and then Vianne turned and walked toward the sun.

CHAPTER 32

The End of a Beautiful Friendship

"ONE OF MY MEN IS missing, César."

"What do you mean?"

Gustave Mignone held the phone an inch or so from his face and felt he was ready to retire, though he was ten years away from the age at which he would receive a full pension. Not that he needed the money, as certain citizens in his jurisdiction had bestowed generous gifts of appreciation upon him over many years in payment for many favors. One of those grateful benefactors was César Duval, and this was just another accommodation that Mignone expected to be remunerated for by his most important supporter.

"A detective named Jouet, Philip Jouet," the inspector went on. "It has been four days since he clocked out of the station, and he seems to have disappeared. This morning we sent a man to his apartment. The furniture was there, but his personal effects were gone."

César was quiet. Now he had a name for the corpse that he and Bernard and Luc had located on the beach. Even with

Vianne's directions, it was by sheer luck that they had found the body later in the evening near where she had told them it would be.

Jouet had been completely covered by blown sand, but one exposed hand still gripped a half-buried automatic and protruded from the dune to mark his temporary grave.

"Where is this man now?" César asked.

Mignone laughed to himself, intuiting from the quality of César's voice that this question was more a formality than a serious inquiry. He chuckled. "You tell me, my friend. You always seem to have a sixth sense about these things."

"We need to have a talk about other things, Gustave." César changed his tone as he altered the direction of the conversation. "When can you give me an hour of your time?"

Mignone was nonplussed. *What's that about?* he wondered. *Better not act too curious or anxious.* "Tomorrow," he said. "Tomorrow we have lunch together." As he said it, an odd feeling came over him that it would be the last time he would ever lay eyes on César Duval.

"I'll be there," César said, and hung up the phone.

The diamonds were hidden on board César's Hatteras, the same boat on which Vianne had come to Corsica four years earlier.

The day after next they would sail for Genoa, where a broker was waiting to take delivery of the motor yacht. Some of the uncut stones would be left with a black market cutter, but the bulk of the diamonds would remain with the Duval family as they traveled through northern Italy and across the border into Switzerland.

Eduard and Matteo would be driving the two cars, and the loyal bodyguards were energized by the prospect of a new life. Both men had seen disappointment and loss over the last few years, and were now pledged to their benefactor more than ever.

When the family crossed the border into Switzerland, they would do so with their new identities and new citizenship papers that César had acquired at an outrageous price from the very accommodating and very corrupt official in Kanton Zürich.

But there were still a few details that had to be taken care of in Corsica before they left.

One of those details he and his sons had already made certain had washed out to sea.

Twenty-four hours later, he and Inspector Mignone were having coffee in the commissary at Ajaccio police headquarters. Gustave wasn't surprised to learn that the man was leaving Corsica. Since the incident with the *Crescent Rose,* he had intuited that Duval had reached a point in his life past which he didn't want to venture. Their world was moving too fast, unraveling too quickly, the distinction between good and evil blurring with greater frequency.

And we're both getting too old for this, the inspector thought as he took a drag on his cigarette and watched the other man's face. He would miss César Duval, a man who stood opposite him on the other side of the law, but ironically on the same side of fairness, of judgment.

It all comes down to people, not laws, Gustave reflected for the thousandth time. *Though my life revolves around law, justice is ultimately best decided by individuals, not edicts. Individuals like me, and like César.*

He chuckled to himself. *And apparently also decided by the man's stepdaughter, Vianne. Her verdicts are unpredictable and her punishments brutal, but she has no hesitation about bringing things into balance.*

He studied the man sitting across the table.

She may have been adopted, he thought, *but to all under heaven, she's surely César's girl.*

Mignone took a last sip of coffee. "Let me know what part of the world you'll be in."

César just looked at him for a long moment. He put his cup down on the table in front of him and said, "I'll contact you in the future, in a few months."

"Well, you won't hear from me, César." Another puff on his cigarette. "That's my going-away present."

César Duval stood up. "You know it was Jouet, don't you, Gustave?"

Mignone smiled. "*D'accord.* Of course. Thank you."

As César turned to walk away, he said, "Don't thank *me.*"

Inspector Mignone knew exactly what he meant.

CHAPTER 33

The Inevitability of the Winds

EVERYTHING WAS READY, THE HOUSE and warehouse were secured, and Eduard and Matteo were making the last preparations to escort everyone into the cars. From there they would head to the pier in Ajaccio and board the motor yacht.

The neighboring Cappucci family had agreed to foster Solomon and Sheba until the Duvals had settled in Switzerland. Then the two German shepherds would be flown there to reunite with the family.

Jacqueline, Luc, and Bernard stood by the cars as César came around from the back of the house. He had resolved that this was the best and smartest thing for everyone. For his sons, for Jacqueline, and for …

"Where's Vianne?" he said.

Luc looked at him. "Isn't she with you?"

César shook his head. "No. And where's Adèle?"

When no one could answer his questions, he sent Bernard into the house to find the two women. Five minutes passed before he appeared from inside the half-collapsed structure.

"I don't understand," Bernard said. "They were here this morning, but I was busy with getting ready and didn't think about it."

"That's odd," César said, and suddenly knew with an unbidden flash of sickening intuition that everything had suddenly gone completely and utterly wrong.

Vianne had walked out to the warehouse and stopped in her tracks. Something was missing. She had been there five minutes previously and was certain she had seen one of the ATV fourwheelers parked at the side of the structure.

Now it was gone.

She found Bernard back at the wreck of the main house and asked where it might be.

"I don't know," he said, but he was obviously busy with some last-minute preparations for their trip. "Ask Luc."

Luc was speaking with Jacqueline in the half-demolished kitchen, and César had yet to arrive from his meeting with Mignone. No one seemed to have had the time or the inclination to move the four-wheeler.

Suddenly Vianne froze. Her inner voice said one word. *Adèle.*

Vianne ran through the other rooms looking for her friend, and then out onto the back lawn. She stood still, all her senses reaching out. Slowly she let her eyes wander up to the villa cantilevered out of the mountainside a thousand feet up.

Without wasting another second she sprinted for the warehouse and one of the two remaining ATVs.

As Vianne approached the villa on the winding road, a cold caution began to envelop her heart. She parked the ATV a hundred yards short of the villa, and quickly and quietly covered the rest of the way on foot.

She saw the other four-wheeler parked outside the front door of the low glass-and-steel structure.

What's gotten into Adèle? she thought. *Why did she come here knowing that we would be leaving within a matter of hours? And why didn't she tell me?*

And what's wrong here? She reached behind her, slid the Beretta from its spot at the small of her back, and held it ready at her side.

She walked cautiously through the front door, past the small modern kitchen, and came to a sudden, sickening stop.

Adèle was lying unmoving on her stomach on the living room floor, a dozen feet from the glass doors that opened to the balcony. A wet red stain had spread beneath her.

Vianne started to run to her but then realized they weren't alone.

She slowed to a stop, but before she could turn around, there was an eardrum-shattering *crack* of an automatic weapon. The insides of Vianne's thighs were instantly slashed with a ferocious sudden burn as a single rifle bullet blasted between her legs from behind. Its trajectory was professionally precise, and had it been just a few inches higher, would have obliterated the base of her spine. As such it had seared the skin on the insides of both thighs, almost setting the legs of her jeans on fire, before crashing through one of the glass doors to the patio, shattering it to pieces.

"Don't," came a single word from behind her as Vianne began to whirl and aim the Beretta.

Vianne resisted an impulse to put one hand down between her legs, and she completed her turn. She froze when she saw the owner of the voice standing at the door through which she had just entered the house.

The shooter was dressed head to toe in a black leather bodysuit with a high collar. Rakishly cut platinum hair contrasted vividly with her red lips, her olive skin, and the dangerously modified, telescopic-sighted assault rifle in her hands.

"Don't," the woman repeated in an even tone, and Vianne's hand holding her pistol stopped moving.

"One move, one tiny move, *Mademoiselle* Vianne, and I will aim the next round straight at your heart. Trust me, you're an easy target."

Vianne's eyes went from the woman's face to Adèle's lifeless body lying a few feet away in a pool of blood.

"Whoever that redhead is, she certainly came in handy," said the blond woman without taking her eyes from Vianne. "I knew I could lure you up here with your now-dead friend, you stupid bitch." She hefted the rifle, aimed it at the center of Vianne's chest, and held it rock steady.

Vianne's eyes narrowed and she didn't move. Finally she whispered, "Mistral."

"At your service, orphan. Now throw your gun to me." Mistral bent her head and sighted down the rifle, making sure it was zeroed on Vianne's heart.

Vianne waited as many seconds as she dared, then carefully tossed the gun. The Beretta sailed across the room, landing on the floor with a metallic clunk a few feet from Mistral.

The assassin walked forward until the muzzle of her weapon was six feet from Vianne, who knew with sickening certainty that the chances of this professional killer missing her heart were zero.

"It's about time, bitch," Mistral said without taking her eye away from the telescopic sight. "When César comes up here, I will be waiting. I'll see his face when he discovers your body chopped in half with bullets. Right here in this little home that you stole from him."

Vianne said nothing.

Mistral snorted. "You aren't surprised?"

Vianne made a careful, microscopic shrug.

"Daniela had flown planes for Miguel since I'd met him," said Mistral. "She was the best pilot among the drug smugglers and one of the keys to Miguel's operation."

The rifle moved slightly, but Mistral's eyes didn't.

"When I gave her the very lucrative job of destroying you in spectacular manner while César was in another country, she not only relished it, but flew her own beautifully equipped plane to Corsica to get it done."

Vianne saw the professional concentration in the killer's face and suppressed a shudder.

Mistral went on. "And she fucked it up, Vianne. Incredibly stupid. Unforgivable. The only thing that turned out not to be stupid was lending her the ring my husband had given me for good luck. Just in case."

Mistral watched for a reaction, but Vianne's face was a closed book.

"*Sí*." The assassin's lips formed a small, almost winsome smile. "Just in case."

But a moment later the smile turned feral. "César Duval, your loving, step-fucking-father, murdered my husband in cold blood. I swore to take everything precious from him and ruin his life in spite of all his power."

Vianne stopped breathing for a second and whispered, "Isabelle."

Mistral laughed, though she kept the gun dead steady. "Of course—who else would be interested in killing a stupid young girl? It made me feel *muy satisfecha,* so worthwhile. Well, for five or ten minutes, at least."

"*Chatte,*" Vianne whispered. She was rooted to her spot, and the insides of her thighs burned mightily. *What's left but to charge at this woman and hope for a miracle?*

As if reading her mind, Mistral stepped back a pace. "The first bullet won't kill you, Vianne. Neither will the second. But you will be pleading—no, *whispering*—for the third one, the head shot. Ha! It will be interesting watching you—*you cannot scream!*"

Mistral let out a short manic laugh and continued, "When I've finished with my fun, I'll do as promised and cut you into pieces right here on this floor." She made a guilty, sarcastic face. "It will be a mess."

Vianne tensed and readied to jump, though she knew the distance between them was too great to reach Mistral before she would fire.

"I see that thirst for blood in your eyes, *coño,* that killing lust," Mistral said, smiling. "I recognize that desire from my own reflection in the mirror. Do you think you are any different from me, Vianne?"

Vianne narrowed her eyes.

"You know that you and I are two sides of the same coin, and that the world can suffer only one of us at a time."

Vianne whispered, "*Va te faire foutre.*"

Go fuck yourself.

"I may do just that when I think of you in the future," Mistral said with finality, hefting the rifle and caressing the trigger with her finger. "*Adiós,* Vianne."

The bullet beat the sound of the shot by a microsecond, and Mistral's shredded right ear exploded off the side of her head.

Vianne froze in confusion and shock, and Mistral turned her face in the direction of the sound.

The smoking Beretta was in Adèle's hands. She had silently slithered the few feet over to where Vianne had tossed it, leaving a wide swath of blood and, shaking on the floor behind Mistral, taken the shot. The pale woman was frozen with fear and pain, and the gun fell from her hand.

Mistral, the side of her head hemorrhaging scarlet, whirled to bring the rifle to bear on Adèle, but Vianne was faster. She leaped at the assassin and the two went down, the heavy rifle between them.

They grappled with each other on the floor, both frantically trying to wrest the rifle from the other's hands. Blood spread in red stripes through Mistral's platinum hair from where her ear used to be, and she screamed in an incoherent rage at the top of her lungs.

Vianne struggled in silence.

Mistral twisted the rifle with the fierce abandon of someone fighting for her life, and it came away out of Vianne's hands.

Vianne fell back hard on the floor and felt something hot and metallic under her back. She twisted like a viper, scooped up the Beretta, brought it in a wide arc to aim at Mistral, and fired. The muzzle of her gun was an inch from that of Mistral's weapon when it went off, and the rifle tore out of Mistral's hands as it too fired wildly, its damaged muzzle exploding between them like a bomb.

The two women were deafened by the blast, and the Beretta rocketed out of Vianne's hand, jammed and useless. They both stumbled quickly to their feet, but Mistral was faster.

The blond killer freed a gleaming, serrated hunting knife from its sheath in her bodysuit as she staggered forward through the shattered glass door and out onto the patio.

Before Mistral could turn to face her, Vianne flung herself at the woman's back and the two crashed into the patio's railing. There was a sickening *crack,* and part of the metal railing broke and swept away from the balcony like a waving arm over the thousand-foot drop. The two women fell together and grasped at the sagging railing and at each other like desperate acrobats.

Vianne managed to grab one of the thin metal struts to keep her from tumbling to her death, but suddenly felt a searing pain in her back as Mistral's knife made a deep, straight cut down her spine.

Vianne twisted hard, let go with one hand, and with her fist punched Mistral's head where the woman's ear used to be.

Mistral shrieked, let go of the knife, and fell, wrapping her arms around Vianne's waist. The extra weight nearly caused Vianne to let go of the sagging railing.

The two women hung over the abyss, Mistral the assassin slowly slipping down Vianne's bleeding body as she held on for dear life. In a few seconds she was dangling with both hands gripping one of Vianne's ankles. The thin drizzle of blood from the gash in Vianne's back speckled her face scarlet.

"Pull me up, you fucking bitch!" Mistral hollered. "I'll leave you alone, you and your shit family, your shit stepfather. You have my word!"

Vianne carefully let go of the swaying metal railing with one hand, and through the colossal pain and the strain on her muscles, reached down with the other. With a movement of her fingers she indicated that Mistral should grab her hand.

Go ahead. Take my hand.

Mistral's eyes gleamed in sly terror. "Are you going to drop me?"

Vianne said nothing, her teeth gritted hard with the strain.

"You will pull me up?"

Just take it.

Mistral let go of Vianne's leg with one hand and reached up.

Vianne grabbed her wrist tightly.

Mistral's other hand came off Vianne's leg, and she hung by one arm, her wrist clasped tightly in Vianne's fist.

I need to tell you something, Mistral.

As Mistral reached up to grab Vianne's arm with her other hand, the railing made a screeching sound, moved a few more inches, and began to finally break off the patio.

"Hurry!" Mistral yelled. But when she looked up into Vianne's face, she knew what was really happening. The tiny splinters of light in the midnight eyes told her a stark, midnight truth.

Need to tell you just one thing.

Mistral held her breath.

Cold stars flashing in her eyes, Vianne finally whispered, "This is for Isabelle."

Her fist holding Mistral's wrist opened.

A long, rapidly diminishing scream echoed out over the valley as gravity took over and Mistral accelerated through the clear Corsican air.

The release of the extra weight was an instant physical relief to Vianne. She watched as far below, Isabelle's killer smashed into a rock outcropping and ricocheted out and down into the valley like a tiny doll that a little girl had thrown away.

I had a doll like that.

Vianne hung by her two hands and knew that her fever of revenge, and the hate that came with it, was over. But she also knew one more, limitlessly sad thing.

I just can't anymore.

She knew that she couldn't climb back up the sagging, dangling railing to the patio. Though she had only two or three feet left to go to reach safety, the pains in her arms and her legs and her back and mostly in her soul were too great to bear.

... Mother?

She tried one last time to pull herself up with the failing shreds of her remaining strength, and almost made it. But then she felt the twisted metal she was gripping finally break off the patio.

And now the stars …

Ashes in a Midnight Sea

———

ADÈLE OPENED HER EYES.

Her body ached dully, and above her she saw tubes and hanging intravenous bottles of blood and clear liquids. Muffled street sounds came from outside a window. She realized that she was in a hospital, and an odd voice inside her said, *I'm alive.*

Her vision cleared a bit, and she saw a man in a doctor's white jacket standing next to a familiar woman with auburn air.

"*Bonjour,*" Jacqueline Murat said softly.

Adèle tried to say something, but it came out a jumbled whisper.

"Don't." Jacqueline put a finger to her lips, and her large brown eyes were a mixture of kindness and relief—and what seemed an oblique melancholy.

The doctor standing at the bedside said, "Don't try to talk." The man had a German accent. "We are going to make you better, but it will take some time until you are back to perfect."

He patted Adèle's hand, smiled, and said to Jacqueline, "She will be sleeping soon and we will be watching her at all times. You must be leaving. Two more minutes."

Jacqueline nodded and watched as the doctor left the small private room. She turned to Adèle and saw the beginnings of blurred questions forming in the light blue eyes.

"You're in a hospital," Jacqueline said. "But not in Corsica. You are getting the finest care in the world."

Drugged puzzlement was plain on the exhausted girl's face.

"You were badly injured, but now you're completely safe."

Adèle mouthed some silent words.

Jacqueline looked away. "You've been here almost two weeks, in what the doctors call an induced coma." She stared at nothing for a few moments, and then looked back at Adèle. "It will take some time, but you'll be back to normal, better than ever."

Through the gauzy haze of the drugs, Adèle tried to say something. But it was only a murmured slur, something that Jacqueline couldn't make out. The woman leaned over until their faces were close, and Adèle finally whispered, "Where's Vianne?"

Jacqueline looked into the girl's eyes with a sad tenderness. After a few seconds she smiled and said, "You're safe now, that's what matters."

Then Jacqueline Murat touched Adèle's hand and stood up.

Adèle heard a small voice inside her say, *Ask her again,* and she tried, but sleep had already enfolded her in its soft wings.

As the motor yacht sailed east and began its slow turn to the north, the lights of the city of Ajaccio faded on the dark horizon and soon disappeared between the blackness of the sea and the starry night sky.

César stood staring out the window of the main cabin. He didn't care to speak, to say anything to anyone.

Behind him, Luc and Bernard sat on a low couch. They too were silent, lost in their own thoughts about how life and the recent events had played out.

Two weeks had passed, and César had decided that the time had come to resume the plan he had put into motion. *Life goes on,* he had said to himself a number of times.

It always does.

He had sent Jacqueline ahead to Zürich on a specially chartered medical jet with Adèle. He wanted someone to stay with the badly injured girl, to be there when she woke up, and he felt an inconsolable bitterness that his life, his power, might have killed yet another young woman. *If Adèle dies as well,* he thought, *I'm not certain what I will do.*

Bernard, his mind simple and clear as always, got up from the couch and walked over to stand beside his father.

"Papa," he said, looking out through the window at the dark sea. "About Vianne—"

"Not now, Bernard," César interrupted him, his eyes stormy.

"But aren't you …?"

César turned to look at his son, knowing that the man's mental affliction had become his blessing. The plain, happy world in Bernard's damaged mind was a state of grace on earth.

As was the heaven-sent gift of Vianne's silence—her most precious possession through all her years. The silence that had guided her, had molded her—had shaped her life in its deep and secret ways.

César continued to look out the window at the night sky, and he thought he could see more than stars.

Bernard stood by him for a few more seconds, then turned, walked slowly back to the couch, and sat next to his brother. He put his head in his hands.

Luc reached over and touched Bernard's shoulder, his eyes finally clear and transparent with truth. "Everything will be fine, Bern," he said, and meant it.

Bernard lifted his head and reflected for the hundredth time on the treasure and the grace and the love that he had in his heart for Vianne …

Her wounded back bleeding in a steady stream, drops falling off her like a red summer rain, her legs burning, and her arms at the breaking point, she hung by her too-tired hands and watched as far below, Mistral smashed into a rock outcropping and ricocheted out and down into the valley like a tiny doll that a little girl had thrown away.

Vianne knew then that she couldn't climb back up the dangling railing to the patio. Though a distance of only two or three feet separated her from safety, the excruciating pains in her body and her soul were too great to bear.

She tried one last time to pull herself up with the failing shreds of her remaining strength, and almost made it. But then she felt the twisted metal she was gripping finally break off the patio

And now the stars—

—and she closed her eyes and let go of the railing.

Instantly, two thick, powerful hands grabbed her wrists, and she swung out over eternity.

In a haze of quicksilver confusion, her eyes snapped open and looked down once at the valley far below and then quickly up and straight into a familiar smiling face. Bernard held her wrists with a powerful and joyful concentration, and she saw that his upper body was halfway off the patio, while behind him Luc held his legs to keep his brother from flying off into space along with their stepsister.

"I have you," she heard Bernard say, and she saw his delight, and not daring to take her eyes from his, felt herself being lifted up—up and away from the stars: the stars that would have to wait a little longer.

"And I have *you*," she whispered back.

She stood alone on deck, leaning on the bow rail of the motor yacht—just her and the dark sea and the spangled sky.

It was the same spot on which she had stood when she first laid eyes on Corsica four years earlier.

She wore jeans and the gift that Luc had given her yesterday for her twentieth birthday. The subtle caring that her older stepbrother seemed to have developed for her in the last two weeks was a pleasant surprise, as was his clear, new respect for her that she easily, finally saw in his eyes.

And she loved the gift. It was a shirt of dark Shantung silk, and she liked that its deeply scooped back exposed her wound to the sea air. The angry red slash began from the nape of her neck and ran down to the base of her spine—the final mark of the woman who called herself Mistral.

The scar would grow fainter with time, but would never fully disappear. Vianne liked that.

She looked up at the carpet of stars above the boat, saw what she knew was there, and listened with calm certitude.

I told you there was a future.

She turned at a soft sound and saw Bernard standing on the deck behind her.

Neither of them moved.

Then Vianne smiled with an uncluttered simplicity, and shook her head once with the élan of a smooth, new freedom.

With a clear, gentle nudge to her subconscious, she emptied the burning remains of vengeance and violence and hatred from her mind, as one would pour cold ashes over the railing of a boat far out in the silent caresses of a midnight sea.

She came and stood close in front of Bernard, not touching.

After a few measured heartbeats she leaned forward and tilted her face up, locking her eyes with his. Her diamond *V* winked in the starlight.

And for just a brief moment, for a single cherished second in the fast river of time—a silent glimmering instant in the un-stopping rush of the world and the stars and life and love and death and the secret things Vianne kept in the well of her heart—touched her lips ever so lightly to his.

Now, said her inner voice.

Now I'm done.

ABOUT THE AUTHOR

A CONSUMMATELY COSMOPOLITAN WRITER, HUNTER Lake has assumed a pen name, not wanting notoriety as a writer of international thrillers to detract from the greatness of Vianne, who deserves to stand in her own right, and in her own light.